S.K. EHRA

Call From The Crossroads

First edition

ISBN: 979-8-9851522-0-3

This book was professionally typeset on Reedsy.
Find out more at reedsy.com

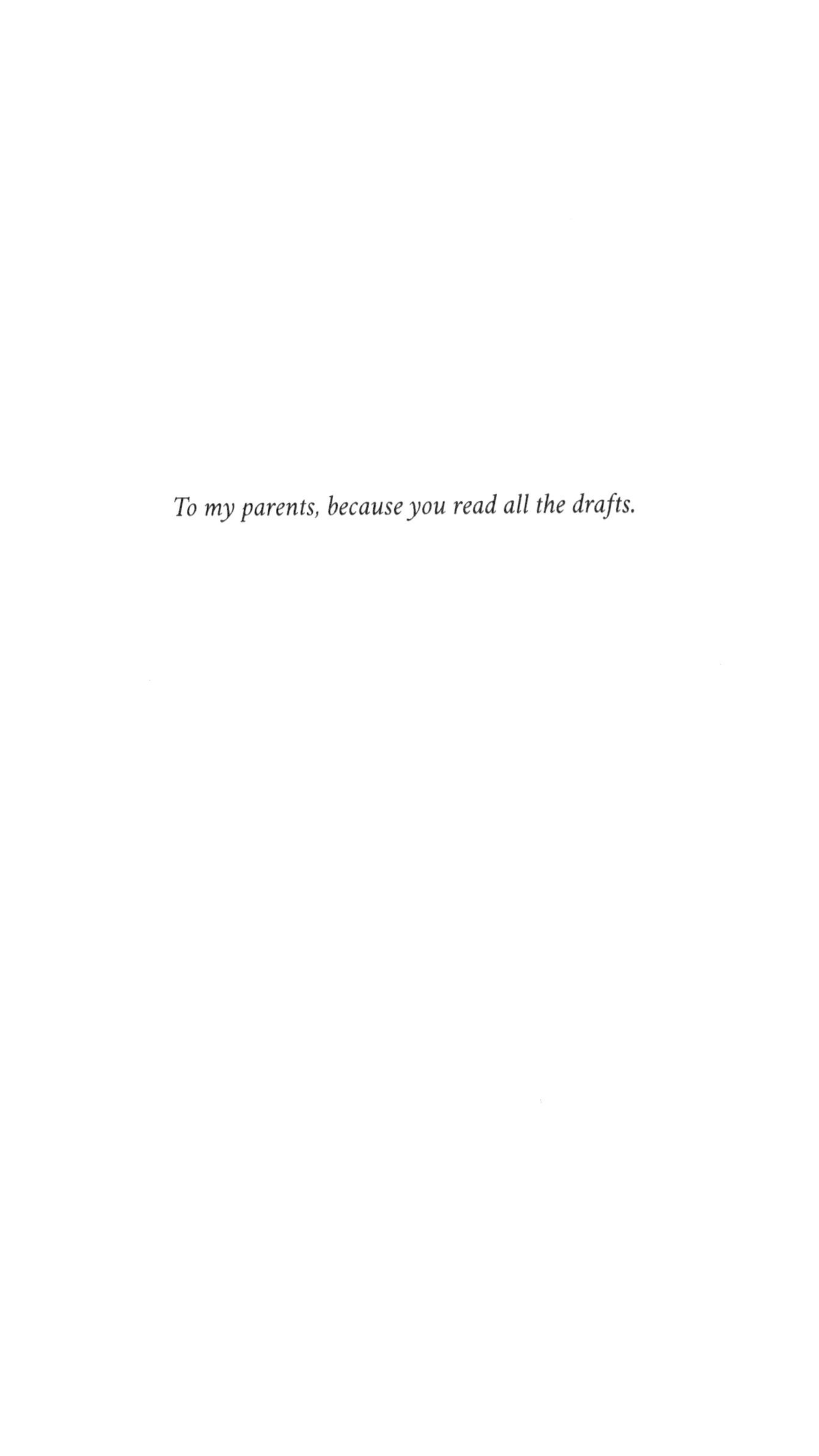

To my parents, because you read all the drafts.

Contents

Chapter 1

Static bursts sharp from the car's busted radio, and the sudden swing from silence near sends my heart straight out my chest.

"Today we're going to—kshkk-kashak"

My hand never moves near the dial, but the radio keeps having fits like someone's fishing for a station playing hard to get. The hiss and spit has all the clarity of the heat mirages rising off this lonely road stretching through cattle kingdom.

With an angry trill, the sought-after station fights to come through.

"A lot to get—kachak—take a look at the rise of violence—kshkk"

The station skips away for a faint guitar strum to play beneath the static. I grip the steering wheel tight and my knuckles turn bone-white. A cocktail mix of agitation and dread pulses through my veins. Someone is trying to tell me something and much as I'd like to ignore it, I've learned the hard way a haunted radio ain't something to be written off.

I keep driving until a recognizable rhythm kicks in. A series of stomps and claps brings order to the radio's buzzing mess and welcomes Cash's baritone promise that no matter how far and long you run, sooner or later God'll cut you down.

I slow as the lyrics shake off the last cobwebs of static and come clear. I cruise for another mile until an ear-splitting crescendo that rattles the car windows urges me to pull over to the roadside.

Cash's chorus line booms on a repeating loop as I idle, listening for anything more definitive than the haunted radio and me sharing a fondness for "the Man in Black." After a half minute, I turn the key. The engine shuts off with an obedient rattle while the radio opts to keep going long enough to let Cash finish his chorus before plunging back into silence.

A Texas summer in full swing greets me in a blast of humid heat as I step out of the car. Insects hum thick in the air under the drowsy afternoon sun, and I can almost hear the pavement threatening to buckle beneath the overbearing stretch of blue sky.

A few buzzards circle lazily overhead in search of roadkill, and it takes less than a minute for the sun to summon up beads of sweat to stick my shirt down my back. A sea of dry scrub flecked by island clumps of oak trees spread out on either side of the road for miles to go without a soul to be seen. There's not even a speed limit sign to break up the monotony.

And a sign is precisely what I'm looking for, just not the mundane roadside sort. I'm waiting for something more than the murmuring hum that always hangs low in the background. Unlike the other voices I hear, I never understand the murmurs. They're a senseless, ever-present tinnitus hiss. And there's an edge to them today: the sibilant chatter that's haunted me since I got back from my final tour in Afghanistan matches my own unease as I stand at the roadside.

Sticking my thumbs into my belt, I rock back and forth on my boot heels. I don't see or hear anything that tells me why I got called to pull over at this empty stretch of nowhere, and it's too hot to be standing out in the sun like this for much longer.

"Well," I say, looking about with no idea what to look for. "Gonna need a hint here."

The summer scene stays silent. That doesn't mean there's nothing here.

I go to grab my hat from the passenger seat to keep the sun from melting my eyes if all I'm going to do is stand all stupid-like by the roadside when I hear it—a man's voice rises above the perpetual chorus of murmurs.

"What are you doing here?"

The radio gives a quick hiccup and I go stock-still. I don't automatically whip around anymore. Don't bother looking for the person the voice should belong to. I know the road will be just as empty as it was a minute ago.

Hand hovering above my hat, I exhale the little mantra as a reminder. "Ain't no one gonna be there. No one's there."

"What are you doing here? What are you doing here?"

The man's voice is muffled. Like it's carrying through the wall of the next room over.

I breathe deep to drill in the habit of composure. There's no need to jump and look wildly around. Ain't no one gonna be there.

At least no one living, that is.

"Shh. Shh. Come on, there ain't no need for that. No one's coming for you."

His mocking purr brings to mind sharp teeth leering wide into a gloating smile.

I pull down my hat and stare out into the fields of scrub and brush, scanning the shady patches of low-slung oak.

"Coming for. Coming . . ."

I feel the first fingers of a cold that could never have survived this summer heat trace down the ridges of my bones by way of introduction. It trickles down my arm and shapes into a hand clasping mine. My skin prickles when it pulls, telling me to follow.

"Come."

I hesitate a second before stepping forward. I'm reasonably reluctant to follow the lead of the dead but know neither of us will get rest until I do. Much like haunted radios, the calling voices and cold hands that reach out to me don't stand for being ignored. I tried doing that the last time the dead-but-not-departed called out to me. It didn't work out.

The grass reaches up above my knees, rustling harsh against my jeans in an angry exhale. Grasshoppers whir up on clicking wings as the cold tugs me toward the nearest clump of trees.

"Come on."

Sometimes I hear them. Other times I hear what they heard. Other times it's something else entirely. The rest of the time I'm still not sure how to describe it. This, whatever it is, won't be limited to fit in my narrow understandings and mortal expectations.

"Come."

I don't know why it's sometimes one way and other times something completely different. The rules of engagement haven't been made clear and I know better than to ask too hard. Ignorance doesn't make a good weapon, but it makes one hell of a good defense against madness.

"Come on."

I check back over my shoulder. My silver Honda Civic is a pinprick of metal shine barely visible over the dry brush and grass. In a couple minutes I'll lose complete sight of that one marker for where the roadway is. A cold sweat joins what the sun has worked up and I can't feel the summer heat anymore. The creeping chill has me full in its grip as it guides me through thickening brush.

The man's taunting doesn't echo out again. A heavy, hungry breathing takes its place. The hairs on the back of my neck stand on end as the insects stop humming. I wish they wouldn't. I don't like it when nature takes pause for the unnatural.

I like coming across the sun-bleached high heel even less. At one time it might've been blue. One of those types of shoes my wife would wear out dancing and that she'd inevitably end up slipping off before having me carry her home at the night's end. I always made a fuss of grumbling over it, but I loved how she looked in the shoes and loved carrying her even more.

Part of the foot remains stuck in the heel. Strips of skin leathered from exposure hold to a splintered tibia bone. Canid teeth left gnawed tracks and divots along the shaft.

The heavy breathing comes louder. It pounds against me in hard, excited gasps.

Six more steps through the rustling grass and there's the rest of her. What's left of her.

The shallow sandy grave did nothing besides serve as a mockery. Coyotes and buzzards left little more than a splintered ribcage, spine, and skull. Dried skin hangs in tears and has rotted into the tatters of her dress. Empty eye sockets picked clean leer wide up at the indifferent bright blue sky. Exposed teeth are cracked open to make it look like she's stuck forever in a shriek not even I can hear.

"No one's coming for you."

Chapter 2

"Coffee?" Sheriff Suarez pours a cup without waiting for a response.

"Thanks," I say. I put the mug on the Longhorns coaster. It's late enough in the day it won't do me any good.

"It's decaf, if that's alright," he says, taking a drink from his own mug.

"It's alright," I say, leaving the mug untouched. There's a proper time and place for coffee and this ain't that.

His office is small and neat, in the corner of a small and neat one-story building, in the center of a small and neat little town. The big white letters of "Welcome to Encrucijada" framed by stenciled bluebonnets greeted us when we drove into the city limits.

Kitty will be less than enthused I didn't even make it past the welcome sign before earning a police escort. Then again, if I can wrap this ghostly business up quick, she might never need to know. And I'd rather get this squared away before showing up at her doorstep, seeing as how it was my previous haunting that got me shipped off here to be her problem for a while.

"Cream? Sugar?" Sheriff Suarez asks.

I shake my head. I prefer to keep things simple.

"I appreciate you taking the time to come down here," he says.

I didn't have much choice in the matter of coming down to the station. Not that Sheriff Suarez threw his weight around when he asked me to. He was nothing short of cordial, even said please which I more than appreciated. But when the sheriff asks you to come down to the station to talk about the body you found in the middle of nowhere, you don't say no. Whether or not he says please.

At least he let me follow him in my own car instead of insisting I ride with him in the cruiser. My radio staying quiet for the rest of the drive into town was an added bonus.

Sheriff Suarez sits down across from me, sizing me up. As proudly announced on the white lettered sign, Encrucijada boasts a healthy small-town population of 42,000. They might want to change that to 41,999 now. Either number doesn't allow for a large enough police department to have someone play both good and bad cop during a friendly chat over some fresh brewed decaf.

Besides, Sheriff Suarez gives off the air he can play both to the nines.

Salt is winning the war against pepper in his close-cut hair. The greying has already conquered his no-nonsense mustache and neatly trimmed beard. It's moved forward in its campaign to flank his sideburns, trimmed with impressive geometric precision to emphasize a forehead made thick from constant furrowing, and the frown lines mapping his brow never fully uncrease. The wedding band around his finger, the family photographs on the shelves and desk, and various school children craft projects peeking from beneath paper work suggest there's a family man beneath the badge. He's at an age I'd wager the enthusiastically colored pages of Disney Princesses are from a grandchild rather than one of his own.

"What brings you out to Encrucijada?" he asks. His current expression near matches the weary frustration he wore in the framed photograph perched on the shelf behind him. A much younger Sheriff Suarez, hair all black and face much less lined, is caught in the moment of failing to get even one of his three boys to look at the camera. I'd guess them to be at a county fair of sorts and the boys appear to have thought whatever was happening around them was far too interesting to stay still for a picture. The youngest boy photo-Sheriff holds is caught mid-flail, arms and legs going every which way. The second son leans to the side as if trying to resist the magnetic pull of his father's authority. The third is turned completely around and taking the first steps of open rebellion to wander off away from the camera.

His wife holds a little girl in her arms and an older daughter beams by her side. They're the only three smiling and are either oblivious or very well-versed in overlooking the struggling sons. The little girl being held waves a pudgy toddler arm at the camera, grinning beneath her pigtails.

A man who frames a picture like that either has a solid sense of humor, or prefers to keep life honest and not waste his time presenting it as posed and perfect. Or his wife really likes that picture and he really likes his wife. My wife held veto power over which pictures got hung up for public viewing, and since we were cursed where only one of us could manage to keep our eyes open per picture, there were a lot of photos hanging in our living room of me halfway through a blink.

"Son?" Sheriff Suarez asks.

"What?"

"What brings you to Encrucijada?"

"Got family in the area."

Sheriff Suarez leans back in his chair. "You visit them often?"

"My brother-in-law says it isn't often enough. My sister says the opposite, so I try to strike a balance."

"Your wife not with you?" he nods at my wedding ring.

"No. She's not," I say. She would have liked Encrucijada. She always was a small-town girl. Never wanted to live anywhere she couldn't say a sincere "hello" to everyone she might run into at the grocery store. Her favorite getaway was a tiny town tucked away in hill country with little more to boast than a church across from a bed-and-breakfast on a single sleepy main street.

Realizing we would have gone there just about this time of year makes my chest go hollow.

"What made you stop?"

"Stop what?"

"At the side of the road," he says. Steam twists up from his mug. He hasn't touched his coffee since he sat down. His hands are knotted into fists. The muscles of his neck are taut, straining his skin slackened by years.

"Saw a coyote."

"You make a habit of pulling over for every coyote you see?"

"No. But when it's got a shoe and bone in its mouth . . ." I shrug. There's not much stretch to the lie. There were plenty of tracks around the corpse and evidence of scavenging that all it needs is for me to sell it convincingly.

Sheriff Suarez isn't convinced. He leans farther back in his chair, springs creaking under his weight. A few decades ago he probably could have wrestled a bull to the ground with one hand while holding his coffee mug. Age has softened him around the edges and he's starting to droop under time.

He stays quiet, arms crossed, waiting for me to say more. I start tapping out Johnny Cash's tune with my boot heel on the linoleum. Not that it's a contest, but I know my reserves of patience run much deeper than his.

He pulls a picture from a folder and slides it over to me.

"You ever see this woman before?" he asks.

I take the photo with all the eagerness of being handed a pinless grenade. A pretty young woman smiles up at me. Straight jet black hair braided over her shoulder, dark skin, grey eyes, and a dimpled smile a guy would make an idiot of himself to be graced by. The image of the hollow-eyed corpse in the field flickers over her face.

"What are you doing here?"

I hold back a shudder and hand the photo back to Suarez.

"No," I say. "Never seen her."

"Where were you April 27th?" he asks.

Oh, that's easy. You couldn't ask for a more airtight alibi than mine.

"St. Jude's Inpatient Mental Health Center." It's just not an alibi that'll shed a good light on me as a reliable citizen.

"That's a mouthful. You work there?" he asks, jotting down what I say on a notepad.

"No, sir."

He pauses and cocks a prompting eyebrow. "Visiting?"

"No, I . . ." There isn't a way to spin it nice and I already used up all the bullshit he'll take on the "saw a coyote" lie. "I was a patient."

The whir of the air conditioner sounds too much like the heavy breathing that chased me to her body for this next wave of silence to be comfortable. The murmurs needle at me and it's hard not to fidget under their harsh whisperings.

Sheriff Suarez's gaze roves my arms. He lingers at my wrists for scars and then checks the veins where drug use would leave its own marks. Not finding any obvious indicators for suicide attempts or addiction, he locks onto my eyes, searching for any crazy lurking behind the irises.

"You mind me asking what for?" he asks.

"I do." I gesture for pen and paper. "May I?"

Sheriff Suarez hesitates a second before handing me a pen, as if giving me anything close to pointed is a calculated risk.

"Here." I write down a phone number and pass him the paper scrap. "If you need to confirm or anything, call and ask for Dr. Joseph Day."

Sheriff Suarez takes the paper, his dark eyes never leaving me. He looks at me different and not in the way I expected.

"Is your family close, or are you still going down the road a piece?" he asks.

"If you know of a motel nearby, I figure I'll just call it a day and get a room for the night," I say.

In truth, Kitty lives about half an hour away, but I'm darkening her door already without dragging a ghost I picked up on the road with me. Best to get this haunting business all cleared up first. Especially as I'm pretty sure if I let this latest ghost drive me as mad as the last one did, my parents are going to send me back to St. Jude's.

"Ranger's Roadhouse on Dove Street." He writes down directions on a Post-it note and hands it to me. "You be sweet to Maybelle and she'll fatten you up with her pecan muffins."

"Thanks."

"There a number I can reach you at, son," he asks, "in case we got more questions?"

I scribble my contact information down on the sheet next to Dr. Day's number.

"Anything else I can help with?" I ask.

He shakes his head, tired and slow. "I suppose I should be thanking you. Be grateful that you found her and called it in."

I stop at the door. "Sir, what was her name?"

"Silvia Lopez."

The rust in his voice answers my next question. He knew her.

Chapter 3

The Ranger's Roadhouse lives up to its name. The oak wood check-in desk looks like a converted bar, and the piano in the lobby corner completes the old-time saloon feel. The Texas state flag, horseshoes, and paintings of cowboys hang from the wood-paneled walls. Fake bluebonnets on the tables made from barrels and the smell of smoked mesquite and pecan tame the Wild West theme roaming the lobby.

"Well, you're an early bird," Maybelle says. A southern syrup of the Georgia flavor coats her words. "Most folk won't be arrivin' 'til tomorrow."

She looks to be on the cusp of clocking out of her seventies. Her cotton-white hair is so perfectly coiffed she could've just stepped out from a 1950s' red carpet gala. Her dentures are just as pure a white and she shows them off with a warm and ready smile.

"What's tomorrow, ma'am?"

"Oh, you ain't here for the festival?" she asks.

"Was just planning on passing through. What festival?"

"Encrucijada's Folk Festival," she says. "Been running every year since before I was born. Happens to be where my parents met. Used to be just in June with only small, local names playin' and maybe a few folks comin' in from Louisiana—"

The murmurings swing up in pitch, heralding his voice.

"Come."

"—but it got so popular over the past few years, they started doing a set in the spring as well as summer. Some of the younger crowd are sayin' they got some big names on the stage this year. If you want to know who that all is, there's a list over on that there table. Lord knows I can't keep them straight anymore."

"Come. Come."

My whole body tenses tight to stop me from turning round to find the speaker. He sounds like he's standing inches behind me, and I keep expecting to feel his breath against my neck.

Ain't no one gonna be there.

"Here."

"Well, I think you might've convinced me to stick 'round, then," I say. "Any chance I can get that room changed from one night to three?"

"Sure thing, hon. You're in luck, I just had a cancellation call in not ten minutes ago," she says and makes a note in her guest book. "Mind you, Main Street runs right opposite us. If you like to go to bed early, you'll need to get some earplugs."

"That work for you?"

"Come. Here. Here."

She slips her hearing aid out and winks. "I got the natural earplugs you cash in on after Social Security."

"Speaking of cash—" I fork over pay for three nights. My folks decided limited funds were the best way to be sure I didn't wander too far off somewhere between their garage and my sister's doorstep. Joke's on them, I still managed to find a dead body and a cheap motel along the way to throw a wrench in their plans.

"You always carry that much cash on you?" Maybelle asks as she hands me the room key.

"Only after a night of dancing with good tips," I say, and she chuckles.

"Up the stairs and to the right," she says. "The pool is out back and closes at ten, but with all the noise that'll be blastin' out from one street over, ya'll get reprieve long as I don't catch any drinkin' out there."

"Here. Here."

"Don't worry, ma'am." I fight down the shivering chill coming stronger each time his voice echoes out. "I'm not much of a drinker."

"Oh, you don't have me fooled, young man." Her grin would be wicked if her eyes weren't so wrinkled from seventy years of incessant smiling. "I know trouble when I see it. Married a man who liked to play innocent as well. Had big doe-brown eyes just like yours. And then I had to raise six boys who were ungrateful enough to take after him."

"Thanks for the warning, ma'am," I say. "Good to know I'm outmatched."

"Come. Come."

My hands shake as I grip the stairway railing. That it's a man's voice I'm hearing doesn't mean it isn't Silvia calling out to me. The little I've pieced together among a whole lot of guesswork on how all this supernatural sensing works leads me to think the man's voice is the last thing Silvia heard.

I've heard the dead echo similar last moments before. There was a nurse at St. Jude's I avoided like the plague. She used to work in an emergency room and had a patient they couldn't save from his suicide attempt. She comforted him as he died and I got to hear that final conversation play out whenever she came near me. I never figured out if she knew she was being haunted. I never wanted to get close enough to her to ask.

"Come. You. Come."

The voice plays in the unbroken loop of a stuck record. There's an urgency there. Not in the man's tone but in the relentless repetition running the words together.

"Here. Here. Here. Here. Come."

His voice aggravates the ever-present murmurs. They stir up into a growl, fighting the new haunting presence for dominance.

"You. Come. Here."

I drop the room key twice before managing to unlock the door.

"Here. Here. Come."

An old-fashioned quilted duvet and plump white pillows sit on the bed taking up most the room space, sandwiched between the wall and a bedside table topped by a horseshoe lamp. The sheer curtains draped over the window offer as much privacy as a stripper's lingerie, and the thin white plaster walls are easily breached by any outside noise.

Living voices come faint from the next room over. The man's voice calls out clearer from a much farther place.

"Here. Here."

The second-story window gives a view over the row of businesses separating the motel from Main Street. The street is blocked off by traffic cones and a woman in an orange safety vest directs a couple of trucks carrying stage equipment down a side road. Skeletons of booths take shape in front of shops, people pitch white tent awnings, fold out tables, and sound tests from the main stage in the park rumble low and muffled.

"Here. Here."

I grab a pair of industrial earphones from my duffel bag and shove them over my ears. The sound tests and the people in the other room go quiet. The murmurs and Silvia echoing the man's voice do not. They would chase me through deaf and dark.

"Come on. Coming here. Here. Here. Come. Here."

"I get it," I hiss, gritting my teeth so hard they could crack. "You can hush up now."

It doesn't stop. My irritated request has no more influence than the earphones. If anything it swells, growing louder to weigh heavier on me. Pressing down, making it a chore to breathe.

Pulling my laptop from the duffel bag sends a couple bright orange pill bottles rattling across the floor—my neglected friends of duloxetine and clozapine. I'd like to say it was common sense that pushed me to ignore the numerous prescriptions thrown my way, that I avoided taking medication because I knew drugs wouldn't cure supernatural impingement. In truth it was a choice of spite. I got tired real quick of being treated like a bag of chemicals and the notion that fixing me was only a matter of people in white coats tinkering around until they found the right ratio.

I shove the capsules back in the bag and out of sight like they're something shameful.

Opening my laptop, a dozen news articles pop up when I search "Silvia Lopez April Encrucijada." She went missing on April 27th, a week shy of her twenty-third birthday and the same week of Encrucijada's spring festival Maybelle mentioned. They found her car in a makeshift parking lot for one of the shows hosted at a local ranch on the morning of the 28th. No one had seen or heard from her since.

I switch to a different article when I reach the sections near the end where family and friends are interviewed. They're quoted talking about their fears and hopes. How much Silvia is loved. How much they miss her and ask for prayers for her safe return. One reporter interviews a coworker of Silvia's at Sawdust, a local bar. The next article went all the way to get the emotional punch and dedicates two lengthy paragraphs detailing how Silvia's mother can't make it through the interview without breaking down into tears.

"Come here. Come here."

I stop scrolling at the image of Silvia's mother standing outside her home. Zooming in on the picture shows the address for the neighboring house numbered on the mailbox in the background: 3417.

I punch the numbered address and "Encrucijada TX" into a search. Three possible listed addresses come up. I find all three on Google Maps, the ultimate spying tool, and drop down into Street View.

"Bingo," I say, finding the house matching the one pictured in the article. And I'll find the Lopez place at 3421 Wild Rose Way.

"Come here."

It's too late in the evening to check out the Lopezes. Chances are Silvia's family will be home and I don't have a good excuse lined up as to why I'd invite myself over at this hour. "I found your daughter's corpse in a field and think she's reaching out to me from the grave" isn't a good pitch for getting invited to dinner.

"Come here. Come."

I skim through the remaining articles and pretend to read a few before looking up Sawdust's address. I'm not sure what Silvia wants me to do or where to go, so starting at the bar she worked at should be as good a place as any.

"Here."

Then again, I can't be completely sure it is Silvia calling for my attention. Ghostly voices aren't real strong on the material evidence front, and I'm taking a leap of faith Silvia's the one sending me a spiritual distress signal. I've got more reason than faith to believe it could very well be something entirely different and entirely hostile.

I pinch the bridge of my nose, pretending that willpower is all it'll take to push back the headache marching forward to a throbbing drum. Billy Davis was much more straightforward in what he wanted done, none of this hanging around after being found business.

I close my laptop and lie back on the twin bed.

It's a hard battle to resist the urge to roll over and shove the pillow over my head, knowing if I do, it's game over for the night and that's where I'll end up staying.

"Come. Come . . . come . . ."

The man's voice drifts farther away and becomes a whisper needling the back of my mind, an auditory Chinese water torture in its constant repetition.

"Come. Here."

"Shh." I hold a finger to my lips. "I'm trying to think, and that's hard enough without your netherworld nagging."

Sawdust is a little over four miles away. Taking a route that puts a more comfortable distance between me and a hospital adds an extra couple miles. It isn't cemeteries or old church yards I've found need avoiding. More often than not, those are the quietest places. Even the murmurings dwindle to near nothing when I'm there.

It's busy highways, hospitals, bridges with histories of suicide, and neighborhoods where violence has bled into the pavement that I have to avoid. As long as fates like Silvia's are an aberration, Encrucijada should be a simple town to navigate through.

Simple. That ain't the same as easy.

"Come. Here."

There's an overwhelming temptation to sink back into the lukewarm stew of despondency. Doing that would be easy. The idea of going out, inviting earthly noises to compete with the unearthly, is draining. Bars and similarly crowded sites were quick to join the list of places to avoid along with hospitals. Nauseatingly overfilled by sound and stimuli. The coping methods I use to tolerate the voices of the dead makes it difficult to deal with more than one living voice at a time. Being in a crowd where the filters of sobriety have been removed is near unbearable.

The thought of it alone sets my skin crawling.

"Come."

The ceiling fan wheeling above me makes lazy *whup-whup-whups* on the lowest setting. I fix on that, something material and rhythmic, to encourage the spectral intruders in this plane to simmer down. If I'm gonna go out, I need a better grip on reality than the tenuous strings I'm grasping right now.

"Come here . . . come here . . ."

Using the mattress as a keyboard, I play out broken bits of piano tunes muscle memory held onto over a year out of practice. The recalled melody softens the background murmurs.

Whup. Whup. Whup.

Following the fan's rotations encourages the sluggish gears of my mind to follow suit, to start moving to make a plan—get up, go to Sawdust, and then what? Solve Silvia's murder? I can't think of any other reason she'd be lingering other than a death-transcending desire to see justice done. Or maybe all she wanted is for someone to find her body and all this follow-up won't be necessary. Being found is all Billy Davis wanted.

"Come."

But if that was all Silvia wanted, she would have left me alone by now.

"Here."

"Two minutes," I say. "Give me two minutes and I'll go."

The voice disappears, leaving me alone with the murmurs.

Two minutes somehow stretches into half an hour before I roll off the bed and grab my car keys. That the voice stayed quiet the whole time makes me think this really is Silvia and not a more malevolent being. Evil forces crept out from the veil don't seem the sort to tolerate my extended brain-dead brooding time.

"Thanks for waiting," I say.

"Come. Come."

I make a point to walk out the door with a little more enthusiasm for life than I feel. After all, a lady is inviting me out to the bar.

Doesn't matter that I don't drink and that she's dead.

Chapter 4

Sawdust's gravel parking lot is near full by the time I pull up. This evening's crowd is most likely larger than usual, swelled by the out-of-towners flocking in for the festival. There's not a single shop on the street that doesn't have some bluebonnet banner, a special discount sign, or "Welcome to Encrucijada" written big and bold with little music notes in the margins hanging in the front window.

Sawdust is no exception. A chalkboard sign out front advertises festival-themed drink specials for each day of the coming week and live music as entertainment.

The wave of noise released when I open the door near convinces me to turn on my heel and leave. A band sporting plaid shirts and artistically frayed jeans strums out a bluesy ballad on a low platform. A handful of patrons, all of them about to round the corner into the midlife-crisis age bracket, know the song well enough to sing along. I take a steadying breath and tap out the song's beat against my leg, finding an anchor of order before wading into the discordant din of the bar.

All the tables are claimed, and I snag one of the remaining stools at the counter. The television screens hanging above the bar are on mute, and the baseball game being played adds a quiet, flickering background noise to the room, the screen's light reflecting off the liquor bottles lining the wall behind the counter.

"What can I getcha, sir?" the bartender asks.

I was hoping the bartender would be cut from the old-fat-guy cloth. The kind who's older than the dirt the town sits on, knows everyone, everything about them, and any reverence he held for privacy is at least two decades expired. Life, however, decides to remain consistent in holding no regard for my hopes. This bartender looks too young to be serving liquor. The black uniform he wears thins his build from scarecrow to beanpole and washes out the little color of the ginger peach fuzz clinging to his upper lip. I doubt he's more than five years younger than me but it's hard to imagine he's even gone to prom.

"A Coke," I say.

"With what?"

"Ice. I'm driving."

"Sure," he says. "Anything to eat?"

I should eat. I haven't had anything since breakfast this morning.

"Nah," I say, "I'm alright, thanks."

Sitting at the counter's far end, back to the wall, gives me a good view of the room. The smart spacing on the open-wood floor allows for unhampered movement between the circular tables. The hardwood bar, booths, and stools provide solid surfaces for bludgeoning, and the tables on the floor aren't nailed down and look light enough to flip or pick up if needed.

Two back doors lead to an open porch area fenced in by a low railing that'd be no trouble to hurdle over in case a quick exit is called for. The hundred feet of open dirt and grass stretching between the railing and tree cover is the bigger issue: it'd leave you exposed for too long. The fire from tiki torches ringing the porch plays off the drinks and laughing faces of those who have spilled out into the night. Little light strands hanging over the open-air seating string back inside along the planked wood walls above framed pictures of famous visitors and favored patrons.

The clink of plates and silverware escapes from the kitchen behind the bar as does the clogging scent of fried foods. A waitress sporting wavy purple hair done up in a ponytail, her bare arms covered in flowery tattoos, balances plates of nachos and fried jalapeños as she floats between the tables with practiced grace. The voices of the living blend into the murmurings, an irritating whine like an insect buzzing too close to the ear.

"You work here long?" I ask Peach Fuzz when he comes back with the Coke.

"Every summer for two years," he says. "You sure you don't want anything with that Coke?"

"Just summers?" If so, he wouldn't have been around when Silvia Lopez disappeared.

"Yup."

"You still in school, then?" I ask. Maybe I should order some food for the chance to talk to Flower-Sleeves the waitress. She might've been working here in the spring. I should've paid more attention to the article that interviewed Silvia's coworker, bothered to remember their name.

"Texas A&M," Peach Fuzz says, "studying chemistry. This is just a summer job," he adds again to be sure I know he's meant for bigger and better things.

"Bet you get a boom with this festival," I say.

He nods. "Yeah, I always make sure I work this week. Really good for tips. Most folk want time off to go see the shows so it's easy to pick up extra shifts."

He goes on about how last year he got a picture with some singer who recently clawed her way up to the national stage of fame. She—and the band she left and hung out to dry to pursue her solo stardom—came into the bar last year, and Peach Fuzz points out a copy of the picture hanging over the bar wall. I nod at the appropriate moments during his story while scanning the crowd over the rim of my glass.

The bar's clientele is a mixed bag. Older men wearing denim shirts holding back beer bellies get foam from their drinks stuck on handlebar mustaches. Their belts and hands look to be made of leather, well-worn and heavily used. None of them look to be packing.

Groups of kids covering the entire college spectrum from bright-eyed undergraduates to long-suffering doctorates talk too loud in their readiness to prove they got something worth saying. They don't wear belts and most have their callous-free hands wrapped around a cell phone.

A man in his late twenties, early thirties, sits in a corner booth. He has a healthy tan and absentmindedly taps his finger against a perspiring beer pint while reading his phone. He shows little interest in the woman sitting across from him. She rivals her companion in disinterest, alternating between swirling the skewered maraschino cherry in her sugar-rimmed drink and flicking a manicured finger across her own phone. Her chestnut hair is pulled back into a fish-tail braid. Her short dress shows off long legs accentuated by white high heels, one ankle crossed over the other, daintily swaying to the music.

Both the man and woman glance up from their screens in mild annoyance when the college kids across from them explode in laughter. One kid stands up in drunken triumph, beer dripping from his face and shirt. Flower-Sleeves tosses him a towel to clean it up. Beer Face starts to protest, then shuts up as his spine snaps under Flower-Sleeves' death stare. She stands over the college students, tattooed arms crossed, until they've finished mopping up their mess.

Peach Fuzz mutters something unprofessional and shakes his head.

I slide my Coke glass back and forth between my hands, less than thrilled that nothing supernatural has happened so far. Sawdust offers no quick revelation as to why Silvia's reaching out to me. Which irritates me because I'd like to get this over and done. I don't like having a ghost hanging over me and the sooner I can get some clear-cut answers as to what unfinished business has Silvia lingering, the sooner I can get her out of mine.

But if there's something to be found here to tip me off, I'm missing it.

An older gentleman drinks his whiskey with a steady practiced rhythm. He stares off into a middle distance and I recognize the expression. He used to have a drinking buddy who until not too long ago sat across from him.

A group of men gather around the pool table in back. One stands with a soldier's forged discipline, has the no-nonsense haircut to match, and his lean, wiry build marks him as a quick pick for a stranger you'd avoid on a dark street.

I never had that hard-edged look that let people know to leave you alone. Even after Ranger training, I couldn't shake my natural tendency to look like a walking doormat. Alec described it as a face girls want to kiss and guys want to kick.

One man keeps tapping his fingers nervously like he's itching for a cigarette. Most of his friends are enjoying the show of a poor sap getting the hell hustled out of him by a five-foot-nothing woman wearing a strategically distracting dress. The man with the soldier's stance is just enjoying the woman. He catches her eye as she lines up a shot and grins. She flirts back by sinking three shots before taking a long pull from her beer, making a science of angling her hips as she circles around the table.

I take a sip of Coke, more and more feeling like Sawdust is going to prove to be a bust. None of the patrons fit what I picture someone possessing the required evil to murder a woman and dump her body for buzzards would look like. No one has so much as a passing resemblance to Stalin, Hussein, or H.H. Holmes. If the murderer is here, he had the foresight to leave his dripping knife and blood-stained clothes at home. And that's assuming her killer being brought to justice is the reason Silvia wants my attention. I can't think of another reason why she would—

A cold tapping finds my shoulder and I freeze, the Coke halfway to my lips.

"What are you doing here?"

There's a woman's voice lurking behind the man's this time. Caught in that tunneling effect death holds over those who linger, Silvia strains to make herself heard through the words that heralded her death.

"What are you doing here. Here. Here. Here. Here."

Strengthened by terror, her voice overtakes the man's whisper until it's only her I hear. The cold tapping against my shoulder shifts to a hard grip on my jaw, as if an unseen hand wants to wrench my head around.

"*Here. Here.*"

I go rigid, unwilling to let the preternatural pressure move me. Peach Fuzz the bartender comes back over and asks me a question, lost behind Silvia's hissing repetition and the murmurings rising up alongside it.

The cold moves to grip my neck and tightens.

"*HERE. HERE. HERE.*"

Panic floods her voice and fear pounds against me. I force myself to take long, deep breaths that make my lungs hurt, and touch a hand to my neck, reminding myself the strangling pressure isn't really there.

"*HERE! HERE!*"

I try to block her out, focus on the rhythm of my breathing and the cool, slick feel of the glass in my hand, ground my senses to stay anchored in the tangible. It's not working. My always feeble grip is slipping and the last thing I need is to lose hold in a public place.

"How much for the Coke?" I ask. The incessant murmurings rustle hard against my senses, coarse sand scraping bits of me away.

I can't hear Peach Fuzz's reply. His lips move out of tempo from Silvia's screaming. Her desperation drowns out all other noise until the entire bar disappears behind a wall of her shrieks.

"*HERE. HERE. HERE.*"

My body stops listening to what I tell it. I can't breathe right, barely managing shallow gasps, the cold causing me to sweat instead of shiver.

"*HERE!*"

Peach Fuzz's face shrivels into a sun-baked corpse. His

watery eyes sink to form empty dried sockets in his skull. A lipless mouth moves to speak.

"HERE! HERE!"

His distended jaw stretches with rot and shapes soundless words. The bar blurs away to a stretch of blue, empty sky above the field that served as her graveyard.

"HERE! HERE! HERE!"

The bar rushes back in a roar that knocks the wind out of me. The patrons clap out a beat and whoop as a band member pours his soul into a harmonica solo. A woman's high laugh pierces through the pounding in my head. Beer-heavy glasses hitting hardwood tables boom too loud. The relentless frenzy of noise keeps me locked in place. I grip my glass tight in one hand while the other holds onto the bar counter to keep me upright.

"Sir." The bartender's face is back. Peach fuzz, acne, and all. "You alright?"

Fishing a ten out of my wallet, I hand it over to him. "Keep the change."

"Sir?" He takes the damp bill from my clammy hands. "You sure you're okay?"

I stagger toward the door. The floor bucks beneath my dragging feet as I push against a cold, dark tide threatening to pull me under. There's twenty feet of frigid water separating me from the rest of the bar. If I reach out, I could touch the nearest person, yet they feel miles away, separated by the murmurings swarming around me.

I can't quite remember how to breathe without conscious effort as I stumble across the parking lot and fall against my car. Tremors make me miss the door handle a few times which adds an unneeded spike of panic each time shutting off the rest of the world is delayed.

I finally catch the handle and collapse into the driver's seat, slamming the door shut behind me. The murmuring voices sound amused when I clamp my hands over my ears in a useless attempt to block them out.

"You stay quiet, you hear?" I say to the radio. The respectful silence is ominous rather than understanding.

My cellphone vibrates and I ignore it. Part of me is terrified I'll hear the man's voice on the other end of the line. Or worse, Silvia's caught in that repetitive loop. There's no one calling me, living or dead, I want to speak to. I have no confidant I can be honest with. Not if I want to be outside of the locked rooms of a psych ward.

Dr. Joseph Day is a good man and a good doctor, but he wanted to cure me of something that wasn't in his scope of practice.

"Son of a bitch." I rest my head against the steering wheel. I'm reasonably sure, despite professional opinion to the contrary, that I'm not crazy. But if these hauntings keep up and I don't find a better way to deal with them, I got a sinking feeling I soon will be.

The keys keep slipping when I try to start the engine. I'm not fit to drive and the radio refuses to stay silent at this display of stupidity. An angry burst of scolding static doesn't let up until I put the keys down on the passenger seat.

"Yeah, okay. You're right," I admit. The radio gives a small huff of static to remind me who wears the pants in this relationship before settling down. My wedding ring feels warm as I turn it slowly around my finger, hands sweat-slicked and shaking.

It takes near twenty minutes for my hands to stop trembling

so I can shove the keys in the ignition. I shoot a glance down at the radio and take its quiet as approval.

Gripping the steering wheel so tight my knuckles are going to split, I drive well under the speed limit. Anything more than thirty miles an hour is too fast for me to handle. Every shadow cast by the street lamps seems ready to take on a life of its own. The smallest hint of movement is a grim warning of larger lurking terrors. The ten minutes it takes to drive back across town to the Ranger's Roadhouse are ten minutes fraught with the peril of imagination and hallucination battling for control of the senses.

New cars clog the motel's parking lot and there's half a dozen people waiting to be checked in. The lobby is decently full and filling as the newly arrived guests get ready to venture out for the night after dropping bags and belongings off in rooms. Most are around my age, yet they look years younger. They seem so light, like if they're not careful their next step won't touch back down to earth.

I on the other hand feel like I'm going to sink down into the ground to join the owners of the murmuring voices. I'm not sure that'd be such a bad thing.

The hallway shrinks in on me under the laughter, music, and excited chatter leaking out from the closed doors. Reaching my room, I jam the headphones back over my ears and go weak from relief when it gives me ringing deafness from the physical world. I'll check out the Lopez place tomorrow and hopefully turn up something more helpful as to what Silvia wants than terrified shrieks and visions of corpses. Until then, I just want some quiet.

Lying flat back on the bed, I watch the silenced ceiling fan's slow spin. I don't bother crawling under the covers. Sleep isn't something that comes easy or has been particularly kind to me of late. It only took one tour in Afghanistan to create a dislike for lying unconscious and vulnerable. A second tour brought this dislike back stateside and a third made it a permanent fixture.

I've almost mastered walking the narrow line between awake and asleep—where I'm not really aware of the world and neither am I subject to the hostile dreams sleep brings. It's a no-man's-land between dreams and thought, where neither one can hold me long.

I never find rest there, but at least it's quiet.

Chapter 5

"Mr. Dalaguerre?" Dr. Keller raised his voice to call back my attention.

It half worked. My gaze did an involuntary flick to the spike of noise before drifting back out the window. The mental hospital's garden was mostly dead and dormant under the dull winter sky.

"Do you regret it?" he asked.

Frustration hissed out between my teeth in a tense sigh. The last few weeks had been Dr. Keller and me talking past the other, a waste of both our times, and I would've bet the farm he'd grown to resent our little chats as much as I did.

"Mr. Dalaguerre?"

"No."

"Mr. Dalaguerre, did you even hear my first question?" he asked, his own frustrated sigh rivaling mine.

"We've already been over this," I said. Blocking out Dr. Keller had become second nature. It wasn't intentional, or at least it wasn't at first. In my efforts to push away the background murmurings, Dr. Keller's constant inquiries about my time serving in the army ended up being what got blocked out. There were only so many times I could say no to if I regretted any of my actions, if pulling the trigger scarred my psyche, if I carried survivor's guilt, or blamed my superiors for being left for dead.

I didn't hold any grudge or grievance, but Dr. Keller never believed my unswerving no's. If anything, he interpreted them as further evidence to support his previously held convictions.

"I asked if you regret checking yourself in to St. Jude's," he said.

That was a new one and it pulled me back. The murmurings gave a painful surge as I abandoned the safety of inattention.

"Yes," I said after a moment's consideration.

Dr. Keller made a few notes and when he returned his focus back to me he looked surprised I had not yet retreated to staring blankly out the window.

"I'm referring you to another doctor," he said, pushing up his horn-rimmed glasses. "Have you met Dr. Day?"

He paused to give me the chance to respond. I didn't. He'd already made it clear what I said didn't matter in his office.

Dr. Keller started to speak and I drifted back out the window, away from the expected interminable sermon on how I needed to learn to trust authority again. A speech of not-so-subtle insinuations I suffered crippling trauma from when the system I'd been a part of almost my entire adult life, that I had trusted and depended on, failed me in a time of crisis. That my disagreement with his assessments was really deep denial I needed to address. That my initial anger when he made these suggestions confirmed the emotional insecurities he diagnosed me with and the severity of said trauma had manifested in a psychosis I would continue to have until I faced what he declared to be the root cause of it all.

I learned a month ago how easy it was to drown Dr. Keller's voice and the murmurings under the sound of the mirror waterfall fountain in his office. It was my favorite part of the otherwise insufferable sessions. The water's soft, rhythmic hush masked the less pleasant sounds haunting me. It turned the room quiet. Not silent.

Silence was Afghanistan, the oppressive emptiness of not being able to hear the enemy as I staggered through the hostile terrain. I had trouble keeping my feet, dizzy and disoriented as I stumbled over rock and thorny scrub. While the world around me threatened to fall away and every next step became an act of conscious will, the sky crept closer down on me. A vast, terrible emptiness ready to swallow me up at the slightest sign of surrender.

Alec stayed silent as he led me down the hellish slopes. I assumed at the time my incomplete deafness was a result of a concussion blast. It had happened before, but not like this. Before, there had been an unpleasant ringing between my ears that faded in time. As I followed Alec, I kept pawing at my ears, trying to claw out the grating din that sounded terrifyingly like voices circling around me just out of sight.

My hearing returned. The voices never left.

***

Hints of dawn peek in through the window. I must've fallen asleep at some point during the night. Probably at multiple points as I moved in and out of uneasy dreams. I don't bother to try and return to fading snippets and shapes of sleep as I watch the motel room slowly shift out of night's navy gloom into the dull grey of a new day.

Dr. Day encouraged me to work on getting back on a consistent sleep schedule. Good advice I struggle to follow as I refuse to use an alarm clock. It's a tool for the weak and undisciplined. A year ago I would have laughed at the thought there'd be a day I'd still be in bed after 6:30. Now I'm either listlessly awake at three in the morning or not bothering to get out of bed until noon.

Looks like today is going to be a listless one.

The vestiges of long-dead discipline tries to roll me out of bed. But I can't move. My fingers twitch uselessly against the cotton sheets. The ceiling fan ticks above me. The rotating blades cause the shadows cast by the weak morning sun to flutter about the room. One rotation I'm staring up at the motel's white popcorn ceiling. The next, I see a roof made of corrugated steel, grey and patched with age, looming overhead.

A door opens to my left, letting a cut of light stretch down the roughly painted slatwall. It disappears as the door snaps shut.

Oh, God, he's here. He's here.

I need to move. I need to move.

Plastic instead of cotton sheets crinkle beneath my feeble shifting.

Move. Get up. Get out.

Wild panic fails to override the block between thought and action, reducing me to a limp doll.

The man moves closer. His heavy booted footfall takes its time. He's in no rush as my heart races. Each step sends me deeper into a terror I can't act on. Looming above me, he reaches down and—

I lurch up and tumble to the floor in a cotton sheet-tangled *thump*.

The scream I couldn't make bursts out in stuttering gasps. Limbs shaking, it takes a terrible effort to force myself up onto hands and knees. My spasming gut would've made a mess on the floor if it had anything in it and the taste of empty bile burns up the back of my throat.

***

"How often does this happen?" Dr. Day asked.

"Not a lot."

"Once a month? Once a week?"

I stared out the window in response to the prompt.

"How about last night?" he asked.

I shook my head. Not last night. It was the night before that was God-awful.

"Are you familiar with sleep paralysis?"

Yes. This isn't sleep paralysis.

"It sounds self-explanatory," I said.

Dr. Day leaned forward and I leaned back, ready to listen and nod as he attempted to explain something he didn't understand.

"Logan, I can't help you if you're not honest with me."

***

Whup. Whup. Whup. Whup.

Rolling onto my back, I steady my shaking breaths to match the ceiling fan's mechanical beat. There's no need to get dramatic over this. Voices and visions, they ain't nothing new, just a rough fact of how life's gonna be. Treat them as occurrences, not obstacles. There isn't a therapy, drug, or technique for it other than toughing it out.

Heart racing, but certain I'm back in full control of my body, I fumble through my duffle bag for running shoes. Being haunted is no excuse to surrender to a sedentary lifestyle and running is the best way to clear the head. If you can't outrun the thoughts refusing to fall in step with shoes pounding on pavement, then you just gotta run faster until you can't think.

Maria tried to break me out of this mindless approach. She claimed running was a quicker way to see a world too big for us to take in with the little time we got. My retreat into a mechanical stride annoyed her to no end. I pretended her tendency to stop to look at every baby in a stroller, butterfly, new flower bloom, and then sprint to make up for lost time until she slowed for another distraction irritated me just as much.

The motel's lobby and reception desk is mercifully empty as I step into the early morning. The air is cool, a temporary respite from summer's heat. In a couple hours it'll be too hot to spit. The murmurings are more grating than usual this morning, leaving my thoughts feeling jagged and incomplete. I pick out points in the scenery that Maria would have stopped to enjoy as a guard against the voices pulling me down into the muttering depths.

Most of our first dates were runs. She liked to pretend we were just workout buddies, and I liked to pretend I let her run a few paces ahead of me out of courtesy and not out of appreciation for her tight running shorts. Her claim soon changed. Mine never did. Even after marriage, all of our runs ended in a race one way or another. Being a gentleman, I never let her win. She won enough of our arguments that it was my responsibility to humble her wherever I could.

***

"You gotta earn it," I said, running circles around her after waiting until the last stretch of road to sprint past her.

She flicked her hand out to bat me away and I skipped out of arm's reach, adopting the shifting dance of a boxer, arms at the ready, staying the barest distance ahead of her until we reached our driveway.

"Alright," she said. The sweatier she was, the thicker her southern drawl came in. I made it a priority to bring it out. "But don't you go gettin' all high and huffed when I say the exact same thing to you later."

I swooped in to take her off her feet, carrying her the rest of the way up the driveway and through the front door the way a groom does his newly wed bride. Her heartbeat was a fluttering bird against me, full and fragile with life.

I leaned down, feigning to kiss her but instead whispered in her ear. "Oh, I know how to earn it."

Chapter 6

My clumsy footfall thumps ugly against the neighborhood's early morning quiet. The winding residential streets are free of cars and barely any of the houses have lights on behind kitchen and sitting room windows. No one's in a rush to get the day started or in a hurry out the door. Even the tabby cat moves at a sleepy pace as she slinks across the street and beneath a garden hedge. Morning birds sing a medley of songs, and I apologize for ruining the peaceful scene as I run through, sneakers slapping on concrete.

In high school I suffered an awkward growth spurt. Half a year shot me up six inches, leaving me still short but with the added bonus of nothing working right. The simple act of walking had me tripping over my own feet and anything of higher physical demand than that was an ungainly disaster. How it felt to run back then, disconnected and disjointed, reminds me of how it feels now. My legs don't remember the proper rhythm and are out of sync with my breathing. My cussing under my breath at how uncoordinated I am doesn't help matters.

I haven't felt this out of shape since completing Ranger School. After two months, a couple of fractures, a hernia

I didn't tell anyone about because I didn't want to be put on medical leave and have to do it all over again, and my metabolism being beaten into an indecisive mess, my body couldn't quite remember how to function normally. I'd suffer through all that again, every day, if in exchange my mind would be my own again and the only voices I'd hear would be my own thoughts.

Give it time, Dr. Day would say. He was constantly reminding me that establishing a working routine was a long-term process and I should be patient. Setbacks were a natural part of recovery and I shouldn't get discouraged or be so hard on myself.

My footfall on the pavement reminds me of the patient *tap-tap-tap* of his pen on the clipboard. To be honest, I don't think I'm hard on myself. The standard I hold for myself is so low a snake couldn't slither under it.

I pick up my pace to outrun the frustration, sustaining the faster step through sheer willpower and the feeble ghost of the fitness I once had.

Dr. Day's advice would have had more impact if I hadn't heard it too many times before I ended up in his office. Friends, family, neighbors, parishioners—they all echoed similar sentiments. I discovered it's impossible for people to offer their condolences without an aluminum foil covered casserole topped off by a scoop of unsolicited wisdom.

Give it time, they'd say and give a sympathetic smile as they shoved another CorningWare dish into my hands.

The old adage of time healing all wounds is complete bunk. Time and waiting don't solve a damn thing.

I'm so busy brooding I almost miss the alarm my overtaxed warning system sends out. My awkward running gait isn't the only thing that's off about this morning. There's a mighty big difference between quiet and silence. Quiet is a good thing. Silence never is.

The morning was quiet. Now it's silent.

The birds aren't singing anymore. The low, insectile hum in the trees is gone. The distant rumble of cars on a far-off arterial has vanished as well, unable to cut through this newly descended hush.

Instinct begs me to run faster. I ignore it, shifting to a slower, more purposeful pace to get a read on the terrain. My hair stands on end as my eyes dart to dark corners where shadows huddle against shuddering leaves that fail to make noise when disturbed. There's no breeze to move them, at least not one I can feel, but they shiver under an unseen presence. The disruption runs a path too straight, too narrow, and too direct to be natural. It's selective in what it disturbs. The wind chimes and flags hanging beside front doors are immune to the approaching force. They remain motionless as the garden leaves and grass beneath them quiver.

I don't have a name for it, but the dead of this world are the least of my hauntings. This is something else—silent, secretive, and unmistakably predatory. It carries all the joy of drinking spoiled milk while simultaneously discovering Lovecraftian creations are escaping their paper and ink prisons.

The grass bends and trees yield away from it as it circles around then falls into pace beside me. Ghosts are unwanted. Whatever this is, it's unholy. And it's no stranger. We're becoming more acquainted than I care for.

I don't remember how or when it started, but I do remember when I could no longer ignore it. The night orderlies ratted me out, thinking me screaming myself awake was a problem.

The doctors asked and I admitted to the growing sense of being not just haunted, but hunted. The white coats took this as part of PTSD and that *thing* took it as an invitation for it to move in closer. Before I admitted to its existence, all it did was creep at the edges of my senses. It's much bolder now.

The suffocating silence grows stronger, shifting the way you feel a change in air pressure as a storm rolls in. A creeping sepia haze settles over my vision, draining distinction out from the world. Greens fade to brown and the blue sky blisters into a lifeless red. Shapes lose clarity and the road in front of me wavers in and out of focus.

Clozapine did nothing to keep this thing away. It isn't something that can be run or hid from. I don't even think it can be confronted. I just hope it can be endured.

Prayers, broken and unfinished, hiss between my chattering teeth. I keep my eyes fixed ahead, convinced that acknowledging it will give it greater authority to move against me. My footsteps falter and I feel it take that second of vulnerability as invitation to move closer. I could stand my ground and announce, "You don't scare me," with a stone-straight face and Eastwood swagger. But bravado only works against physical adversaries. It and I both know different and there's no point in pretending otherwise. While I don't know what this entity is, what I do know is enough. I know it's evil. And it's intelligent.

Something dark and fast darts out of the corner of my left eye, stopping me cold. I'm stupid enough to pause and stare down the now-empty street, clotted by the reddish-brown hue its presence brings. A dark form silhouetted against the drained, colorless world lurks just far enough to be obscured, close enough to make its presence known.

While I may be stupid enough to make eye contact with evil, I'm not so stupid to investigate it. I force myself back into an even run, as if by acting normal it'll get bored of me. A pointless pretense, I've already expressed too much interest in it for that ploy to work. It coyly picks at the edges of my senses, delighting in slowly wearing me down. It's never shown itself like this before, content to remain a phantom plaguing the corners of my mind.

It matches my step, moving with a loping animal grace, each flicker of movement demanding: *Look at me. Look at me.*

My gaze strains in morbid want to fix on the dark form edging ever closer, causing the sepia veil to darken.

Look at me.

As if guided, my head turns toward it. The sharp screech of rubber on asphalt whips my head back the other way. Unforgiving steel barrels down on me. Seconds stretch out and I see the truck driver's face. His eyes widen, slow motion, in shocked surprise that must mirror my own. The horror of realizing something—in his case, someone—was there much too late.

Asphalt shreds my skin and clothes. I skid and roll across the street, barely missing the truck. The breeze off the swerving vehicle pulls at me as if trying to suck me under the wheels.

Screeching tires burn a trail of acrid rubber as the driver stops the truck in a half-spin onto the nearest lawn.

The world returns in a rush of noise and color. The sepia curtain lifts and life bursts back through. Birds sing from trees returned to their natural soft green. Cars rumble in the distance and a gentle burbling tells of a nearby creek.

"Holy shit!" The driver stumbles out from his truck. "Holy shit! Are you okay?"

He's the textbook example of an Average Joe. Middle-aged, average height, average weight, wearing a collared button-down and work jeans faded by time. On the scale of one-to-threatening, he looks to be about a rung or two above spilled vanilla. He definitely doesn't fit the profile for the kind of guy who purposely tries to put a couple of tire tracks over an unobservant jogger.

Average Joe rushes over and pulls me to my feet as if that will erase the last nine seconds. His hands are rough from a career of blue collar work and are shaking so bad he rattles me.

"Oh God, I'm so sorry! I didn't see you," he says, wide eyes bugging out of his skull behind thick-framed glasses.

"Yeah, I didn't see you either," I say, brushing blood and grit from my legs. While Average Joe is about to have a stroke, I'm on the verge of laughing. The adrenaline rush coupled with the return of life to the world has me on a giddy high. There's nothing quite like flirting with the Pale Rider to make you feel alive.

Average Joe left the truck engine running when he rushed over. The country song playing on the radio is losing the battle against the angry roar of static crashing through.

"Are you okay?" he asks again. "I didn't hit you, did I? Oh God, you're bleeding. I can call an ambulance or drive you to the hospital if you want."

The lyrics buzz out in a flare of white noise, and a familiar voice comes through.

"Today's news cycle is a massive dumpster fire of gshkk-gshkk I'm Maria Ch-shkkshkk-"

"Nah, it's fine," I say to both Average Joe and the radio. "My fault. I wasn't paying attention."

"I just . . . I didn't see you," Average Joe says. His wide eyes narrow as his brow knits down in confusion. He looks around and I know he's trying to figure out how he missed me until I was almost kissing his bumper. The road is straight. No corners, trees, or shrubs hamper visibility. The sun isn't even in the right place to cause a glare.

"It's no big deal." Emboldened by the world turned right and against better judgment, I look around for that dark shape. It's nowhere to be found. The front door to the nearest home swings open and a woman in her bathrobe runs down the driveway toward us, slippers slapping against the cement.

"Are you boys okay?" she asks, cell phone clutched in hand, ready for dialing.

"No, we're—"

"Fine," I say to her. Average Joe is so pale he looks like he was the one who almost got turned into road paste.

"I didn't see you," he repeats, more asking for an explanation than giving one.

I shrug. "You alright?"

"Yeah, yeah," he says, "I . . . are you sure you're okay?"

"It's fine," I say again before jogging off. Average Joe and Slipper Lady call out after me and I wave without looking back, hoping the gesture was appropriately polite for whatever they said.

Hot bloody rivulets mix into the cold sweat running down my leg. They drip down to the street and leave the perfect trail for my dark stalker to follow.

Chapter 7

I manage to cover the remaining distance between me and the Roadhouse without any ghosts, ghouls, or other incorporeal creatures seeking my company. That gets me daring to hope the day might improve. It doesn't seem too much to ask, and there's plenty of room for upward mobility.

No one is at the front desk to see me stagger drunk-like in to the Roadhouse. The stairs are stacked miles apart as I climb up to my room. I'm halfway up the flight when adrenaline peters out and can no longer suppress the murmurings. A skin-crawling wave of whispers washes over me and drags me back down into the standard sensation of feeling half-drowned. I've given up on trying to keep a clean divide between imagination and reality so I can't be sure if the derisive edge to the murmurings is an actual change or just me.

I freeze when I find my room unlocked. Standing in the hall, my hand gripping the door knob, I frantically try to remember if I left without locking it. I listen through the mocking chorus of murmurs, certain I'll hear footsteps or something more sinister moving behind the thin wood door. I don't hear any physical presence but the incessant whispering voices following after me don't do anything to help my paranoia.

Muscles bone-snappingly tense, I push the door open and am greeted by a motel room in the exact disarray I left it. Nothing is missing and nothing, not even a hallucination, is where it shouldn't be. I check under the bed and in the closet, and am met by nothing more sinister than dust and empty hangars. Just to be sure, I leave all the lights on despite the bright and plentiful summer morning light streaming through the window before turning on the shower. There's a fresh sweat clamming my skin as I step under the water and my ribs feel like they're digging into my lungs I'm wound so tight, waiting for the man's or Silvia's voice to find me again.

"Come on." I thump my head against the shower wall's tiles. "Get a grip."

Being jackrabbit skittish isn't going to do anything except give me premature heart problems.

I thought I was past every unexplained noise, small movement, and slightest chill putting me on edge. I hoped that I was past questioning if every sound without obvious source or shadowy shape out of the corner of my eye was imagined.

"God, help me," I plead in the flat tones of a prayer given with no expectation of an answer, thumping my head against the shower wall a few more times.

I used to think that if a shower sans wife took more than nine minutes it was life wasted. Now, I'm more than ready to hide here for a few hours. Beneath the pattering stream I can pretend the murmurings are nothing more than an echo of the falling water.

Self-disgust eventually motivates me to turn off the water. Steam from the shower has blurred the mirror over so there's only a vague familiarity to my fogged reflection. Wiping away the condensation would remove that vague familiarity and reveal a complete stranger. I don't bother to shave. The five o'clock shadow nicely matches the dark circles blossoming beneath my eyes that give me the look of a man who got into a fistfight with the Sandman and lost.

Cooling water drips from my too-long hair. I push it away and the damp strands immediately flop back over my forehead. Once out of the army, I abandoned the aggressive buzzed clip I'd worn for the past three years. Now my hair is long enough that it needs pushing back and not quite long enough to stay there. It's the perfect length to be an annoyance while not being worth me mustering up the energy to do anything other than be irritated by it.

As I step out of the bathroom, my fingers do an involuntary twitch at the motel room's state. The bed is unmade and the sheets lay in a heap on the floor from my graceless awakening this morning. Somehow the single duffel bag of my belongings has exploded its contents across most of the limited floor space. The disorder irritates hard-taught habits but it can't quite inspire action.

I pull on yesterday's clothes sitting crumpled on top of the bed because pulling out my second and only other pair of jeans and a new shirt requires more effort than it's worth. I used to not have to belt the pants and the shirt's cut is meant for a healthier man.

Muffled voices reach out to me and I flinch before realizing it's only the people in the next room over. Their laughter sounds more alien than the murmurings.

The temptation to fall back into bed and lie there is fierce. The mattress is right there. I'd only need to fall sideways down onto it. I grab the sheets off the floor and throw them over the pillows in a half-hearted effort to make the bed if only to stop me from crawling back in. I toss my duffel bag on top as well for good measure, making it another thing I'd have to move before I could give in to the desire to hide from the day.

This time when I leave the room, I lock the door, check the door, unlock the door, open the door, relock the door, and check to be sure it stays locked before heading back down to the lobby.

"Did you lose your key?" a woman asks when she sees me fiddling.

No, ma'am, I didn't lose the key. I just lost my mind somewhere in the Hindu Kush mountains.

"Nah, the lock just sticks a bit," I say and give a smile that probably looks as strange as it feels.

Maybelle sits behind the reception desk, reading a paperback with a worn down cover suggesting it's an old favorite. A platter of fresh pecan muffins sits on the counter and the gospel song "Peace in the Valley" preaches lyrics on persevering through tired weariness from a set of travel-sized speakers. She looks up as I try to walk out giving her only a brief nod in greeting. She doesn't let me off that easy.

"Good morning, Mr. Dalaguerre, I hope you had a good night's rest," she says, doing a more amusing than accurate imitation of how I speak. The overly stiff formality doesn't survive her smile. "Would you care for a muffin, hon?"

"Thank you, ma'am," I say without taking one.

"Call me May," she says. "My boys only called me 'ma'am' when they knew they were in trouble. Speaking of trouble, your parents and your sister left messages at the front desk. They've been trying to reach you since last night."

"Oh," I say and don't add the second part of "shit." Looks like ignoring those phone calls coming in last night wasn't my greatest idea, but being harassed by the dead has a tendency to distract me from keeping in contact with the living. I got a good idea of what played out when I didn't show up as scheduled at Kitty's doorstep—she called our folks, they called the police to find out where their mentally disturbed son had wandered off to, got a hold of Sheriff Suarez and then all but set the Ranger Roadhouse's phone afire trying to get a hold of me.

"They sounded pretty worried," Maybelle says. "I told them you were fine and I'd tell you to give them a call. Is everything alright?"

"It's nothing," I lie. In attempting to avoid bringing a mess of ghosts and hauntings to Kitty's doorstep, I've gone and pissed off the people who have the power to decide whether or not I take another trip to St. Jude's. Seems like every time I try and step over a pile of shit, I trip and fall into a bigger one.

Maybelle's blue eyes narrow behind her grandma glasses as if she's really seeing me for the first time and it ain't a pretty sight. "You sleep alright, hon?"

The radio sings out the chorus of an eventual peace to come. Someday.

"Like a dream," I say, "but I'll be needing a cup of joe if you know a good place to grab breakfast."

The fortitude bestowed only by the power of morning coffee is a must before plunging into the fray of damage control and returning family phone calls. And it gives me an excuse to put it off an hour more. I'm hearing enough voices as is, so I'm in no rush to invite more into the conversation. Particularly those of disapproving parents and an angry older sister.

"Donna's Corner," Maybelle says. "Best hash you'll ever have."

"Perfect. Would you be so kind as to direct me?"

"Oh sure, it's just down the road a piece. Go north, take a left and it's on Chinkapin Oak Drive. Can't miss it."

"Thank you, ma'am."

"You sure you're alright? It wasn't too noisy for you?" she asks.

"Quietest night I've had in a long while," I say, halfway out the front door.

"Mr. Dalaguerre," she calls after me.

She holds up the largest, top-heavy muffin of the batch and arches her eyebrow in an expression approaching admonishment. "You forgot your muffin."

***

The summer sun has already beat morning into sweltering submission. A thick-leaved oak shading a generous portion of the parking lot spared my car from being turned into an oven and it only needs the air conditioner on the high Arctic setting for a few minutes before I can hold the steering wheel and not chance third-degree burns.

"Good morksshkkshh gang. This isshhhk . . ." the radio greets me before fizzling out into a quiet that I doubt will last long.

"If you start up this early in the morning, I'll borrow one of those rifles Maybelle has hanging on her walls and blast you to kingdom come," I say as I pull out of the parking lot.

The radio busts out some laughing static.

"Yeah, I know," I say, "I don't take me seriously either."

"Peace in the Valley" sings out for a quick, encouraging chorus before the radio fizzles into quiet.

Turns out I could have walked to Donna's Corner, less than a mile away from the motel. The diner's air conditioning on full blast creates an ice box oasis escape from the summer heat.

Red vinyl booths and bar stools lined in white and chrome atop a checkered floor ensure the restaurant would be at home in any decade within living memory. Bacon and sausage sizzle on the griddle, adding another layer of grease to the diner already richly saturated in the scents of coffee, batter, and syrup.

The speaker system plays out a Benny Goodman number. Enthusiastic clarinets sing out over the *clink* and *clank* of cheap silverware scraping on cheaper plates, relaxed conversation, cooks calling out readied orders, and an overtaxed griddle's incessant spit and snap.

A few customers have settled into booths, buttering toast and pouring ketchup over their hash brown and eggs. Aside from a mother and her two toddlers, the people who've chosen to sit down for a meal belong to an older crowd who have a taste for the slower pace of life. The customers who order coffee and breakfast to go from the counter are younger, dressed for work in slacks and ties, scrubs, and a smattering of uniformed shirts sporting business logos.

I make no effort to hide my disapproval as a woman busies past me, sucking down her coffee with vampiric relish. She doesn't notice. She's too busy bumping her nose against her phone screen, thumb working furiously.

"Coffee black, please," I say, when I reach the counter.

"Sure thing, for here or to go?" The young lady behind the counter asks with the chipper sincerity that only comes from someone who genuinely likes people.

"For here," I say firmly. Taking coffee to go is a sin against all that is good and holy. Coffee in the morning means you're confident that you not only have time to brew it, but time to drink it in a civilized fashion. It's not some IV caffeine fuel drip. It's a self-assured declaration that for at least half an hour, no one is going to shoot at you or try to otherwise disrupt your existence in a manner that'd stop you from finishing a simple drink of brewed bean juice in relative peace.

Anyone who behaves otherwise goes against every principle America has fought for.

"Sure thing!" Chip says. The ponytail peeking out from beneath her diner cap bounces from barely contained zeal. "Anything else? Bagel? Breakfast sandwich?"

Her enthusiasm is too earnest to disappoint, so I grab an apple from the basket on the counter to add to the order.

"Alright, you have a good one!" Chip's grin defies human anatomy to stretch a few extra inches. I like her.

My wife's work day began early. Her first show kicked off at six-thirty in the morning and I refused to let the early hour eliminate a proper morning ritual. She liked to grumble every time I woke her up at 4:15 a.m. to have coffee and breakfast with me. I was never fooled and took savage pride when I overheard her bragging to her coworkers at an office Christmas party that her husband made the best damn banana pancakes. Because I do. The trick is to use buttermilk and vanilla.

I take a seat a safe distance away from the two toddlers and their battle-weary mother to ensure I'm out of range. The kids look close to breaking down into a scrambled-egg throwing temper tantrum and the mother has that beaten look where she knows prevention is a lost cause and cleanup the impending inevitability. Already she's gathered all the napkins within arm's reach. Resigned but ready.

The chatter of the people in the diner pricks at me like windblown sand scraping over skin. I turn the mug around in my hands, retreating away from the diner to a different place and time. The brush of the unseen murmurs in my head and the living voices in the diner roll off into the distance. I can hear the frogs and mockingbirds Maria and I listened to as we sat on the back porch. Feel the creak of the swing, swaying slow and easy. Her curled up against me, petite frame lost in the oversized T-shirt she stole from me. The floral smell of her shampoo. The way she'd sigh before tucking her head beneath mine.

Gravel crunches impossibly loud to jar me back to attention. An old, well cared for pickup pulls into the parking lot. Combat boots followed by ripped leggings swing out and a young woman, early twenties by the looks of her, follows.

She must have decided her dark brown hair was too pretty to be left alone and reduced it to a choppy rebellious cut completed by bubblegum-pink streaks toward the front. The short, nearly shaved side of Rebel Girl's hair shows off an ear containing more piercings in it than I'd allow a daughter of mine to have total. A silver barbell pierced through her eyebrow shines above eye makeup so thick it makes molasses look watery. Her sleeveless shirt hangs loose and shows off arms sporting a couple New-Age-mandala-like pattern tattoos that she definitely did not clear with her mother before she got.

The piercings, hair, and tattoos almost distract from that she is very pretty, and very, very pregnant. The slack shirt has nowhere near the needed bagginess to hide that she's well into her third trimester. All the loose shirt does is emphasize that she looks far too petite to be carrying around the extra weight.

The bell at the front door dings as she enters and she bites her lip in concentration, digging deep into the oversized bag hanging off her arm. Instead of finding the elusive wallet or phone she's searching for, she drops her car keys. They clatter to the diner floor, an impossible distance for her to reach as she's thoroughly blockaded by her baby bump, and she stares down at them the way a man stranded at sea looks at the hole in his boat.

"Here," I say, getting up to retrieve the fallen keys for her.

"Thanks," Rebel Girl says. Her hand absentmindedly drifts to rest on her stomach. When she sees me looking she jerks it away and blushes. In a second the blush is gone as her face pales as she does a rapid double take over me. Her mouth opens and quickly snaps shut before she drops her eyes from meeting mine to stare down hard at the checkered floor. The skittishness doesn't match her bold attire and seeing her up close gives a better look behind all the makeup, tattoos, and piercings to show her age is south of what I originally guessed. She's probably closer to seventeen or eighteen.

"Don't worry about it, ma'am," I say when she moves to get in line, eyes fixed on the floor. "You go ahead and sit down. Just tell me what you wanna order, I'll take care of it."

She looks back up at me as if I'm some sort of alien species who crash-landed in her backyard, her black-lined eyes saucer plate wide.

"Are you alright?" I ask.

"Oh, um yeah . . . I'm fine." She shakes her head, my offer finally registering. "You don't need to do that."

"Humor me, I insist."

"The breakfast sandwich with peach tea instead of coffee, please," she says, handing me a ten and a five.

I take the bills because I know she'll protest if I don't. I return them to her when I bring over the breakfast to the booth she's claimed.

"I . . . thanks," she says. "You didn't have to do that."

Her nervousness complicates what was supposed to be a simple gesture of basic decency.

"I've seen four of my sisters go through this," I say. "Trust me, they'd tan my hide if I hadn't."

"Wait! Wait! You can sit down if you want!" she calls after me as I start back to my table. She bites her lip when I don't move either way. Her face is soft, sweet, and I bet without the makeup and piercings she'd look too young to drive.

"I'm not expecting anyone. Well, you know"—she motions to her stomach—"except him. And I mean, only if you want to."

I hope my discomfort at the thought of trying to carry on a conversation with a teenager who I probably got nothing in common with doesn't show. One of the advantages of marrying my wife was she handled all conversations with strangers. Matrimony allowed absolute delegation of the art of small talk to my better half.

My mind kicks into overdrive to find a way to turn down the invitation and not be rude—difficult as Rebel Girl looks so desperate for company. Remembering how thrown off she seemed by an attempt at kindness, my heart sinks, and it's pity instead of courtesy that convinces me to join her. Poor kid.

She's equal parts thrilled and surprised when I grab my poor excuse for breakfast and sit down across from her. Fortunately, she proves much more graced than I am in the art of striking up conversation.

"So you have four sisters?" she asks.

"Five," I say, planning out possible topics of small talk and how they can lead to an early escape that doesn't seem rushed or rude.

"Older or younger?" All her shyness has evaporated and I wouldn't be surprised if she started bouncing up and down from excitement.

"Older."

"Wow. I thought I was bad off with three older brothers. So you're the baby of the family, yeah? Me too," she says, easily working around my rusty conversation skills. "I got an older sister too, but we didn't have a lot in common growing up so it was more like every girl for herself. We get along a lot better now, but my mom says all her grey hairs came from us, not the boys."

"Huh," I say.

"Do I know any of your sisters?" she asks then shakes her head, "No, I don't."

"My sister just moved here not too long ago, so probably not," I say. I can't imagine Kitty mingling in the same social circle as the kid sitting across from me. "I didn't even know this town existed until she told us her new address."

"So why are you staying at a motel instead of with her?" she asks.

I stare and Rebel Girl trips over her words as she tries to backpedal and explain.

"I saw the key when you got out your wallet to buy my breakfast, which thanks again for that, you didn't have to. And I'm not trying to be creepy or anything, I just saw it and my dad's a cop so we kinda grew up being told to pay attention to these sorts of things."

She says this all like a very rushed apology.

I don't have a response so she charges back in to rescue the endangered conversation.

"So how long are you staying in town for?"

"I was thinking of checking out the folk festival," I say to redirect the subject away from me.

"Yeah?" Her eyes light up. Her eagerness to chat with a total stranger makes me wonder if the baby she's carrying is the closest thing she has to a confidant. I want to ask where the father is, but despite her hands being bedecked in rings I don't see any that look like one from a wedding or engagement.

"COME ON."

Instinct whips my head around. The tables behind me are empty.

Dammit, I thought I had worked through being so jumpy.

"Come on . . ." Silvia calls again, urgent and harsh.

"Logan, are you okay?" Rebel Girl asks from miles away.

The swing music playing over the sound system drops out in the middle of a clarinet solo. I glance around. None of the other patrons or employees seem to notice the sudden shift of the sound system playing more static than music.

No, that's not static. It's breathing. Low and rasping from an eager, feral hunger.

"You alright?" Rebel Girl leans forward, fascinated rather than disturbed by my behavior.

"Here."

I swipe my hand over my eyes, blurring under a pulse of sepia, and it's no longer Rebel Girl sitting across the table. It's Silvia as I found her. The diner drops away and I'm staring down at the empty-eyed husk in a dry field beneath a spinning blue sky.

"Logan?" Lips stripped away can't close over the exposed teeth as they speak my name. The coffee in my stomach turns to battery acid. It's not the sight that makes me nauseous. It's that I'm seeing it at all.

"Here. Here. Here."

I shake my head and Rebel Girl, healthy and whole, sits across from me.

"I just remembered," I say, "I was supposed to call my sister last night. Gotta go."

She says something I can't hear over the murmurings pounding in my ears. I force myself to finish my coffee. Hallucinations and hauntings be damned, I'm not going to let that break the morning ritual that holds Western civilization together. I'm already crossing a line with my irreverent rush of downing the last of the mug.

Rebel Girl keeps talking at me, head tilted to the side as her brow furrows. At least she looks concerned and not terrified.

"It was great meetin' you," I say, already halfway to the door. "Might see you 'round."

She stares at me through the diner window, wide eyes unreadable as she watches me round the diner's corner and out of sight. The car radio is on before the engine. A voice masked by static cuts in and out before fading over to Cash's country tune.

Stomp. Clap. Stomp.

"What?!" I bang my fist down on the dashboard. "What do you want?"

The volume surges then dips, reprimanding me for the emotional outburst.

I lean back in the car seat, rubbing the dark circles beneath my eyes. "Just tell me what you want. Please."

I learned to lie about hearing voices. Trained myself to stop startling every time an unseen mouth spoke. To pretend the noises haunting me at all hours had faded away. To lie to anyone who asked and say that prescriptions and men in white coats writing on clipboards had solved it all. I mumbled, nodded, and agreed my way through the psychiatric evaluations until they believed they'd made the necessary progress. Other than Dr. Day, a system founded on academic self-congratulation wasn't too hard to figure out and work.

I used to wish for days when there would be no haunting voices. Now I wish for days when it will be just the voices and no cold fingers running up my arms, taps on the shoulder, or stalking presences breathing down my neck. No motel rooms slipping into rotted shacks, living faces turning into rotted corpses. And I would take all of that, the voices, the visions, suffer all of it every day if it meant never having to see that entity—

I shudder and grip the steering wheel as if it's a life ring.

The flicker of Silvia's desiccated face over Rebel Girl's has me more rattled than the episode at the bar last night. I'm not much of a natural ghost whisperer so I don't have any great insight into what it means other than that Silvia is dead and wants to talk about it.

That the field I found her in keeps cropping back up alongside her repetitive chorus of "here" could mean she wants me to go back to where I found her. There might be a clue of some sort, some damning evidence her killer dropped when he dumped her. Or maybe since her body was sitting there so long, her haunting station gets the best reception out there and a clearer message can come through.

Or it could mean none of that and my literal interpretation of the limited bits of vocabulary she has in death is not at all what she intends. She might not even want me to find her killer and I'm just jumping to conclusions. Maybe she has a message for a family or friend she never got to say. I don't know. I don't speak ghost very well.

"Any suggestions?" I ask the radio. The station dial skitters up and down but emits no sound.

I exhale through pressed lips. I'm a simple man with enough miles on life to know it ain't an easy trip. So for the sake of consistency, I'll always pick the simple over the easy. I choose to run with the simple idea Silvia is trying get through to me and I'm too thick to put it all together, over the easy excuse I'm suffering psychosis and all the complications that brings.

I'll check out the Lopez home first. It's closer than where Silvia's body was and might give me better context to understand what she's trying to get across. I'll wait until it's dark before driving out to the field just in case it's still being treated as a crime scene. Sheriff Suarez doesn't strike me as the kind of guy to tolerate meddling mediums tromping around an ongoing investigation. Particularly ones who are fresh out of the psychiatric ward.

My cellphone vibrates for a seventeenth missed call and voicemail from Kitty, reminding me that my line to Rebel Girl wasn't just an excuse to leave. I really do need to call my sister.

"Hey, Kitty. Wh—"

"Where the hell are you?" Her tone is teeth-cutting sharp and spells all manner of trouble. She usually reserves this short a fuse for when she's losing at Euchre or when her oldest daughter reminds her that she is very much her mother's child.

"I'm fine. How are you?"

"That ain't what I asked, Logan."

"I'm in Encrucijada."

"Yeah, I heard. From the sheriff."

"So then you know I'm checked into a motel and everything is fine."

"And you didn't think to call and tell me or Mom and Dad this because . . .?"

"Because I didn't think to call and tell you."

"Logan . . ." I can hear her fighting back the chewing out she wants to give me. And, to be fair, the one I deserve.

"Where are you now?" she asks.

"In my car."

"Oh, God, you're not driving right now are you?" Kitty's enforcement of no phones while driving became tyrannical after her husband backed her new car into a basketball pole while taking a call from a client.

"No."

"When're you getting here?"

I don't answer because I don't have one she wants to hear. Accepting Kitty's offer to stay under her roof means accepting her rules and that won't work at all with Silvia determined to hang around.

"Are you at the motel right now?"

"No."

"Alright, tell me exactly where you are and you stay there," she says. "I'm sending Mark over to get you."

"No. You're not."

"Don't take that tone."

"I'm not taking any tone!"

"Then why are you shouting?"

"Kitty, you need to stop treating me like I—"

"Like you were let out from a mental hospital a month ago and then didn't show up last night like you said you would and didn't tell me where you were and then ignored all my calls?"

I was going to say "like I'm fucking four," but she put it better.

"I didn't check my phone," I say.

"You realize Mom and Dad were calling the police to file a missing person's report when the sheriff told them where you were." Her mom voice is gone. Her I'm-the-oldest voice is roaring in with gale force vengeance.

"Well, I'm not missing. I'm right here." I stab my finger into the driver's seat to emphasize the point. "And I'm fine."

I'm not sure if she's exaggerating about our parents being on the verge of sending everyone from neighborhood watch to the National Guard out looking for me. It's safer not to stick on that point.

"Watch your sass, kiddo. And no, you're not," she says. "You are certifiably not fine."

"Point," I say. She's right to call me out on that one, but what's wrong with me isn't something that can be fixed. Not by nodding shrinks and another prescription. It gets pretty damn irritating when everyone is jumping in to fix a problem you don't have. The living and the dead would cause me a lot less grief if both of them paid me the simple courtesy of minding their own business.

"I booked a room for a few nights," I say.

"Logan—"

"I'll come over after."

"Logan—"

"I'll call you when I check out."

"Do not hang—"

I hang up the phone, feel guilty about it, hold out for ten seconds, and then redial. She picks up on the first ring.

"Why're you doing this?" she asks.

"I . . ." I can't string anything together. There are points in life when you're not told *why*, you're just told *do*. I'm doing this because I'm supposed to. I don't think Silvia would be asking for my attention this hard if there wasn't something I could do about it. Even if she wasn't reaching out to me, I don't think I could let this go. I just don't exactly know what *this* is so I don't have an answer that can be articulated.

"I need time," I say lamely. "Everything since . . . everything keeps happening and I can't . . . I just want to be away from it all for a couple days."

There's enough truth in that last part to get a pass from her.

"I don't think you should be alone," she says.

Oh, trust me, Kitty, I wish I was.

"Look, I haven't had any time to myself since . . ." I can't say it. No one's left me alone since Maria. . . . "I'm twenty minutes away. I just need to get my bearings. It's just a few days."

"Are you taking your medication?" she asks.

No.

"I've got more pills than an octogenarian," I say.

I've got to tread carefully around Kitty. She's always had a bullshit detector strong enough to sift out the smallest grain of a white lie. Having five kids has only heightened this. There's no tattling in that household 'cause her sixth sense knows her twelve-year-old did something wrong before he slinks in through the back door.

"Do you want Mark or me to come see you? I can stop by, just to make sure everything is alright. I'd only be in your hair for five minutes, if that."

"No. Thanks, but I'm okay. Really. I'll call you tonight. I need a few days where no one is checking in on me every hour. I'd like there to be more to life than pills and therapists."

"Fine. But you can't ignore your phone. When I call, you pick up. And you need to tell me where you're going and what you're planning on doing today."

"I was thinking about checking out the folk festival," I say.

"Yeah, that might be good for you," she says. "Okay, call me tonight. And Logan, if you don't call . . ." She lets the sentence hang for me to come up with my own threat.

"I'll see you later," I say.

"Call me tonight."

"Sure thing."

"I mean it."

"Wait, Kitty," I say before she can hang up.

"What?" she asks, and I can hear her four-year-old making incessant demands for juice in the background.

"Could you call Mom and Dad to tell them I'm alright? And not tell them I'm not there with you unless they ask?" I say, acting like I'm sixteen instead of twenty-six. "I don't want them to worry."

"Oh, kid." Her laugh is absent of humor. "They are way beyond worrying about you."

I hold the phone to my ear long after the call disconnects. Rebel Girl waddles out of the diner and clambers into her pickup. The radio hiccups out static as she sits in the truck cab, engrossed in her cellphone, and Silvia's voice calls out to me.

"Here. Here. Here."

Chapter 8

I accept that a shaded parking spot being available at the Ranger's Roadhouse is one of the better things that'll happen to me today and enjoy it for all it's worth. My earlier hopes that today would improve have shifted down to a more realistic desire that at the very least, the day doesn't get too much worse.

Guitar strumming and the festival crowd's growing babble carry over from Main Street. By afternoon it will be a roar as the number of attendees swells.

Maybelle is sitting on the shaded front porch with a couple of women in their late teens. They may be old enough to vote, definitely not old enough to drink. A perspiring pitcher of sweet tea and a platter of pecan muffins sits between them.

"Whatcha doin' back here, son?" Maybelle calls out. "There's a whole world to see outside this dusty old roadhouse."

"Just dropping off the car," I say. "Town's small enough I don't need it."

"Main Street ain't the only place to find some fun," Maybelle says. "A fair number of ranches 'round the area help to host and have shows of their own, but most of those are later in the day 'round evening. I've got brochures listing the places and times at the front desk if you'd like. But all you gotta do is drive out down the road a piece and you'll run into one sooner or later. You might be able to hitch a ride as well—with so many folk going out and back that way you can always find a lift."

"Thank you, ma'am," I say. "I'll check it out."

"Son," Maybelle says sternly, "ya'll know that smilin' ain't a sin?"

The two young women sitting with her giggle. They're both wearing cutoff shorts, oversized sunglasses, and the invincible confidence that dries up after you turn twenty-four.

I smile at her to show I do know. The two women giggle louder.

"Might want to practice that smile some, hon," Maybelle says and I feel sincerity creep into my stiff grin.

"Now that's the ticket," she says. "Care to join us for some sweet tea?"

"Yeah, come and sit with us," one of the girls says. Her friend giggles, either at the thought of me joining them or at how eager her friend sounds.

"No thank you, ma'am. I've just been told there's a whole wide world out there and I suppose I'm overdue to see if that's so." I tip my hat at the women and head south.

3421 Wild Rose Way is only a few miles away and I intend to use the time the walk will take to come up with a plan. The ideal scenario is the Lopezes won't be home. Maybe they'll be at the sheriff's office, receiving the news their daughter's body has been found. Or maybe they already know, Sheriff Suarez called them soon as he could last night, and the family is out making arrangements now that they finally have something to bury.

I wonder if relief outweighs grief in this situation or if it just rips all those old wounds open again.

The feeling of being followed plucks at my paranoia strings as I walk through neighborhoods of brick paved driveways and streets lined by oak and crepe myrtle. The presence doesn't radiate malice like the entity does so I ignore it, reminding myself I probably won't see whatever is haunting me. And if I pretend I don't know it's there, it might leave.

By the time I turn onto Wild Rose Way, I have nine terrible stories and excuses that might get me through the front door but more likely will get it slammed in my face. Turns out, like most of my planning and thinking, it wasn't necessary. A few cars are parked off the Lopezes' front lawn and the front door is wide open. A woman in her late forties, early fifties, hovers at the front step. Her grey hair is twisted away from a face carved by long-standing grief. She's not wearing any black, having mourned long enough for her daughter that such shallow displays are no longer needed.

Mrs. Lopez greets a woman carrying a cake pan smothered under tinfoil. The earlier arrivals who came by to offer condolences are visible through the living room window, standing in loose, limp circles. Every once in a while one will clasp a fellow's shoulder or solemnly pat another person on the back.

The feeling I'm being followed nudges harder at the back of my neck. I turn around and frown. No cold touches, ghostly whispers, or dark formless haunts writhing at the corner of my vision justify the growing suspicion there are eyes on me.

I time my approach to the house to tail after what looks to be a husband, wife, and their adult daughter. The woman I guess to be Mrs. Lopez greets us in a mechanical fashion, shaking hands, thanking us for coming. Her dark eyes are clouded over and miles away. She barely glances up at me as I take my hat off and she shakes my hand, murmuring hollow gratitude for my being here.

The family of three adds their casserole to the growing pile on a credenza before turning into the living room to join their neighbors. Like Mrs. Lopez, hardly anyone is wearing black, and all look more tired than stricken. I blend in seamlessly with this beleaguered gathering. The little snippets of conversation I catch lean towards business over consolation, offering help with funeral arrangements, prayer services, setting a time to come by and help around the home.

I half expect to feel cool fingers tug at me and lead me to something, some room, some secret hidden beneath a bed that would bust this case wide open or at least give me a direction to run.

I get nothing. No cold caress or whisper. None of the faces in the crowd twist to mirror the rotted state I found Silvia in. No crackle of white static from the radio clock sitting on the kitchen counter gives any indication of what Silvia wants me to do.

"Not even a hint?" I ask under my breath to anyone dead who wants to listen. No one, dead or alive, bothers to answer.

I make a cursory pass through the living room, pretending I belong here while looking over the family photos. The smiling faces frozen in frames look more out of place in this home than I am. Silvia, no older than seven, chases bubbles with her younger sister. The two girls are older in the next picture, wearing matching pink and yellow dresses at an Easter egg hunt. Silvia beaming wide in a pink chiffon quinceañera dress, a silver crown in her curled hair. At her high school graduation, arms flung over two friends on either side of her. Silvia and her father at a baseball game. Fishing with her grandparents. Grinning to show off missing front teeth, wearing a soccer uniform of unidentifiable color beneath layers of mud.

A woman pats my arm and smiles sympathetically at me as I stare at the pictures. I give a grim nod and it convinces her I don't want to talk. She leaves me to brood over the photos, but her gesture of kindness is a reminder I have a limited amount of time until someone sniffs me out as an interloper. Already a grandfatherly man with Santa white hair is giving me a suspicious side-eye. It could just be because I haven't shaved and look like a halfway house's black sheep resident. More likely it's because he's got the wisdom to sense I don't belong here.

The murmurings hissing in my ears blend into the gathering of mourners, and after two minutes of dodging through them I get uncomfortable, feeling irreverent in my trespassing on the Lopezes' grief. After four minutes of hovering on the edges of clumps of people talking in low voices, trying to avoid Suspicious Santa, and hoping no one attempts to bring me into a conversation or realize they've never seen me before and ask me how I know the Lopezes, I'm leaning toward the idea coming here was straight up stupid and disrespectful.

To make sure visiting the house wasn't a complete waste of time I decide I'll peek into Silvia's room before heading out to stop sullying the mourners through my inept snooping.

With the age-old bathroom excuse ready in case of questioning, I casual-as-you-please walk up the stairs. Four rooms make up the small second story. The master bedroom, a seaside themed bathroom, a playroom that's been converted into a mash of an office and exercise room with lingering pink fairy-ish décor on the wall trim suitable for a house that raised two daughters, and a second bedroom with a similarly girlish feel.

The bunk bed's sheets are both pink, one covered in stars, the other with white flowers across the bedspread. The beds, the two small desks in the corners along the window wall, and the few articles of clothing hanging in the mostly bare closet look untouched. The single dresser is empty save for a pair of running shorts, socks, and a couple of sweatshirts.

"The bathroom is down the hall."

I turn with all the dignity of a rabbit caught looking at porn. Rebel Girl leans against the doorway. She's got her arms crossed atop her baby bump and is trying so hard to look intimidatingly cool and in control that I instantly relax.

I lean back against the bunk bed and cross my arms in imitation of Rebel Girl's body posture. All it takes is for me to wink and grin, and just like that, she's flustered.

"What are you doing here?" she asks. A breathy nervousness cracks her words.

"Paying my respects. What about you? You wouldn't happen to be following me, would you?"

The last question was supposed to be a joke. A means of lightening the tension. It achieves the exact opposite when Rebel Girl stutters and blushes.

Oh my God. She was following me.

"Silvia was a friend, I was going to come here anyway," she says defensively, "but I saw you walking—"

"Saw me walking where?" Has she been following me since the Roadhouse?

"Just a couple miles from here."

So essentially yes, she's been following me pretty much the whole time. I understand I'm partly to blame in this. How the hell did I miss her truck creeping behind me for two miles?

"Why're you—"

"What were you doing at the sheriff's office yesterday?" she asks.

Oh shit. Now I'm flustered.

"What?" I blink.

"You were talking with the sheriff yesterday," she says, her words tripping over each other as she speaks faster and faster. "You're the one who found her body, yeah?"

I have no idea how she would know that unless I have sorely underestimated the power of small-town gossip. At the very least I have seriously underestimated Rebel Girl.

"What?" I blink again.

"Don't play dumb. How did you find her?" she asks.

"I never have to play dumb," I say.

"Look, I saw you at my dad's office—"

"Your father is Sheriff Suarez?"

"Yeah, that's what I said. Anyway, I see you there and then next thing you know, they finally find Silvia's body. And then you just happen to know where Silvia's family lives, even though you're not from around here, and then you start looking through her room." Rebel Girl takes a deep breath and I hold mine. "So what are you doing?"

I open my mouth but Rebel Girl is too excited to wait. She's shifting from one foot to another, incapable of staying still.

"You think she was murdered, don't you? You do, I know you do!"

I shrug.

Rebel Girl chews her lip with a furious passion and I can almost hear the gears to her brain grinding to strategize a way to get what she wants while she has the advantage.

"You know, she moved out of her parents' house years ago," Rebel Girl says. "If you're looking for clues, you might find them where she actually lives . . . I mean lived."

"For Silvia being your friend, you don't seem too broken up about finding out she's dead," I say.

"I knew she was dead a long time ago," Rebel Girl snaps, and she sounds genuinely offended. "I'm just mad everyone wasted time pretending she ran off or something and were too busy praying she'd come home, when they should've been looking for the guy who killed her!"

"Knew how?" I ask.

"I . . ." Rebel Girl bites back whatever she was about to say. "I just knew, okay? Silvia wouldn't have run away like that. And I could feel it, you know? Besides, Dad always says after 72 hours he starts looking for a body. But even after a couple weeks, people were still trying to pretend she was just lost. Like she took a wrong turn driving home and would be back any minute or something. It took you finally finding her for people to admit she was dead and someone killed her."

"I'm sorry, who are you?" I ask. Maybe it's her connection to the police, or that she followed me for two miles, or maybe it's just that she's brimming with barely repressed excitement in a house of mourning, but Rebel Girl raises my hair almost as much as when I'm woken up by the lips of the dearly departed pressing against my ear.

"My name's Glenny." Her handshake has a strength you wouldn't expect from such a small hand with fingernails painted cotton-candy pink.

"That short for something?"

"Glen Ellen," she says. "But only my mom calls me that. Did someone hire you?"

"Hire me?" I start working out an escape route. Aided by her baby, Glenny is doing a top-notch job of barricading the door. If worse comes to worst, the bedroom window is within sprinting distance and if I remember correctly, there is a flower bed beneath it to cushion the fall.

"You know, like a private investigator, to find out who killed her?"

"Oh, no," I say. "My sleuthing services are only of the pro bono quality."

"But someone did ask you to solve this, yeah?" she presses, and the question is obviously leading.

"Uh, sure, I guess you could call it that," I say.

Glenny the Rebel Girl grins. "You should come to my place."

"Excuse me?"

She rolls her eyes over a blush. "Not like that. I mean, come to my place 'cause it's Silvia's . . . well it was, her place and . . ." She shoots me an angry look like it's my fault she's rambling. "Silvia and I were roommates in a house across town. All her stuff is still there so, I don't know, maybe being there might help you sense and"—she wiggles her fingers like a spider reeling in web—"find something?"

That's the best lead and possibly the weirdest unintended pickup line I've ever received, so I nod. Why not?

From her reaction, you'd think I had agreed to marry her. She claps her hands together and does a little dance.

"Okay, wait here, I'll be right back," she says.

"What're you doing?" I ask.

"Well, I actually did come up here to use the bathroom." She points at her bladder-crushing belly. "The one downstairs was being used and I really had to go. But this was more important."

So maybe the shifting from foot to foot wasn't because she was antsy. She just really needed to go.

"Don't leave. Please," she says before closing the door to the bathroom at the end of the hall.

I shove my hands into my pockets and let out a tight-lipped sigh. I get the feeling I'm making a mistake when I do wait for her. Not just because she registers in the red for weird on my very liberal spectrum, but that involving a pregnant teenager in my half-baked quest to avenge a murdered woman who I only met after she died might be a terrible idea.

Glenny opens the bathroom door slowly, peeking out as if preparing to be disappointed by the sight of an empty hallway. She looks close to tears of relief when she sees me waiting for her.

"Oh my God. Thanks for not running away. Come on." I wince at her choice of phrasing, unsure if her echoing what Silvia whispers out to me is a sign or an uncomfortable coincidence, as she grabs my hand to lead me down the stairs. Half a step later she stops, and next thing I know she whirls and shoves her face into my chest, her body shuddering with sobs.

My look of surprise and discomfort must've been a good enough pretense for grief because Mrs. Lopez barely blinks when she rounds the corner. Her deadened eyes, bruised purple and bloodshot, slowly move from Glenny sobbing into me, and then to me too late trying to make it look like I'm comforting her, before sliding back into a middle distance.

"Sorry," I mutter to Mrs. Lopez, and gesture at Glenny's shaking form. "She wanted to be alone. We can go."

"No, no," Mrs. Lopez says, voice as flat as her expression as she walks past us to the master bedroom. "It's okay. I know."

Glenny keeps up her crying until the sound of the bedroom door clicks shut behind Mrs. Lopez. She gives an apologetic look up at me as she wipes away tear-stained makeup. "I figured no one would chew us out for being up here if one of us was crying."

"Better you than me." I wriggle out of her hug and vow to wriggle out of this odd partnership as soon as possible.

Chapter 9

"And you know I didn't mean anything, like I expect something *more* with you coming here," Glenny says for the millionth time as we drive farther out from the nicer parts of Encrucijada. "This is strictly professional. I'm not that kind of girl."

I nod to show sympathy for her pregnant-teenager-identity crisis. She takes a right turn off the arterial onto a residential street.

"Who's been paying Silvia's rent?" I ask.

"Her parents. I told you, people kept acting like she was coming back. I mean, I don't blame her mom for that. I guess that was easier than admitting she was gone."

"And who else lives with you?" I ask.

"Nicole and Adrienne are my other roommates," Glenny says, obediently pausing at an empty four-way stop before continuing down the street rowed by small, one-story homes where chain-link fences separate yards filled by cracked paint buckets and dead grass.

"But don't worry about them," she says. "They're both at work. Oh, and they didn't kill her if that's where you were going with that question."

"Shouldn't that worry you?" I ask.

"Why would I be worried about living with people who didn't kill her?"

"You just invited a stranger to your home and then bragged that there's no one there," I point out.

"Oh my God, you sound like my dad. And I know self-defense," she says.

I raise an eyebrow at all one hundred ten pounds of her. Based on her mass distribution, she only poses a minor threat if she tries to hip check me.

"Besides," Glenny continues, "you're hardly a stranger. We've cried together."

"You're misremembering that a bit. And you don't even know my name."

"Yeah, I do. It's Logan."

I frown. I set up that line to give a fake name complete with a fake origin story if she pressed. I'm sure I made a point of not giving her my name when we were at the Lopezes' and I wrack my brain for when I would've let it slip. Did I introduce myself at the diner? I seem to recall her saying my name there. Or maybe it was Silvia who said my name. Jeez, I can't even keep track of whether it's the living or the dead talking to me.

"Logan?" she asks.

"What?"

"You kinda spaced out there for a second so I thought maybe you were going into a psychic trance or something," she says.

"Nope, I just have limited brain power so I gotta operate on power-save mode."

Glenny's lip chewing can't bite back her questions. "So does it help to be in physical contact with something the person owned in life to get in, like, spiritual contact with them?"

"Excuse me?"

Glenny looks over at me like I'm being deliberately dense. "Isn't that why you wear it?"

"Wear what?" I don't know where these questions are coming from and like even less where they're going.

She points to my wedding ring I've been fiddling with. "Your ring. She died, like, a year ago, right? So why else would you wear it?"

I stop playing with the ring as my hands clench into fists.

"What did you say?"

The question was quiet but Glenny winces as if I'd shouted.

"Forget I said that. I didn't mean . . . sometimes I forget and it just slips out," she says, words hurried and rushing into one another.

"How did you know?"

The alarm bells that I ignored when she knew my name and the warnings I tuned out when she showed up at the Lopez house are blaring with a vengeance.

"Who told you?" I ask.

She covers her mouth with one hand and shakes her head.

"Who told you?" I repeat.

"I didn't mean it," she says through her fingers. "Just . . . just forget I said anything, okay?"

And I decide it's time to punch out. I don't need supernatural intrusion to convince me to drop this can of worms unopened. Common sense is enough.

"You mind pulling over for a second?" I ask.

Confusion yanks Glenny's brows together as she brings the pickup to a stop and puts it in park. She turns to me to launch into apology or explanation, but my mind's already made up.

"Hey! What're you doing?" She moves to lock the car doors too late. I'm already unbuckled and off like a prom dress.

Car still running, Glenny throws herself out after me. The truck dings indignantly from the keys left in the ignition and both doors hanging open.

"Wait, Logan, wait!"

I keep walking at a pace fast enough she only gains for a moment before the pregnancy waddle drags her down.

"What're you gonna do? Walk back? May's place is more than five miles away!" she calls after me.

That additional slip of her knowing where I'm staying convinces me this whole escapade was a huge mistake ended none too soon. I'm gonna go back to the motel, grab my bag, and put this weird-ass investigation with preternaturally nosy pregnant girls and chatty dead ones behind. Sorry, Silvia, but there's too much strange sauce in this dish for me to handle. And here I was lecturing Glenny on stranger danger without considering the shitstorm I might be walking into.

I ignore Glenny's pleading for me to stop, to slow down, her saying she's sorry. That she didn't mean to. That she can explain. For me to at least let her drive me back to the Ranger's Roadhouse. The radio in her truck starts humming out a tune I recognize but am too far away to place.

I ignore that as well because I'm done, done with it all. I should never have even played with this business of ghosts, dark entities, and muffled voices. Shouldn't have even gone out to find Billy—

Cold, angry nails dig in to me. They claw and tug me back toward the pregnant girl chasing after me.

"Logan, please!" I can hear the tears making her voice tremble.

If I hadn't seen her put on fake waterworks less than fifteen minutes ago I might've stopped.

"It's okay! I know you're like me! You know things too!"

The murmuring voices pitch up into a shattering din. Just keep walking, I tell myself. You're done with this. Keep walking.

The clawing cold cuts in harder. The murmurs grow louder.

Ignore it. Keep walking. I've walked through worse. Go back to the Ranger's Roadhouse, pack up, and hide in your sister's guest room. Enough playing detective. Leave the dead alone, even if they won't return the same courtesy.

Unearthly voices press down hard, closer than just the murmurs. There's an intelligence to it beyond the base emotionalism of the whispers and my skull creaks under the unintelligible din.

"Logan, wait!"

The cold grip shifts into a harsh blow, swift and sudden. I double over, gasping for air. I clutch my stomach, surprised it's still there. It feels like someone shot icy shrapnel through me.

The dirt bucks beneath me and I clutch at it on all fours. The hot summer day is gone, replaced by a barren nothingness. I can't find my feet. Every time I move to stand, the frozen force runs me through and keeps me down.

I can't breathe, my lungs are numb.

"Stop," I beg whatever is causing this. "Stop."

Silvia's voice cuts through the dissonant chaos of the clamoring things lurking behind this world's veil. There are no words to hear. It's an oppressive shriek of fury and frustration. My vision spins as she echoes through my mind and with a heaving retch I splatter the ground in a mess of coffee and apple.

Fingers, warm with life, tentatively touch my shoulder.

"Logan," Glenny says. She's brought the truck around. The radio keeps playing as it idles a foot away. "Are you sure you don't need a ride?"

Chapter 10

aria moved a hand up my back to tease along my shoulder. I rolled away, half asleep, and wholly irritated.

"Stop," I mumbled into the pillow. Her hands were like ice and I knew she was only doing it to annoy me.

She cupped her hand over the back of my neck, fingers tapping against the base of my skull.

"It's not funny," I growled. "Knock it off."

The clear fluid had finally stopped leaking from my ears but the headaches clung on tight, making me testy. Especially when someone drummed their fingers against my skull.

"I said stop."

She didn't stop. She kept tapping, cold and steady.

"Maria, stop!" I yelled, throwing off the covers.

I blinked in confusion at my gloomy surroundings. I forgot I was in the guest room, not in our bed. My tossing and turning kept her up, so most nights I dragged myself to the spare room to ensure only I was bleary-eyed and exhausted in the morning.

A light clicked on in the hallway, firing sharp blinding shots through my pounding head.

"Logan?" Maria stood silhouetted in the doorway, a

bathrobe hanging loosely from her.

"I . . . sorry." I rubbed the back of my neck. "I didn't mean to wake you."

The drumming on my neck continued beneath my hand. Cold creeping strokes down my arms and chest joined in with the invisible drummer.

"Was it a dream?" she asked.

"No, it's . . ." I was so unsure of what it was I couldn't even come up with a lie for it.

"Are you okay?" she asked.

"I don't know" was the right answer. Instead I nodded as she sat down next to me. I could explain away the whispering voices as some weird form of tinnitus. The doctor said it might continue for a while. Even the odd shapes that kept flickering in the corners of my eyes could all be part of the vision blurring. But I had no idea what was causing the cold spells. Or why they felt so intelligent.

"Is it your head?" she asked. She cupped my chin, gently tilting my head to check my ears. Her hands were warm.

"It's just a headache. I'm going to see if I can get an appointment for tomorrow," I said. Pulling the heavy duvet over me did nothing to keep away the cold. "Make sure it's just a cerebrospinal fluid leak."

Maria pursed her lips.

"What?" I asked.

"It took me weeks to convince you to go to the doctor when you had fluid dripping out your brain," she said. "It must be something real serious if you're going to the doctor without me nagging you."

"Just want to make sure," I said, lying back down.

"Make sure what? Logan, please, what's wrong?" she asked.

Shaking my head hurt.

"I don't know," I admitted.

She leaned forward to kiss me on the forehead. That didn't hurt.

"Come back to bed," she said.

"I don't want to keep you up," I said.

"Logan." She took my hand, hers warm, mine shaking. "Come on."

***

"Come on."

The phrase repeats with each pound of my head.

"Is it always like that?" Glenny asks. She sits a safe distance away on a chair that looks like it was a stray rescued from the roadside where the previous owner abandoned it. The futon I'm lying on is of similar ilk, old, used, and sporting a few strange stains not completely hidden by the black fabric.

Despite my valiant efforts to display a manly toughness in insisting I could walk back to the Ranger's Roadhouse, Glenny ended up driving me to her place, arguing it was closer. Tiny as she is, she did a remarkable job of navigating me through an entryway choked by enormous bags hanging from coat racks and booby-trapped with sinisterly spiked high-heeled shoes into the living room.

"That was a first," I say. The ice pack she offered me sits neglected on the coffee table. I'm not terribly fond of cold sensations at the moment. Too many are still plucking at me. I ignore the blankets she piled at the foot of the couch as well. Accepting one seems like too much of a commitment.

"So it's not normally that bad?"

"I don't know what 'it' normally is."

"What do you mean?" she asks.

"It's not consistent. The moment I think it's one thing, something else happens." It's hard to say what something normally is when you're still figuring out *what* it is.

"Like what? Sorry, I mean, if you want me to be quiet, I can."

I doubt that.

"No, it's fine," I say. "It's helping." Hearing her talk helps push the haunting chatter into the background again.

Glenny goes quiet.

"Glenny?"

"I don't really know what to say."

"You were doing fine before."

"Yeah, but then hearing I was helping put pressure on me and now I got nothing."

The ceiling painted an off-yellow has stopped swooping in and out of focus so I can turn my head to look at her without being pitched back into dizziness. She grins at me, a teasing Cheshire smile, and pushes the mug full of steaming tea closer.

"It's ginger. It helped with my morning sickness," she says. "I know what you got going on is different than pregnancy but you never know. I've also got chamomile, honeybush, and rooibos if you want."

The tea isn't the only offering she's made. A bowl of sliced watermelon, plate of crackers, and a couple of sports drinks accompany the steaming mug.

"I'm fine, I just need a minute," I say. My head pounds as I sit up and I automatically touch my ears, feeling for any leaking fluids. "You wanna tell me how you play into all this?"

"Yeah, I've been trying to tell you since pretty much when I saw you in the diner," she says, giving a long-suffering huff, "but I didn't know how to do it without freaking you out, and then you did freak out so you gotta promise not to freak out this time no matter how weird it sounds. Okay?"

"I never freak out. I'm the model of cool rationale."

"Yeah? Then what was that at the side of the road?"

"I was perfectly calm."

"You were vomiting everywhere and could barely stand."

"Despite all appearances, I was perfectly calm through that as well. There's a significant difference between losing your cool and losing your lunch."

"Okay, fine." She rolls her eyes. "If you promise not to have a panic attack—"

"I don't have panic attacks."

"Will you shut your lying mouth long enough to let me finish?" she snaps and I grin, finding myself liking her a bit despite us getting off on the wrong foot and then taking a few running steps. Life is weirder than I thought, and I'll be a lot better off once I reassess my normalcy bias.

"God, people already think I'm trash," she says, "now the neighbors are gonna think I was dragging my boyfriend back into the truck after we had a fight because he was too drunk before noon to walk straight."

"Let's not get carried away. They won't think I'm your boyfriend. You're way out of my league."

Glenny's snort is too large for a girl that small.

"And you don't strike me as a person who gives a damn about what other people think," I say.

"Well, it's different because I usually end up knowing what they think anyway. Even when they don't say it." She shakes her head, punk hair cut swaying around her over-pierced ears. "I just . . . there are just things that are obvious, you know? Like I can just tell these things. It's like it's written on people even if they don't say it."

"Like what?" Considering my own claim to strangeness, my skepticism of her "knowing things" borders on hypocritical.

"That's how I knew in the diner you were having some sort of, like, a psychic episode."

I'm not too crazy about being associated with having a "psychic episode." But it's a personal peeve, not a legitimate complaint, so I settle for frowning instead of arguing the point.

"Anything else?" I ask.

Glenny pulls at her lip. "You promise not to freak out? Please?"

"Only if I'm still allowed to have a panic attack."

Her grin is nervous and fleeting. "Okay . . . um, well, I didn't know you were married until you started playing with your wedding ring in the car."

I stop fiddling with the silver band.

"But then like that"—she snaps her fingers—"I just knew she was dead—I mean, she was gone. Like I had known the whole time. And just so you know, I'm usually a lot better about remembering to wait for names but you started acting all weird in the diner so I forgot."

The silence stretching between us breaks Glenny first.

"You said you wouldn't freak out, remember? Don't be mad, please."

"I'm not mad."

Glenny is going to gnaw a hole through her lip if she doesn't settle down. "You don't believe me."

I don't. I'm running through all the possible ways she could have gotten that information. Maria's radio show and podcast were well-known and her death made national news. Even I made national news not too long before that after my last tour in Afghanistan. A soldier being left for dead during a fire fight and then him stumbling out of the mountains a few days later while sporting a bullet wound and head trauma is a good story to kick off the evening news.

And while our being married wasn't overly broadcast, it wasn't a secret either. A few news stations ran the tale of my Afghanistan camping trip again as a tag-on to the story covering her death. With a little legwork, Glenny could have gotten most of her info from those reports. As for knowing I was the one who found Silvia, her father being the sheriff explains that away. She already said she saw me at the sheriff's office. She could have been listening in as well and small-town gossip might be able to fill in any remaining gaps.

Yet try as I might, I can't make it work. Occam's razor comes swooping in to shave the feeble connections I'm trying to string together to keep all explanations unextraordinary. The hardest one to sell is the idea Glenny is a scheming mastermind, plotting and weaving a net of information to serve some ulterior motive. If Glenny has an ounce of cunning in her, it all belongs to her baby and is entirely the father's contribution.

"Do you still need me to keep talking or no?" she asks. "Is it helping with whatever you have going on? Or do you need it quiet right now?"

She's so frantic to please it hurts. I don't have to know things, like Glenny claims to, to figure her out. She's a stranger in the small town she was born in and is desperately lonely for it.

"Please don't be mad," she says.

"Why would I be mad?"

Glenny shrugs. "People get mad at me all the time. I don't always keep straight what people have said and what they haven't."

I wonder if that's why the baby's father looks to be out of the picture.

"Oh no, that was just me getting really drunk and making a lot of mistakes one right after the other in super quick succession," Glenny says. Her face scrunches up in disgust at the memory. "And I'd rather say I got no idea who the dad is than admit it was him. I don't know if it's a good or bad thing everyone believed there were too many possibilities for who the dad is to make a fuss over finding out. I thought *my dad* was going to make me take a paternity test and then arrest every guy in town until he found a match. But I think he's still torn on finding the guy and shooting him or pretending none of this happened."

I stare and Glenny's hands fly over her mouth too late to halt the oversharing exodus.

"Well," I say, pretending not to see the thick blush spreading up her cheeks behind her hands, "you've convinced me you got a knack for knowing and saying things that are better kept quiet."

From behind her hands she says, "See, I told you."

***

"Anything?" Glenny asks. She walks backward as she leads me down the narrow hall to be sure she doesn't miss it if I have a sudden "psychic episode." Her playing tour guide is unnecessary. The house she rents is a small one-story with the living room and kitchen immediately off one side of the entryway and a small narrow hall lined by five doors on the other.

I marvel at the miracle that the house is still standing despite all four girls having to share one bathroom. My parents chose another mortgage over loss of sanity and moved into a house with three bathrooms. Really all that did was shift the fighting from taking too much time in the shower to taking all the hot water. I learned pretty quick it was easier to brush my teeth at the kitchen sink.

"No," I say.

The small bounce in her step isn't stifled by my lack of spiritual sensitivity. As we come to the second room on the left, Glenny darts forward to slam the door shut.

"Your room?" I guess.

"Yeah," she says. "It's kinda messy right now so . . ." She shuffles across the hall to the opposite door. "This is . . . was Silvia's room."

The flimsy wood door scuffs over the shag carpet as Glenny pushes it open for me. There's no obligatory creak to mark the room as haunted. No frost gathers on the window glass, no cold spots lurk about the bedroom. Aside from the constant hiss of murmurs that never fully fades, no spectral sounds answer our stepping across the threshold.

The room is still completely furnished. Nothing has been packed, moved, or even disturbed. The hope that Silvia was alive and would return preserved this room to commemorate her last moments here. A nursing textbook lies open on her desk next to a ringed binder, the page halfway filled by notes in neat, feminine handwriting. A few more books of anatomy and pathology are stacked to the side beneath a desk lamp with pink glass flowers encircling the light bulbs.

I don't pick up anything other than a thin layer of dust as I run a couple fingers over her desk.

"Anything?" Glenny asks again.

I open Silvia's closet instead of answer. The full length mirror in the door reflects a woman's face right behind me. I freeze and then whistle out a low hiss between clenched teeth. It was just Glenny.

"Nothing." I cut Glenny off before she can ask, "Anything?" again.

Sundresses, light spring coats, and an umbrella hang above the shoes on the closet floor arranged in neat rows. Her dresser is just as tidy, everything folded and sorted. The books on top of her dresser, mostly romance and fantasy novels alongside a few more nursing textbooks, are alphabetically grouped by genre.

I sit down on Silvia's bed. The blue throw pillows are perfectly arranged and match the floral pattern blooming on the white comforter. The bright orderliness to the room can't mask the lifelessness of it all.

"Anything?" Glenny asks, scooting across the floor in the rolling desk chair to sit across from me.

"Nope," I say and go back to staring around the room.

"Then aren't you going to do some more investigating?" she asks.

"I have to do my contemplating first."

She rolls her eyes when she figures out I'm being flip. "Is that hard for you?"

"I've been known to leak brain fluid from my ears if I think too hard. And I don't perform well under pressure," I add when she rocks back and forth in the chair expectantly.

A corner of a black box beneath the bed catches my eye. I pull out a case for an Ouija board followed by a séance kit.

"Is this yours or Silvia's?" I ask and already got a good idea on the answer. The black ochre box and old-fashioned stenciled engravings doesn't match the rest of Silvia's taste in décor.

Glenny makes a sheepish *meep* noise. Her pixie face smeared by makeup from her fake crying is a mix of apology and apprehension.

"Okay, look, I had to do something," she says. "I wasn't trying to be ghoulish or just randomly contact Silvia out of morbid curiosity. I was trying to get a clearer connection, that's all."

"You think Silvia has been trying to contact you?"

"I don't think. I know." She takes a deep breath and launches into a story at a pace that would make a toddler on a sugar high dizzy.

"Okay, so when Silvia didn't come home after work the night she disappeared, I thought it was weird and got worried. But Adrienne and Nicole just said she was probably out at the spring festival, which if they knew her at all—which they didn't because they're awful—they would've known she wouldn't have stayed out that late because she had a test coming up the next week and had been studying pretty much every waking hour she wasn't at work."

I give her to the count of fifteen to get somewhere relevant with her story before I'll cut in and ask for the abridged version.

"So I go to my dad to say, hey, something's up, and he says probably not but if she isn't back by morning he'll check it out. So Silvia doesn't show up the next day and no one can get a hold of her. People finally started taking it more seriously, like I told them to, when they found her car but no one knew where she was. And then that night I'm lying in bed and I suddenly get this weird feeling, like something heavy is pressing on me and this really awful sense that everything is wrong."

I sit up a little straighter as her soliloquy starts to tie in to my ghostly mystery plot.

"And all of sudden it's gone, but it left this lingering sense of wrong and I just knew, you know, that Silvia is dead. And that was…I don't know, but I've never felt worse than that."

It only takes one deep breath for her to gain her composure and return to her rapid fire storytelling. "And that made sense 'cause that's how most of these disappearances end up, you know? With the woman dead. But even with all the missing women statistics on my side, no one believes me when I say I know Silvia's dead and my dad gets super mad at me and we have this huge fight over 'my feelings' being just 'feelings' and how I need to grow up, and how I only do this for attention—actually I don't think he said that but I know that's what he was thinking—and how he blames my grandma for putting in my head the idea I had spiritual sensitivities, he did actually say that—"

Telling Glenny how uninterested I am in her dad drama would only derail the story more so I sit through it. Fortunately the segue is just a minute of her letting a bit of pent-up resentment for her parents boil over.

"—and then things started getting weird."

She looks at me and I give the encouraging nod she needs.

"I would hear noises coming from Silvia's room but when I looked in there was no one there. Her light would come on at night and I asked Adrienne and Nicole if they turned it on, but they always thought it was me doing some prank or whatever. They thought I was pretending the house is haunted and so they got totally mad when stuff actually started moving and they started yelling at me, telling me to cut it out. See, I've always kind of liked that occult stuff, so when I started telling people I knew Silvia was dead and her room was haunted, they thought, well they thought . . ." she trails off.

"That you were an attention-starved teenager desperate to

validate her interest in the occult so was seeing patterns and evidence where there wasn't any?"

"Yeah, that, but meaner. They stopped blaming me when I was gone for a weekend on a family thing and the lights still kept coming on and stuff kept moving, so now they just ignore it. And me."

"Anything else strange happen?" I ask.

"Doors kind of swing open and shut when no one is near them. And this is a crappy house but the doors didn't do that before so I know it isn't anything stupid like the foundation is bad or whatever. Furniture will rattle around, if you check behind the headboard you can see the dents in the wall, and I've seen the drawers to Silvia's desk open when I'm walking by and"—Glenny scuffs her feet nervously against the carpet—"and I can hear this knocking on my door at night."

"Do you ever answer it?" I ask.

She shakes her head, face a little pale. "No. It's different when you're alone in the dark, you know?"

I do know.

"And I could just feel things, like there was someone there but not really. I thought it was Silvia but I had no idea what to do or know anyone to even talk to about all this stuff happening. Everyone thought I was just looking for attention. Well, except Josie—"

"Who's Josie?"

"My sister. But I know she doesn't really believe me either. She thinks it's all pregnancy stress making my imagination overactive. She tried to get me to move in with her earlier instead of waiting for the lease to end. Then a couple weeks ago I started getting these weird feelings, like angry, you know, but not like normal angry, it was an injustice sort of angry, like I needed to fix some wrong. And I thought, maybe that's Silvia, she's angry and I can feel it."

Skepticism wants me to jump on the bandwagon of Josie's theory. But if Glenny is just a desperate liar I might as well toss in the towel and call me just crazy.

"I tried talking to her, to Silvia, whenever I got the weird feelings or would hear things at night. But nothing happened, I mean I never got a real answer or anything. So I got out the Ouija board and séance stuff that my grandma had—don't tell my dad, he doesn't know I took it when she died—and tried a few times using that."

Glenny stops to chew her lip again. I guess that habit is the only thing stopping her from getting it pierced.

"And?" I prompt.

"Everything stopped," Glenny says. "No more noises. No more lights. No more moving furniture. Nothing. Until last night."

She looks at me, waiting for a response.

"You got me at the edge of my seat, kiddo," I say. "Cut the suspense and tell me what happened."

She shifts in the chair, bottom lip pinched between her teeth.

"Glenny, I believe you," I say. "I'm not setting you up and I'm not going to make fun of you no matter what you say."

"And you won't get mad or freak out?" she asks.

"I won't get mad, and we already agreed I won't freak out as long as I'm allowed panic attacks."

The small smile stops her from devouring her lip. "Okay, so it was completely quiet, for like two weeks, and then last night I had the weirdest dream in the history of dreaming. Well, not my weirdest, but it was at least top five, and I don't remember it all but—" Her lip goes back between her teeth and her voice quiets to a nervous plea. "I'm not making this up, okay?"

"I know."

Glenny takes a couple false starts to speak and shakes her head. "I need to show you."

Her rising from the chair looks overly complicated with her swollen belly but she doesn't take my hand when I offer to help.

"I'm fine," she says, stealing my go-to lie as she leads me across the hall to her room.

Cardboard boxes, most of them filled, cover the floor. Her closet is open and empty save for a jacket and a couple of lonely hangers. Small holes in the walls mark where decorations used to hang. Judging from the number of black dots in the white plaster, the walls were once nearly covered.

She pulls open her secretary desk, barren other than a sketchbook, a couple loose leaf papers, and a pencil.

Glenny starts to riffle through the sketch book. "You can sit down," she says.

"I'm fine."

"Well, you should sit down 'cause your standing is making me nervous," she says. Finding the page, she waits until I sit on the bed before handing it to me.

And it's a good thing I sat down because I was not prepared to stare down at a perfect life-like pencil drawing of me. The exactness is bone-chillingly eerie, and that is not a word I throw about lightly.

The jeans are shaded to match the fading of the ones I'm currently wearing. My shirt in the drawing is the spare sitting on the motel room floor and that hat is the one I hung on the entryway's coat rack. Glenny's closet doesn't have a full length mirror hanging on the door but if it did I know the shadows beneath the eyes and dark stubble on the chin would be an exact match.

To make it even better, the accuracy of the rendition isn't the most unsettling part. In the drawing I'm carrying a woman's corpse, dessicated, dry, teeth drawn with obsessive detail to capture the mouth cracked open in a scream. Behind us isn't the field I found Silvia in, it's a mass of blurred penciling and stark eraser slashes to give the effect of a world burning.

"Don't be mad," Glenny whispers.

I'm not angry. But madness is thick on the ground and I have no control over it.

"This was your dream?" I ask.

"Yeah. It was all so clear, like seared into my brain. When I woke up I was full-on panicking. Not from the dream but by this sort of sense, like I had seen you before and needed to find you. And then when I saw you at the diner I recognized you and then remembered I saw you leaving my dad's office but you were far enough away I didn't realize it was you from the dream then and . . . you believe me, right?"

I nod. "You're an incredible artist."

I look up and Glenny's brows are a tight, angry knot.

"That's it? That's all you got to say?"

"It's obvious you're very talented and I'm not well-versed enough in art to give more specific feedback."

"I tell you about all this ghost stuff that's been happening that all leads up to a dream about you—"

"Women dreaming about me is nothing new."

"You said you wouldn't make fun," she snaps.

"I'm not making fun, I'm making light."

"Well, don't. You . . . oh." She nods slowly as comprehension smooths away her irritation. "You're freaked out—"

"I'm not freaked out." That would be an overstatement. I would, however, admit to being a hair unsettled.

"—and this is how you cope. Got it."

"Do you mind if I look through the rest?"

"You're not in any of the other drawings," she says.

Which is a relief to hear. For one, it's creepy to have someone draw you before you meet them. For two, I'm hoping her ability to "know things" has provided her more interesting subjects than me carrying dead bodies around.

I flip through the pages. Some pictures are studies of people, birds, landscapes, and still-lifes. The mundane drawings are beautifully done but lack the devoted detail of her more imaginative pieces. That greater level of dedication belongs to the drawings that dive into the disturbing. A young woman with a smile pulled wide by fishing hooks sinks into the floorboards. There's eyeless faces with lips sewn shut. Hands coming out of blackened borders reach for a small, pale figure with distorted, stomach-churning anatomy curled up in the center. A corrugated steel roof drawn from the perspective of someone lying flat on the floor looking up at it.

"When did you draw this?" I ask, holding up the drawing of the roof.

"Oh." Glenny pales at the memory. "That was the morning after Silvia disappeared and . . . wait, do you recognize it from somewhere?"

"No," I lie.

"You're lying. I know you're lying."

"No, it seems familiar but I don't recognize it from anywhere I've been," I say and Glenny relaxes in what I hope is indication she's buying the amended fib.

I flip through the rest of the book.

"Anything else?" Glenny asks and I shake my head. No other drawings catch my eye as obviously relevant to my personal hauntings.

She lets out a heavy sigh. "Oh well. You know, at first I was kind of worried when you didn't pick anything up in Silvia's room that this was gonna be a complete bust and maybe I really was imagining all of this or it didn't mean anything but if you recognized that roof, that could mean something, yeah? Do you wanna try a séance? I haven't been able to get it to work but it might be different if you're there. You seem like you're already a conduit for Silvia."

"Is this the first time something like this has happened to you?" I ask, ignoring the séance invitation.

"Not like this. It was never this extreme before," she says. "You?"

Yes.

"Not like this," I say.

Chapter 11

I was a month out of St. Jude's and desperate to keep it that way. And if that meant risking smothering myself with a pillow at night to muffle the shivering sobs, so be it.

His voice came as it always had for the past three weeks.

"Please. Please. Someone find me. Help me. I'm here. Here. Here."

I felt the words more than heard them and suffered all their desperation. At first they had a sense of hope, expecting against all odds to be saved. By the end of the night that hope was gone and the voice echoed hollow and forsaken.

"I'm here. I'm here."

I tried everything to escape it. I avoided the stretch of country road where I first heard the pleading cries with a religious fervor. The voice still found me. It came to me in the car whenever I drove. I stopped driving. The voice kept coming.

I even gave clozapine another chance. All that did was make me dizzy and nauseous. The voice came at night, sporadically at first, and then it never left. It pleaded and begged for hours, unbroken in its hopeless recitation.

"Here. I'm here."

I curled into a tighter ball when the pulls on my arm started up. They had joined the nightly voice the previous week. Cold fingers reached deep into me, unchecked by skin, muscle, or bone. They wrapped around and tugged to move me off the bed.

If my parents hadn't heard me tossing and turning or the muffled sobbing I was reduced to after another sleepless night, they couldn't miss the morning listlessness. They saw how detached I was and becoming more so by the day. My mother had begun to drop heavy hints I should schedule more appointments with Dr. Day. And I hated how broken my father looked whenever he saw me. He looked as helpless as the voice sounded.

"I'm here. I'm here."

The cold hands pulled and the voice begged.

"I'm here."

I rolled onto my back to stare up at the bedroom ceiling.

"Here."

I was at a crossroads and a choice needed to be made—go forward with this, or go back to St. Jude's. Doing as the voice asked embraced the madness. Ignoring it was resignation to a slower descent into insanity.

"Please. Someone find me. I'm here."

"Fine," I sighed. "I'll be crazy, then."

I tried to be quiet as I fumbled my way into a jacket and sweatpants, skipping shoes altogether. I dropped all attempts at stealth when opening the garage and driving off into the night. I didn't bother looking back at my parents' house, knowing there was no way they missed the garage door rumbling, their room being right over the carport. My mother would be at the window staring after me, my father either beside her or running down the stairs in pursuit. Dr. Day didn't mince words when informing them on the suicidal behaviors to watch out for.

The voice called me back down dark and unfamiliar roads to where I first heard him—a lonely country road winding along a steep drop to a dried creek. He spoke to me as I left the car parked on the roadside and pushed my way down into the dry brush. Each step I took brought a little more hope back into his voice begging to be found.

"Here. Here. Here."

Driving home from a night out at the bar with friends, Billy Davis had been too drunk to keep his car on the road. No guardrails protected the curving way, leaving no evidence as to where he had tumbled off, car rolling into the trees and disappearing into the brush. After nearly a month it was impossible to tell how long he had lived after the crash. How long he lay at the bottom of the ravine, if he heard cars driving on the road above, oblivious to him dying.

All he wanted was to be found and I was the only one who could still hear him.

Turned out my father did chase after me. Seeing my car parked on the side of the road near a cliff, he feared the worst. I think it was the only time in history a father was glad to find his son barefoot and standing over a car wreck with a decomposing corpse inside.

***

"So what now?" Glenny asks.

I shrug. All my leads are of the paranormal variety and those leads are really me being led. I'd been expecting some supernatural revelation to creep out from a closet or grab my ankle from beneath the bed, pointing me where to go next. I told the Billy Davis story in a Hail Mary attempt to stimulate any spiritual energies or whatever Glenny would call them. Talking about previous supernatural experiences always seems to summon the climatic one in the movies. No such luck here.

Sensing I'm figuring out a way to politely leave, Glenny offers lunch and leaves me the two options of accepting or feeling like a dismissive jerk for the rest of the day.

The kitchen is too small to fit all the different cooking equipment for four, now three, women. The counters are buried beneath coffee grinders, waffle makers, electric skillets, and utensil racks. The little counter space left is in hot demand for the house's residents to claim as their own, creating a clash of varying tastes in décor. Sunflowers compete with pottery, vases against knickknacks that may or may not serve some culinary purpose.

The table is crammed so tight into a corner only two of the four seats can be comfortably used at the same time. I'm doing my best to sit perfectly still to stop my knee from knocking into Glenny's. She's already powered through her sandwich and is eyeing mine with predatory hunger.

"Are you sure you don't want to try a séance?" she asks.

"I don't think it works like that."

"Well then, how does it work?" she asks.

"What?"

"You know, your abilities," she says. "Did you hear Silvia calling to you or something so you drove out here?"

I shake my head. My parents had the best intentions in trying to break my habit of seeking out the dead but they misunderstood the relationship. I wasn't the one doing the seeking.

After the Billy Davis incident they decided a change of scene might do me good and Kitty volunteered to take me in. They thought there'd be less a chance of me stumbling over lost roadside corpses in Encrucijada. Little did they know Silvia was waiting en route for me.

"Do you need to go into a trance or something?" Glenny asks. "Or would it help if you slept in Silvia's room? I know that sounds really weird but people do that on the paranormal shows all the time, you know, sleep in the room being haunted. You'll need to do it soon, her parents are probably gonna start moving her stuff out now that . . . well, you know, they know what happened. Oh, and you don't have to sleep in her bed if that's too much. I have an air mattress you can use."

"I'm gonna pass on that one." Sleeping in a dead woman's room doesn't do it for me.

"And you haven't figured out where you saw that roof before?" she asks.

"I have no idea where that would be."

"Do you think that's where she was killed?"

Yes. "Can't say for sure."

"If you recognized that roof, do you think you'd recognize her killer if you saw him?" Glenny asks.

"What makes you think her killer is a guy?"

"Statistics. And I think it's like, one-third of women who are murdered, it's done by someone they're intimate with, so chances are she knew him," Glenny says. "So if you saw him, do you think you'd know it was him? Would Silvia tell you? I could get out a yearbook or we could go through her photos."

"I don't know." I push my plate over to her.

"You don't like turkey?" she asks.

"I'm not hungry."

"She had a boyfriend," Glenny says. Somewhere in the space

of that statement she inhales half of the second sandwich. "Well, they were more like friends with benefits. Actually, maybe not even friends, just benefits."

"And you think he did it?" I ask, working on a way to leave without upsetting the delicate balance that is Glenny's feelings. I don't think I'm going to get anything of substance by continuing to hang around here. If any divining of the dead was to be done I'm pretty sure it would've already happened. Silvia hasn't shown much shyness about being heard when she wants to be.

"He has an alibi but you never know. They were always fighting and he could have been involved somehow," she says. "So if you saw him or just a picture of him, would you be able to know?"

"I said I don't know and I don't think it works like that."

"Well, how did it work before?" she asks.

"How did what work?"

Usually my being deliberately dense gets folks to give up. Not Glenny. She's undaunted.

"When I asked if you had something like this happen before, you said 'not exactly' so you at least have some sort of experience to go off of," she says.

"I already told you about that," I say. Billy Davis and Silvia Lopez are almost parallels of each other. Driving along in my car, minding my own business, radio acts up, spirit acts up, I find a corpse. Except in Billy Davis' case I tried a lot longer to dismiss it as imagination or a hallucination. And while Billy Davis left me alone after we found his body, Silvia doesn't think our date is done yet.

Glenny frowns. "But you finding Billy, that happened after you got released from the psychiatric hospital."

"What's your point?"

"So"—she rolls out the word like I'm being purposefully dense, which I am—"that's not the thing that got you committed. That wasn't your first, that's just when you decided to stop pretending it wasn't real. How did it all start?"

"I don't remember."

I had not realized Alec was dead. I didn't have time or energy to spare on the thought how strange it was he never spoke as we walked through hostile territory. That he only ever pointed, or motioned for when I should run, wait, or hide. How his movements were unnaturally smooth and that he never tired. I assumed the wrongness lay in my senses, not in what they were seeing.

My insistence that Alec had been alive with me was dismissed as a result of physical and mental stress. And eventually I bought into that assessment. For a while.

"Yes you do remember," Glenny says. "Was it when you were on tour?"

"It's not worth talking about."

"Why?"

"Because it's not," I snap.

"Sorry, I didn't mean to—hey, wait, where're you going?" Glenny comes after me when I stand to leave.

"I'm not sure yet."

"You can't just quit," she says. "Nothing's happened yet!"

"My thoughts exactly," I say, rescuing my boots from the massive mound of shoes piled in the foyer. I wouldn't call this whole venture pointless. There's some significance to Glenny having dreams of me toting corpses through fiery fields and drawing that corrugated roof. But I'm too tired to spare the needed energy for the deserved curiosity.

"You didn't even try to talk to Silvia or find something!"

"I'm sorry my paranormal detective skills aren't up to snuff," I say.

"Wait, don't go! I'm . . . I'm sorry, I didn't mean to pry!"

A warning cold flushes over me. After the episode at the side of the road earlier today, it doesn't seem Silvia is going to let me off easy. So my best play seems to be to bumble my way through until Silvia becomes so frustrated by my ineptitude she'll go poltergeist and spatter the answers on the wall in ectoplasmic ooze or whatever ghosts do.

"Could you please just try to talk to her? Or something? Please?" she begs.

I pause, one hand on the door knob.

"Please, I don't know, sit in her room or something and she'll talk to you," Glenny says. "I know it."

She grabs my hand. "She's my friend."

Probably her only one.

"Please."

Chapter 12

"I don't know how to do this," I say, "so how 'bout you just tell me what you want?"

The creaking springs of Silvia's bed are all that answer. For simplicity's sake, I'm going to hold to my original guess that she wants the guy who murdered her brought to justice. But that's going to be a bit more complicated than I think she'd like. Even if Silvia names her killer in the fashion of King Hamlet, I'm going to want physical evidence to back that up. I can't go around exacting vigilante justice against every Joe Blow the voices in my head say is guilty of murder. There's got to be some sane standards in all this madness.

"To be fair, if I just shot the guy who killed you, I'd probably end up back in a mental hospital instead of jail," I say. It wouldn't be as friendly a hospital as St. Jude's and the duration would be for significantly longer.

Not even creaking springs answer me this time. It's so quiet I can almost hear Glenny's impatience as she waits in the living room.

"Alright, Silvia." I clear my throat. "We're gonna lay down some ground rules. This playing hard to get has gotta go. If you want my help, you ask nice and don't go running off expecting me to chase after you. You also don't get to sucker punch me on the side of the road and then give me this silent treatment."

I check the mirror hanging on the closet door as that seems the cliché place for a ghost to appear. Nothing.

"You need to take it down a couple notches," I say. "I get being murdered has got you riled, but we'll make better headway if you tone it down."

No voices. No cool touches.

"Is that a yes?" I ask. If I really am crazy and I'm doing nothing more than talking to myself, I'm simply too good at being crazy to not go forward with this. So I wait, sitting on a dead woman's bed, waiting for a sign to take that final damning step into the world of spirits or insanity.

"I am going to help you," I promise.

Fingers strum over me, moving across my neck, down my arm. The mirror shows an empty room except for me as a cool hand closes around mine and squeezes. A strained voice breaks through the ever-present background murmurs.

"Come on . . . here . . ."

A door slams and I leap off the bed. Footsteps creak over the floor, and I imagine Silvia's ghost, rotted and torn as I found her, treading down the hall toward me. A living woman's voice calls out a dismissive greeting to Glenny, breaking the morbid spell.

The pressure on my hand doesn't let up from this intrusion of the living. It holds steady when I step out from Silvia's room and head back toward the kitchen.

"Do you know when you're moving out?" the new woman asks as she unloads groceries from bag to counter. "Not that I'm trying to rush you or anything, I just need to know when I can list the room as ready to move in. I already have a couple inquiries so really, sooner would be better. And do you know anything about what Silvia's family is going to do? Because I'm gonna need to know when that room is available too."

The woman startles when she turns and sees me standing in the hallway.

"Oh, sorry, I thought you were Glenny." She smiles nervously. "Are you a friend of hers?" She trips over the word "friend" like it doesn't belong in association with Glenny.

I nod. "Helping her pack and move."

"Oh, good," she says, relaxing and moving her hand away from the knife block. "I mean, not good that she's leaving, but good someone is helping her. I'm Nicole, by the way."

Glenny peeks out from the living room. I give her a thumbs up and she grins. What macabre creatures we are, delighted to hear from the dead.

"I told you she'd talk to you," she says.

Nicole blinks, looking between the two of us. "Why wouldn't I talk to him?"

"No, not you," Glenny snaps with enough venom in her voice to drop a horse. She grabs my arm and pulls me back down the hall. "So, what did Silvia say? Or did you see her?"

"I didn't see her."

"But she talked to you, yeah?" she asks. "So do you know who killed her?"

"No."

"Well, did she say where the killer is?"

"Nope."

"What about how to find him?"

"Uh, no."

Glenny stops outside Silvia's bedroom door. "You're a pretty shitty medium."

"Yep." That's what I've been telling her and Silvia this whole time. "And don't cuss in front of the baby."

Glenny stomps over to the bed and slides the séance kit out from under it.

"I'm not using a wheezy board," I say.

"*Ouija* board. Why not?"

"Because this isn't a high school slumber party." This is a serious murder investigation conducted by a psychiatric patient, his plucky pregnant teenage partner, and led by the murder victim herself in all her cryptic-voice-from-the-great-beyond glory.

"You don't need to make me feel like a kid," Glenny says.

"You are a kid," I say.

Her hackles go up. "I'm eighteen."

I drag a hand over my stubble-rough chin. I'm pretty sure a wooden board and alphabet has no sway over spirits. Ghosts and all else that lurk beyond that sepia veil don't play by the natural laws, let alone a board game. While I'm pretty sure an Ouija board has no power to contact spirits, I am absolutely certain that intentionally calling out to spirits begs for trouble. Ghosts are the least of what haunts the physical world and while I can't stop whatever moves behind the thinning curtain from knocking, I sure as hell ain't opening a door for them.

My skin crawls, thinking back to the stalking entity. The unceasing murmurs darken, grow harsher to grate against me. Their whispering feels like pulls, testing fingers brushing across my soul searching for purchase.

"Logan? Did you hear me?"

"What?"

Glenny's looking at me like a normal person should, confused and slightly perturbed.

"Are you alright?" she asks. "You're shaking."

"Yeah, I'm fine. What were you saying?"

"That you . . ." She stops and shakes her head. "Never mind. I'll take you back to May's."

***

"So what's it like? Did you see Silvia or something back there?" Glenny asks. She spends more time glancing over at me than watching the road she's driving down.

"No."

"You were kind of in a trance for a bit there. Was that what that was?"

"No." I'm beginning to buckle under the weight of terrible sleeping habits and Glenny's unending spring of questions.

"Then what was it?" she asks. "Was it like a vision or something? You do have visions, right?"

I do my best to sink in and let the truck seat swallow me whole but it doesn't seem to be hungry.

"Do you know what you're going to do now?" she asks.

"Sleep." The cool pressure on my hand courtesy of Silvia hasn't let up and it feels like it's slowly cutting off the tenuous connections I have to wakefulness.

"Oh, do ghosts talk to you in dreams or do you just see things like I do?"

"I hope not," I say. "I'm just really tired."

I expect Glenny to roll her eyes in disappointment for how boring I am. She gives a solemn nod instead. "Yeah, you do look super tired."

She pulls into the Roadhouse's parking lot and lets the engine idle.

"Can I help?" she asks.

"Help with what?"

114

"You know, when you go investigating or doing whatever you do. Can I help?"

I have a feeling there's only one right answer to this but I'm not sure what it is and no matter what I say it'll be the wrong one.

"I think you need help," she says.

She's not wrong.

"Yeah, sure," I say more to end the conversation than because I think she'll prove to be a supernatural sleuth protégé. To be fair, I don't think I'm much help to Silvia, so one more person of questionable usefulness can't hurt. And I could use someone who has connections to the town. Someone who's familiar with the lay of the land and the natives. Glenny is far from the best fit for that role but she's better than nothing. "But we're not using the wheezy board."

Glenny smiles and I wish she had a life where she'd smile more. The grin stays strung out across her face as I give her my number and promise to check in with her by tomorrow at the latest.

"Shouldn't you have known my number without having to ask?" I ask.

"No, but I knew you were a smart-ass without having to ask."

She drives off and a little spark of hope I'd been holding onto flickers out. The whole time I was in the truck, I waited to hear something from the radio, ready for a sign or a static crackle of reassurance. But it stayed stuck on the same country station. No static, hiss, or even the smallest sputter. And that small normalcy invites the festering loneliness to dig in deeper.

Silvia's unseen hand gives mine a gentle squeeze. If it was meant to be reassuring, it was anything but.

I turn to walk into the motel and the pressure on my hand becomes a painful tug. Apparently Silvia isn't impressed by my "sleep" strategy.

"We talked about this," I warn.

The grip lightens and the tugs become soft but insistent.

The poor girl was murdered so it seems tactless to complain about the problems in my life when she no longer has one. But walking up the flight of stairs to the motel room sounds terrifyingly exhausting. Chasing after killers demands a much higher level of functioning than I can pull off right now.

"An hour. Can it wait an hour? Please?" I ask and flinch when the sensation moves from my hand to my forehead, like someone running a hand over to check temperature, and then it's gone. No ghostly pressure, just me and the always present murmurings.

I feel closer to the dead than the living, separate and disembodied from the world around me as I mechanically shuffle across the motel lobby and up the stairs. I'm not sure if I manage to close the door to the room entirely shut behind me and don't care to check. I drop onto the bed, shove the duffel bag off, and for once find sleep quickly.

Chapter 13

I know it's a dream. The soft edges to my vision and the weightless disconnect give it away. This awareness doesn't give me any control of it. I can't wake up to escape the corrugated roof looming overhead. I can't even rise from the plastic tarp I'm lying on. My head barely turns, my fingers only twitch.

The door to the room opens and the heavy step of his boots comes closer. A chair scrapes across the hard floor and I feel him sitting inches from me.

"I never knew any of their names," he says. "You're a first."

The real horror of his hand brushing damp hair from my face is how human his skin on mine feels.

"It's a breath of fresh air."

The hand moves to my throat and clamps down. Red crowds out his face as I spiral into burning terror. I can't breathe, can't—

I can't move as fast as I need to. The Hindu Kush terrain is rugged and unforgiving. I'm weighed down by the sluggishness that traps you in dreams. Alec motions for me to hurry. They'll find me if I don't. Silvia stands beside him and while Alec waves for me to follow, she points a warning finger at what lurks behind me. I can't move fast enough and her hand is cold as she grabs mine, her lips moving in soundless pleas.

I feel the entity drawing soundlessly closer as Silvia tries to pull me away from the ugly, black presence of rotting malice. When it reaches a hand around to trace along the side of my face, there's no chance I'd mistake it for human.

I don't bolt upright when I wake. I stay locked in place on sweat-soaked sheets. My breathing catches on a constricted throat as if an unseen hand presses down on it. It takes too long for my senses to resurface from the depths of the murmuring chorus.

The motel room is empty as is the hall outside the door I left open. I'm shaking so hard, I can barely walk over to shut it. The detached sensation of the dream hangs on, making it feel like I'm treading chest deep through water.

I lean against the locked and bolted door and the cool pressure on my hand moves up to grip my arm, like she's trying to pull me up before I drown.

"Okay, okay," I say, rubbing my temples to push the dream further away. "What do you need?"

The window across the room slides open to let in more fully the sounds of the music festival.

"Now?" I ask.

The cool pressure takes hold of both my hands and tugs.

"How do I know you're actually Silvia and not something else leading me into madness and doom?"

She chucks me under the chin before pulling at me with a little more force.

"You dead girls sure make for pushy dates."

"Come on."

***

Main Street is a hot mess of people, sound, and fun. The

road is closed off to cars and the swarming mass of pedestrians is undaunted by the summer sun. Tall oak trees and tent awnings provide sufficient shade for the outdoor revelry and the shops provide air-conditioned retreats for those who need temporary escape from the heat. Just looking at the people packing into the street sets me on edge. Their voices are foreign and unintelligible. I start to itch from the phantom sand and dust sticking to my skin. My hand drifts down to my right hip, and the empty air in place of the holster isn't a damn bit of comfort.

Crowds have always made my skin crawl. It used to be because they were too easy a place for a physical threat to hide in. Our evolved ability to read facial expressions, notice small changes in body language, failed to keep up with our change in lifestyle. While fear and anger are easy to recognize on one face, those subtle cues of danger get lost in a crowd, making it damn difficult to detect threats disguised among the many.

Now, much like everything else that sets me on edge, crowds get me jumpy for very different reasons. They look to me the way the murmuring voices sound. Their movement is a noise of its own, discordant and jostling. There's too much that can hide in the shifting throng of people, too much that celebrates the dark murmurings and brings attention to them.

Standing this close to the pack of people incites the murmurings to a louder pitch. I swipe at my ears, trying to clear away the incessant whispering. The bustling chaos invites the murmurings to become more than a background hush, and they manifest into dark shapes moving beneath the turbid waters of the stream of people. They creep forward from being unseen voices to shift among the living, vague shadows teasing at the edge of visibility as if moving behind blurred glass.

The dark flickers are so faint and fade away so soon I can't be sure if I only imagined them. Which isn't very reassuring either.

"Come on."

Whatever happened to ghosts directing people to empty cemeteries or abandoned towns? I'd much prefer that to plunging into this tossing sea of people and murmurings.

I take a testing couple steps away. The cold tug on my hand urges me back toward the crowd.

"Here. Come on."

It's not just the crowd that's overwhelming. Not knowing what I'm looking for, this blind blundering about, goes against every grain of my being. I'm marching off into unfamiliar terrain to face an unknown enemy with only a dead nursing student as a guide.

"Come on. Here. Here. Come."

I should pick up a local paper instead, check out the morning news. See if Silvia's remains being found has been publicly announced. Retreat back to the motel room and read up more on her disappearance. Sift through her social media for red flags, look up any similar disappearances in the county, find a pattern.

Or maybe I should get an Ouija board like Glenny did and demand more direct spiritual intervention.

The crawling terror the entity brings quickly convinces me otherwise. Leave that door shut.

"Come. Here."

"Be warned, I got no idea what I'm doing," I say to Silvia and any other listening haunt. "You might be better off looking to someone else for help."

The door to the nearest shop opens and Cash's tune follows

the man out. The door closing fails to fully muffle the strumming guitar and rhythmic stomp and clap. If coincidences are supposed to be spiritual puns, this sort of humor escapes me.

"God help me." With a deep breath, I plunge into the swelling crowd. The small pat on my back would have been comforting if it had belonged to someone living.

I stay close to the little white tents lining the street. Hanging out at the edges and skipping around the clusters of customers is easier than attempting to move through the turbulent stream of bodies. Sweat and sunscreen marinate the air already perfumed by the scent of frying bread and sugar courtesy of the troop of food trucks.

A few musicians stand on a street corner a respectable distance away from the main stage and twang out tunes to passersby. They're pretty good and I drop a couple of dollars in the guitar case as I walk by.

A horde of people slowly expands to conquer the lawn in front of the main stage. A band boasting mediocre ability and even more mediocre dress sense is doing their best to boost the confidence of the group scheduled to follow them. Their discordant chorus is clearly intentional but sacrificing harmony for originality ain't doing their music any favors.

Blue T-shirts with VOLUNTEER emblazoned across the front and back direct the crowd and herd the overly curious a safe distance away from the stage.

The out-of-towners are easy to pick out. They've got that excited, nervous air about them that infects folk whenever they're some place new. The people from out of state are even easier to spot. They wear open-toed shoes, promising blisters and bruises by the end of the day. The women wear shorts less modest than my briefs and the men are in thin cotton T-shirts sporting dark sweat circles blooming beneath their arms.

The wiser folk know better than to try and stay cool. They wear longer pants and hats faded from use for protection against the fast approaching midafternoon sun.

A light touch, almost tentative, chills my hand. Only after I pause in response is there the feel of a tug.

"See, that's better," I say and the invisible hand gives mine a soft squeeze.

The cops stationed around the stage and at street intersections in their pressed uniforms stick out like yellow at a funeral. Spines held rigid against the melting heat, they hang to the sides, eyes hidden behind sunglasses, sweat trickling down the sides of their faces. The police seem a little thick on the ground for such a small town and I'll bet a fair few of the cops are called in from surrounding localities. This level of security may be typical for the festival and have nothing to do with Silvia's remains being found yesterday. Or that she disappeared during the spring festival a couple months prior.

Yeah, right.

The lead vocalist of the band delivers his song in a rhythmic narration in place of real singing. A stronger chorus makes up for it when the woman on the guitar joins in to harmonize on a lament for days gone by. I decide to give the band a second chance. They're not as mediocre as they're trying to be.

"Ah, get outta here."

The grip on my hand goes hard and shoots ice up my arm. It takes me a moment to clear the sudden wave of secondhand panic to realize I actually heard the voice and that the speaker is physically nearby. My hands ball into fists. I've become all too familiar with the sound of that man's voice not to recognize it.

He's laughing alongside a muttonchopped cowboy who claps

him on the arm. It's not just his voice I can now place but his face as well. He was at Sawdust, the man on the phone sitting with the woman with the fish-tail braid. She's standing next to him, joining in the laughter. Dressed in tan, fitted jeans, a red plaid button-down shirt, and hair plaited back in that same style she wore the night before.

I check her arms and face, not finding any signs of bruising or even the smallest scratch. Not only is there no sign of physical abuse, she doesn't look a damn thing like Silvia. I don't even have the television-taught trope that murderers have a predictable type of victims who all conveniently look the same. Her hair is a dark, maple brown instead of black. Her eyes are hazel, not grey. Complexion olive, far lighter than Silvia's honey brown.

Seeing the man in better light shows I completely misjudged his age—he's closer to forty, the dim bar lighting hid the faint edges of aging. The stretch to his wide smile shoots laugh lines out from the corner of his eyes and his dark hair has a few glints of silver. Straight nose and square eyebrows match his equally square and straight jaw. His muscular build speaks to a well-used gym membership and there's an easiness to him that makes you want to like him. Makes you want to be sure he likes you.

I instantly dislike him. Silvia might've biased me some on that score.

"See you, 'round, Clark," he says to Muttonchops before heading off with the woman. His hand circling around her waist makes me want to throw him through the nearest window.

The man stops to look at a booth selling beer glasses shaped as cowboy boots. When he turns to move back into the crowd

I bump into him. He doesn't say anything. The brush isn't anything more than to be expected when pushing through this many people. He probably would've said something if he bothered to check his now-empty pants pocket.

Opening up his wallet, I'm met by the dark-haired and well-tanned Carl Burns staring back at me from his driver's license photo. Forty-one years old, no restrictions listed on the license, and an organ donor. Another ID card of him grinning up at me, this time in a suit and tie, lists him as a volunteer at the local hospital.

The rest of his wallet is just as painfully innocuous. A couple of loose bills, credit cards, health insurance, car insurance, and the predicted gym membership. There isn't even a crumpled up receipt of some shameful purchase lurking among the cash or a sordid picture hidden between his health and car insurance he wouldn't want the woman accompanying him to see.

The cold burrows down deeper than bone and rage rides heavy on the sensation. I don't tell Silvia off. She's got every right to her anger.

"Hey, you!" I call after Burns. I shove my way through the crowd after him. "Hey!"

A few people turn around. Burns joins in and does a double take when I hold up his wallet.

"You dropped this," I say and slide my way through the remaining line of people.

He isn't subtle about checking to be sure all the cash is there when he takes the wallet back.

"Thanks, buddy," he says. He sounds genuine, humanizing him and shaking my confidence to make me think that rather than chasing a monster I'm tilting at windmills instead. In following my ever-shrinking worldview as a madman, I'm twisting evidence free of reason to turn a man as innocent as his wallet into a murderer.

Burns says something. His words are lost in the rushing din filling my ears as the murmurings swing up in pitch. Burns isn't a windmill. There is something off about him. Superficially he looks normal but there's a stain, like teeth yellowed from substance abuse, clinging to him. I can't quite make it out and have a feeling I'd see it better if I wasn't looking for it.

"You alright?" he asks again.

"I thought I recognized you from somewhere," I say. "Couldn't place it."

Burns' smile is warm and paternal. It's bizarre how human he seems. "You probably have seen me somewhere. I'm Carl Burns."

He extends a hand to shake. I take it and only feel warm, living skin and none of the sinister sickness clinging to him.

"It's ringing a bell," I say, "but I still can't place you."

"He's the hot new life coach," the woman says, running an affectionate hand over his arm. Her teasing tone stands atop a pedestal of admiration. "You've probably heard of his podcast, *Burn Out*, or seen one of his interviews. He recently had a new book come out, *The Empathetic Mind and Heart*."

They wait for me to give a reply and the woman's smile falters when I don't.

"You know, I'm doing a live recording tonight at the Rodney Ranch," Burns says. He claps a hand on my shoulder and I shove my hands into my pant pockets to stop myself from strangling him. "You should come on by for tonight's show. I'll buy you a drink after. I owe you one."

He passes me a business card, the information for the event written on the back.

"I'll swing it so you can be backstage, don't worry about the admission price," he says. "By the way, I didn't catch your name."

"Logan," I say. Giving a fake name is a needless complication.

"Great." His teeth aren't as sharp as they should be, belying his nature when he smiles. "Just tell my staff you're 'Logan the wallet guy' and they'll know to let you through."

"Thanks," I say, "I'll be there."

He gives me another genial clap on the shoulder. "See you around, Logan."

I watch them walk away, wondering if doing so is letting the woman walk her way into a shallow grave. He glances back over his shoulder and gives a wave. His final look of longing wasn't necessary. Our separation won't be long-standing. We'll see each other again.

After all, I know where he lives.

Silvia doesn't approve of my more reserved tactics and demands I go after him. Cold rakes at me with only slightly less violence than it did earlier on the roadside. I shiver, letting her express her displeasure. I'm conflicted about it all as well. It seems stupid to behave by convention, to want tangible evidence when you're being guided by an intangible spirit. But if Silvia really wants justice, she'll have to be patient with the mundane means of the living.

My mind and senses are far from reliable and I can't trust them to the point I'll blithely toss away the restraints of civilized strictures. I need more proof than disembodied voices to gain the confidence of proper law enforcement.

A familiar pink-streaked haircut in the crowd catches my

eye. I'm about to tell Glenny off for following me when I see I'm not the guy she's tailing. She doesn't even know I'm here.

The man she's following is kind of tall, kind of freckly, and very much aware Glenny is dogging him. He keeps glancing back over his shoulder so Glenny will pretend to look away into a consignment shop window, be fascinated by hand-crafted jewelry for sale, or hop into one of the food truck lines. She's got the right idea on how to tail someone but the hilariously overacted execution, her pink hair highlights, and ballooning pregnancy are neon signs begging for her to be noticed.

She doesn't notice when I fall in step behind her.

"Looking for someone?" I ask.

Glenny doesn't startle. She just arches her pierced eyebrow as she turns to face me.

"I thought you said you were going to sleep," she says.

"I did say that."

"Well you're not doing a very job of it."

"That's pretty judgmental and discriminatory against som-nambulists," I say. "Why are you following tall, blond, and gawky over there?"

Glenny blushes. "That's Penn, Silvia's boyfriend."

"His name is Penn?"

"It's short for Parnell."

"Going by Penn is now justifiable." I can relate to having an unfortunate first name. I wasted no time in trying to butcher the atrocity my parents gave me into something presentable and skipped right over to going by my middle name instead.

"He goes by Tom. His last name's Thomas. Wait, what's your first name, then?"

"Then why do you call him Penn?"

"Because it annoys him," she says.

"Whatever you call him, he already knows you're following him, so you may as well call him over to talk," I say.

"He doesn't know," Glenny hisses, her blush reddening.

I point to the unfortunately named Parnell-Penn-Tom-Thomas. He's staring straight back at her. Both he and Glenny hurriedly glance away when they realize they've both been made.

"Okay, fine he knows," Glenny snaps. "But you gotta admit he looks super guilty."

"Or maybe he's just uncomfortable that he's being overtly stalked by a pregnant lady. That would make most men a might uneasy."

Glenny gives a derisive snort and rolls her eyes.

"Do you know Carl Burns?" I ask.

"Oh yeah, he's like a local celebrity. He has this podcast where people call in, talk about their problems and he gives them counseling and all that. He gave a talk at my high school once and Nicole has, like, all his books and keeps saying I should read them because my life is a mess. She gave me a couple of his books but I haven't read them. I think he's a bit of a creep, I don't know, he just has this weird vibe. You know, I met him at the spring festival and he offered me a ride home 'cause there was something wrong with my truck but Silvia came to pick me up instead. My dad doesn't like him either, he says Burns is anti-cop and...why?" Her eyes narrow then widen. "Oh. My. God. Do you think one of his clients did it? He still has his practice in Encrucijada. Hey, he's doing a live show tonight, we should go! Silvia's killer might be there, yeah?"

Her killer will most definitely be there.

"Was Silvia one of his clients?" I ask.

"No, I don't think so. But I know they knew each other from the hospital. He volunteers there and does bereavement counseling and all that other stuff. Was Penn one of Burns' patients?"

"Penn didn't kill her."

"Oh." Glenny frowns in disappointment. "Are you sure?"

"Positive." I get the feeling she's just looking for reasons to warrant her dislike of the guy.

Glenny makes a sound like a grumpy cat being stepped on. "Well, I don't like him. He cheated on Silvia and he's like a dark alley where conversation goes to be murdered."

"Why'd she go out with him, then?"

"I told you, it wasn't really going out-out, they were more like fake friends with real benefits—"

"Can you cheat in that kind of relationship?" I ask.

"Well you can be a dick, that's for sure, 'cause he is," Glenny says.

From what I've seen of Silvia, I still can't figure why she'd hang around a guy like Glenny describes Parnell-Penn-Tom-Thomas to be.

"Because his family is rich, he has a really nice pool, and . . ." Glenny holds her hands a fair width apart.

I don't want to know how she knows that.

"You know," she says, "that we keep running into each other is probably like a sign that we're supposed to work together."

"A sign from whom?"

"I dunno, the universe?"

"I don't believe in the universe."

"Do you always go out of your way to be a pain in the ass?"

"I never go out of my way. It's effortless."

Needling, insectile chills skitter down my arms. From the corner of my eye, shade shifts as if its source was disturbed by a sudden breeze, and the edges of my vision clot into that sepia color. It's all gone as fast as it came. Not quick enough Glenny didn't pick up on it.

"What happened? Did you have a vision?" she asks. "Was it Silvia?"

"Do you need help moving?" I ask, desperate for a reason to get her away from here.

"Um, probably." Glenny's ability to shift gears with the sudden subject change is impressive. "I'm not super good at heavy lifting right now but my brothers were going to come next week to do that."

"Tell you what, I help you move and you let me go through yours and Silvia's stuff," I say. Glenny may have had a point about searching through Silvia's belongings after all, and I think the sooner Glenny leaves the house of dead and sneering roommates, the better for her. And doing something semi-normal sounds real appealing right now.

"Deal?" I ask.

"Ha"—Glenny points at me—"I told you handling the possessions of the dead would help!"

Chapter 14

B eing back in Glenny's room confirms what Dr. Day told me months ago. This was going to be a slow process. For every two steps forward there'd be one step back. Maybe this isn't quite a step back. More like a step sideways. I've got a name and a face to go off of so I'm not shooting blind. But after going through Silvia's desk, turning out all her pockets, and rifling through her dresser a half dozen times, I think I'm shooting at the wrong target. I couldn't find anything that linked Silvia to Burns beyond her own volunteer badge at Encrucijada Hospital.

Despite Glenny's claims of the home being haunted, I find supernatural impingement to be delightfully minimal at her place. Even the murmurings sounded quieter while I rummaged through Silvia's belongings. They faded back to little more than a distant hush and have been barely a whisper since.

Glenny was disappointed I gave up so quick on trying to "sense Silvia's energy." She's even more disappointed that I'm making her repack all her moving boxes.

"God, I never would've placed you for such a neatnik," Glenny grumbles as she reorders the box filled by books and cooking utensils. I find the couple of books written by Burns and leaf through the pages. *The Empathetic Mind and Heart* runs the risk of my fingers sticking to the pages it's so saccharine.

"You've almost halved the number of boxes by packing right," I say, waving a hand at the relieved boxes thrown in the corner. The only box she bothered to pack well held memorabilia from her grandmother. The séance kit, Ouija board, a quilt, and a few framed photos. She and Glenny have the same round faces ending in pointed chins, large eyes, and impish grins.

"Yeah, but now all of these ones are heavier," she says. She keeps trying to sneak over to see what I'm reading. Whenever she does, I scoot an unfinished box between us and roll away on the desk chair to the other side of the room. Neither of us are being subtle and truth be told, we're both enjoying the game.

"You said you were going to help me move."

"I am." I close the book. Seeing Burns smiling back up at me from the back jacket cover stands my hair on end.

"Sitting around and mansplaining to me how I need to pack better isn't helping me move," she says.

"Yes it is. And then you 'girl-bossing' me on how the boxes should be carried and loaded into the truck will make us even," I say.

I squeeze *The Empathetic Heart and Mind* back into the book-filled box and slip out the framed photograph that is an exact copy of the one in her father's office: the Suarez family at the carnival. Glenny must be the little girl in the pigtails.

I move the family photo to a box free from any books by Burns. Having the picture and anything a derivative of that man share the same box seems sinful.

"Does your sister know to expect you?" I ask.

"Yeah, I called her. I could hear her grinding her teeth when

I told her a guy I met earlier today was going to help me move. She doesn't think I make good choices when men are involved."

"Wonder why."

Nicole is sitting on the living room futon, reading a paperback with a mug of tea on the side table. She spares us a couple glances over her book and makes no offer to help as we shuttle the boxes out to Glenny's truck.

"Oh, you're moving out today?" she says after we load up the last one. "Do you need any help?"

Glenny rolls her eyes so hard I expect bits of brain to be smeared across the irises when they come back to front.

"No need to be that way," Nicole calls out after Glenny stalks off. The front door slams shut behind her and the door to the truck after that.

"So do you know if she's going or not?" Nicole asks me as I reclaim my hat and boots from the entryway. "I just want to know for sure when we can rent out the room to someone else and Glenny is impossible to get a straight answer from."

"She'll be back tonight," I say. "Move the bigger furniture out tomorrow."

"And then she's gone?"

"God, I hope so."

I shut the front door a tad more gently than Glenny did.

She sits behind the wheel to the truck, keys in the ignition. She's not crying but she's close to it.

I open the driver's door. "Scoot."

She doesn't protest and slides over to the passenger seat with more grace than you'd expect in the cramped cab from anyone, let alone someone in her third trimester of pregnancy.

"Is it what she said or didn't say?" I ask, braving the risk of brewing up an emotional storm.

"It's what you didn't hear," Glenny says. She's not chewing her lip, just biting it so hard the skin has gone white.

"Don't come back here, then," I say, "I'll break down the bed tomorrow and move it and the desk. Stay at your sister's and be done with it."

Glenny shakes her head. "I need to clean the room and take pictures of it when all the furniture is out. I don't trust them not to dent the walls or stain that carpet after I'm gone, claim I did it and make me pay for damages."

"You're kidding."

Glenny shrugs. "I don't know. I just got a weird feeling, you know? Some of my stuff has gone missing lately too. It was happening before Silvia . . . you know, when she was still here. My clothes would disappear and I knew I had hung them up or put them away. I had this really super cute yellow top that I know I hung up in the closet, but Nicole and Adrienne only got mad when I asked them about it. They accused me of making it up for attention. Take a left at the end of the street and follow it until you reach the stoplight."

She stays uncharacteristically quiet as we pull out of the residential area and drive past a series of strip malls and businesses. We don't have anything in common that doesn't flirt with the macabre so I can't think of any material for lighthearted banter to cheer her up. Her turning on the radio and dialing up the volume tells she's in the mood to keep to herself anyway.

While Glenny may be glum, I'm in an unusually good mood. Which is odd, as today consisted of awkward talks with the dead, almost getting run over, crashing a wake of sorts for a girl murdered months ago, vomiting all over the side of the road, and then topping it all off with meeting the murderer.

And yet all in all, I'm feeling pretty good.

Maybe Dr. Day was right. Getting out and doing things does make a difference.

"What?" Glenny glares at my small smile like it's obscene graffiti scrawled over a church wall.

"I'll let you know when I figure it out," I say. It seems my mood is more contagious than hers. She stops slumping and turns the radio volume down to where conversation can be had.

"Take a right at the next light," she says, "and thanks."

"Sure."

"No, not for helping me move," she says. "For actually caring."

***

Glenny's sister's house is the quintessential southern-style home—pale brick, white wood, and sash-windowed dormers peeking out from the second floor. A white fence encircles the yard to meet at a trumpet vine covered trellis over a stone pathway leading up to the bevel window door topped off by a "Welcome" sign complete with woodcarvings of yellow and white flowers. The porch has a cushioned swing, and a couple of toy trucks are tucked under the white wicker chairs.

"I know," Glenny says, looking at it in the way I would St. Jude's, "it's like what you'd get if Andy Griffith eloped with June Cleaver."

"I like it," I say. It's much better than the rundown room she was renting and I'll bet the roommates are a step up as well.

The front door opens and the warden to Glenny's suburban Alcatraz steps out. She's taller than her sister, has a thinner build, darker hair, and faint rings under her eyes that mark her as a parent of small children.

"Hey, Josie," Glenny says. Josie's greeting is much warmer, a hug, a kiss on the forehead, and insistence Glenny sit down and have some fresh made sweet tea while she and I handle the unloading.

It's only after greeting and fussing over her younger sister that Josie can turn her full attention to me. She gives me a once-over, dark eyes taking me apart as neatly as a surgeon's scalpel. Judging by her expression I don't ace the assessment but get a passing grade as she gives a nod for me to start moving the boxes.

"Go ahead and sit down," Josie insists when Glenny chooses to pout on the porch, standing with arms crossed instead of sitting in one of the wicker chairs. "We'll take care of this."

"I'm pregnant, not helpless," Glenny snaps. The rudeness doesn't throw Josie at all and half a minute later Glenny is grumbling into her glass of sweet tea, Josie and I are unloading the truck, and the two boys who were shyly peering out the front door are showing off their toy trucks on the front lawn by crashing them into one another.

"By the way, I'm Logan," I say.

"I know," Josie says. "Glenny told me."

"She did?"

"Oh yeah," Josie says, looking over me again with a little less wariness than the first time. "She spent almost twenty minutes talking to me about you on the phone earlier today."

"Twenty minutes, that's impressive. I've known myself my entire life and I wouldn't be able to stretch that conversation to five minutes."

I'm a might bit edgy over what material Glenny used to fill that twenty minutes talking to her sister. Between chatting to the dead and crashing a wake, very little of my time around

Glenny has been anything that'd earn me a good impression in a sane person's judgment.

"Not as impressive as you'd think. Glenny likes to tell the same story multiple times in the same conversation," Josie says.

Whether it be from what Glenny told her about me or that I'm a complete stranger, Josie is understandably reluctant to let me traipse into her house so I deposit the boxes on the front porch, deciding not to walk in without explicit invitation.

"You always this easy?" Josie asks as we unload the last of the boxes. "Only got to know a girl half a day before she's got you so wrapped around her finger you're helping her move?"

She's relaxing her guard. If I keep up the good behavior I might get house privileges.

"Hey now," I say, "it's the twenty-first century, you need to be a bit more broad-minded. It's not just the girls."

Josie's smile is the same as her sister's.

"Glenny'll be in the guest room. She can show you where that's at," she says, granting me the coveted house privileges.

Glenny lurches to her feet, ready for purpose. "Come on."

"And the bedroom door stays open," Josie calls after us.

Glenny confirms the low confidence in her maturity is deserved by blowing a raspberry as she shows me up the stairs. "She thinks no one is capable of running their life unless she's got one hand on the wheel."

"I like your sister," I say. "She reminds me of mine." She and Kitty would probably be thick as thieves.

"She's worse than my parents," Glenny says, then sighs. "No, you're right, that was ungrateful."

"I didn't say it."

"Yeah, but you were thinking it real loud, weren't you?"

"Couldn't have been me. I never think above a whisper."

Glenny laughs as she pushes open the door to the guest room. The furnishing matches the Cleaver-Griffith coupling Glenny finds so distasteful. There's a neat little bed, a bassinet at the ready, and a small closet with rose carvings in the wood. The ceramic lamps on the bedside table and glass vases on the dresser were clearly put in here to spare them the destruction two little boys would bring upon them.

"It's not that." Glenny flounces on the bed, resigned to the terrible fate of having a sister who is happy to take her in and help raise her baby. "It's that . . . you know, I want to be on my own. Independent. I don't need her help."

"Yes you do," I say and catch the throw pillow she chucks at me. Josie may want to move those ceramic lamps to a different room. Her sister could outdo her sons in terms of destruction.

Save for a couple smaller boxes, the baby is all Glenny can adequately carry so she follows after me, puppy-like, as I move the larger ones to various locations in the house. Seeing the same photograph of the Suarez family at the fair on the mantel place gets a grin out of me.

Most of the boxes end up stored in the garage, Josie refusing to mix in Glenny's plastic and chipped kitchenware with the higher class ladles and spatulas she uses.

"You know, I was kinda thinking that you had some secret motive for this," Glenny says as I pick up the last box. "That you were getting psychic vibes or something from my stuff and this moving was just a pretense to be around it more."

"Sorry," I say, "I'm not that clever." I wanted you out of that house, to stop obsessing over your friend's death, and get you and the baby clear of this morbid business.

"No, that box can go in here," Glenny says, redirecting me

away from the guest room to the one across the hall.

"See, you're girl-bossing. We're square now."

She pushes the door open to a nursery. The walls are bright blues and yellows, and hand-painted birds in Glenny's detailed style wait in ready flight above the prepared crib. Bottles of baby powder stand expectantly on the nightstand, the toy basket and books with cheery pastel covers lay ready beside the cushioned rocking chair.

Neither my wife nor I had the artistic talent to make a nursery like this. We never even got the crib assembled.

***

"It's just a desk," I said.

The offending furniture stood in the place where the crib should have been. One of the white crib legs stuck out of the opened box that featured a giggling baby in the arms of a smiling mother.

"This isn't supposed to be an office." Maria spoke to the room more than me, glaring at the desk in distaste.

"I'll move it if you want."

"We could've put it in the basement," she said.

"The lighting is terrible down there." This wasn't our first rodeo for this exchange and I didn't miss a beat dropping the practiced line.

I gestured out the window to show the view of the backyard, the reason I fought tooth and nail to close on this house. The five acres of golden-green grass, which would become a palette of wildflowers come spring, dropped off into rolling hill country of oak and juniper.

"You work from home enough you should at least enjoy the home," I said.

Maria crossed her arms, lips pressed into a tight frown.

"This isn't supposed to be an office." Tears eroded the steadiness to her words.

It wasn't just a desk to her. The furniture unrelated to a baby was nothing short of admitting defeat. Two years of negatives, a miscarriage, this latest false-positive, and my constantly being gone for months on end turned the desk into a symbol of a future absent of children and a half-there husband. The unassembled crib was back in its box in the corner. When I left last time, it had been out. Ready to be put together.

"Babe . . ."

She stepped away when I moved to hold her. I settled to stand by and stare out the window with her.

"I can't change that I'm shipping out next week," I said.

"Are you going to reenlist?"

I didn't say anything. I didn't know the answer yet.

"What if we have a baby?" she asked.

"Is that all you think about? You just want me as your studhorse."

She wasn't in the mood for teasing. In nearly four years of marriage I'd only seen her cry once before.

"We'll try again. When I get back."

Her frustration rolled down in quiet tears.

"Hell, we can try again right now." I stupidly went back to teasing. I'd rather have her angry at me than disappointed in herself.

"I want a baby. I want a family," she said, the sincerity of the desire weighing her voice down into a whisper, "and I want you here for it."

***

A chill ripples along my arms and leads me back to the now.

The mobile hanging above the crib's side twists without

tangible touch. White clouds and yellow striped hot air balloons rotate slowly about.

I told myself maybe it was better we never had the baby. Or that she wasn't pregnant when she . . . when it happened. It didn't help.

Glenny is looking at me and I pretend not to notice. She doesn't fall for it. I flinch but don't pull away when she takes my hand.

"I'm sorry," she says.

Chapter 15

"Stay at your sister's tonight," I say.

"Why?" Glenny asks, shifting the truck into park.

Moth wings flicker in the lights lining the Roadhouse's porch. Carefree laughter and splashing comes from the pool out back.

Reaching the motel took more time than I thought. Traffic was thick on the streets as people struggled to find parking close to Main Street. Despite the heavy load of cars, Glenny managed to snag a parking spot right outside the Ranger's Roadhouse, a bit of fortune leading me to believe God likes her more than me.

"Did you have a vision or something?" Glenny asks.

"Yeah, I saw how your roommates treat you and you deserve better," I say.

Despite being in a bear of a mood, Glenny took her sweet time getting me back to the motel. First she said I had to help her unpack all her belongings under the pretense I might pick up psychic energies from it. Then Josie invited me to stay for dinner and Glenny insisted, through clenched teeth, that I had to stay.

Josie only asked a dozen times if I got enough food when I didn't eat much. She wasn't fooled at all by my artful pushing of food around on the plate. I endured the offended looks she kept sending my way but when they changed to concern I started to squirm.

Fortunately Josie's husband, Jacob, the less intuitive of the J-Squad, saved the day by making everyone uncomfortable. He spent half the dinner assuming I was the father of Glenny's baby, and the next half trying to backtrack, apologize, and dodge around the questions his two young boys started asking about where babies come from.

It got even better when they asked what I did for a living.

"I just got out of the army," I said.

"Oh, thank you for your service," Josie said.

"What made you decide to leave?" her husband asked.

I paused a second too long. "Health reasons."

Josie had the sensitivity to not pursue that line of conversation. Her husband did not. He eventually got the message to change subjects after Josie kicked him under the table hard enough to get the silverware rattling.

And after all that, Glenny was still reluctant to be rid of me. She dawdled, found numerous last minute tasks that she needed help getting done. It was only after she realized I was getting too chummy with the J-Squad and we had entered the dangerous waters of childhood stories about her that she decided it was time for me to go.

"I'm a big girl, I can make my own choices," Glenny says, tapping her pink painted nails on the steering wheel. "You think something bad is gonna happen, don't you?"

"Don't sound so excited about it," I say, "and no. Not in the way you think. It's nothing supernatural."

She shoots up a skeptical eyebrow. "I'm not stupid, Logan."

I agree but don't offer a reply.

"Are you doing anything tonight? What're you doing tomorrow?" she asks.

I shrug.

"Can I see you?" she asks.

"If you stay at your sister's tonight, I'll help you move the bed and desk tomorrow."

"Okay. I gotta take all my food from the fridge and pantry too. Josie probably won't want much of it so you can help me eat most of it. It feels kinda bad having to throw it away, that's probably what Nicole and Adrienne will do if I leave it. I guess we can donate the cans and nonperishables, yeah? But what about Silvia?" Glenny asks.

"The ball is in her court," I say. "All I can do is wait so I might as well do something useful until I hear from her."

"You'll tell me if anything comes up though, right?"

"Depends what it is," I say.

"Here. Here. Here."

Glenny sighs. "Ugh, fine. You know, you're like, the most milquetoast spirit medium I've ever met."

"Milquetoast medium is my brand," I say, sliding out of the passenger seat. "I'm gonna put it on my business card."

"Here. Here." A cold hand tugs at me as if trying to reel me back inside the truck.

"Hey, Logan," Glenny calls after me.

I turn and the cold all but shoves me back towards her.

"Here."

"Do you . . . I . . . um . . . I'll, I'll see you tomorrow," Glenny says instead of whatever she meant to say.

As per my usual routine, I turn on all the lights and do a quick sweep of the motel room. I don't expect to find any monsters lurking under the bed or ghostly visitors hiding in the closet, but these checks are my way to prove to them I won't be caught off guard by clichés. It's worked so far.

"Here. Here."

I waste a couple minutes wondering if it's worth the energy to change my shirt. It isn't. But putting on a fresh layer of deodorant is a step in the right direction for me.

Sharp, chilling needles dig into me, the murmurings are a mess of hisses, Silvia's voice is a medley of frustration.

"Here. Here. Come here. Come here. Here."

"I'm going, I'm going," I tell her as I turn off all the lights and lock the motel room behind me. I've got a little less than an hour to make it to Burns' live show. I don't intend to take up his offer for the backstage pass. In fact, I don't really know what I intend to do once I show up. I'm already sure he killed Silvia and if I'm looking for proof, it won't be there. Not unless my presence will somehow compel the spirits that be to besiege him into such throes of guilt he breaks down and confesses to his crimes in front of the captivated audience.

I'm willing to try it. I'm willing to try next to anything to get Silvia to settle down from the tear she's on. She almost gets me to trip down the stairs she's making me shiver so hard.

"Come here. Here."

When I step back out into the parking lot I'm surprised to see Glenny's truck still there. My pondering over new-shirt-or-not should have been more than sufficient time for her to have driven off.

She sits in the cab and while I can't see her face, I can imagine she's wearing her glum-Glenny expression.

"Here. Here. Here. Here. Here."

A couple pieces click into place and I can't believe it could be this simple.

It's only when I make to leave Glenny does Silvia start getting feisty.

"You want me to stay with her?" I ask under my breath.

The piercing cold softens to a cool pull.

"Christ, you could have just said so."

"Here."

Glenny jumps when I knock on her window.

"Did you hear from Silvia?" she asks, rolling down the window with such enthusiasm she should've snapped off the manual crank.

"How late does the festival go at night?" I ask.

"Um, I think it goes to about ten on Main Street but there's always something going on until maybe midnight at least," she says.

"Do you wanna go?"

"Right now?" Glenny asks. The dim glow cast by the motel's porch light catches in her widening eyes. "I mean, yeah!"

She clocks me with the door as she jumps out of the truck. It's worth it to have the chill lift entirely. I didn't realize how warm the night was.

"Is this for the investigation or—"

"No, it's for fun," I lie. "Call your sister first. Let her know what you're doing."

"She's not my mom," Glenny says, "and I'm old enough to make my own choices."

I don't budge until she lets Josie know she'll be back later.

"Happy?" she asks, pretending to be upset but can't stop grinning as she leads the way to Main Street. That she's so delighted by having my poor quality company fires up my sympathy on all cylinders. She's gotta be the loneliest kid I've ever met.

***

I used to go to concerts. It wasn't too long ago I could enjoy music without having to hear it through haunted radios. And I'm resolved to prove I still can. Walking down Main Street to appreciate the festival for what it is, a festival, and not the backdrop to my most recent haunting won't harm anything. It might even do some good.

It doesn't. It all feels fake as I move among the late-night festival goers. New food trucks have replaced the old ones. A solo singer takes the main stage and busts out a bluesy ballad ripped from the records of my parents' generation. The younger folks in the audience are confused by the melody. It's fast enough they want to dance, slow enough they don't know how.

Dr. Day said something about enjoying moments such as these. He gave advice on what to do when they came along. I can't remember what he said. The murmurings are a dam to those memories.

Either fireworks or mortar rounds boom in the distance. It doesn't matter which. It's all so far away. The murmurings mix in with the babble of the living and rather than blurring together, they become more starkly defined as I move through the crowd. My fingers find the wedding band and slowly turn it round and round. The realization of how far I've removed myself from the living should hit me harder. For the past year, the dead have dictated my life more than the living.

"There's more to life than what's been lost," Dr. Day said.

"Logan?" Glenny's hand is warm when she takes my arm. I'm surprised she's stuck around this long, dull, drab company that I am.

"If you like the music we can find some seats," I say.

"What do you want to do?" she asks.

"Or if you're hungry I can get you a burger or something."

"A burger sounds great," she says. "But I'll get it, you go get seats."

At the end of the song, there's a minor exodus as younger audience members look for different entertainment than the throwback singer.

I snag a recently vacated picnic table, brushing away crumbs left by the last occupants, right as Glenny catches up and plops a hamburger in front of me. A couple of fries jump out of the basket as it hits the table and the burger is only prevented from toppling over by the enormous toothpick skewering the multilayered monstrosity.

When I make to move the food back across the table to Glenny, she throws her hands out as a blockade.

"Nope, nope, nope. It's yours," she says. "You hardly ate anything at dinner, don't try and argue, I saw. Oh, and you made Josie think that they had offended you or something over dinner and put you off your appetite. You didn't hear, but she totally laid into Jacob for asking all those personal questions and for being so clueless it was making you uncomfortable."

"You don't—"

"Oh, and I bought the burger with my own money so not only would it be really rude for you not to accept it, but I also don't have a job right now because I'm about to bust out a baby so I don't have a lot of money so that on top of how you made Josie feel should be more than enough to guilt you into eating it."

"I'm not—"

"Say, 'thank you for this thoughtful and wonderful gift, I will show my appreciation by eating it,'" Glenny says.

"How am I supposed to eat this when I'm sick from all the guilt you've put on me?" I ask.

Glenny's response is to drown the French fries in ketchup.

"Tell you what, we'll make a game of it," she says.

"I don't like games."

"Good, because you only do things you don't like anyway." She takes one of the fries and points the ketchup-sodden end at me. "I ask you a question. If you want to answer it, you do. If you don't want to answer it, you have to take a bite."

"So is there a point system to decide the winner or is to the death?" I ask.

"To the death."

"Glenny, I spent half a year of people asking me all manner of uncomfortable questions. If you think you can make me—"

"What's your first name?"

Damn. She's good. I take a bite.

"Favorite childhood memory?" she asks.

"Going to my grandparents' on Sundays after Mass."

"Most awkward high school moment?"

"Freshman year to senior year."

"That's not a real answer," she says.

"It was a very long moment."

"Fine, most embarrassing moment. Ever."

Glenny is too young and pure for the answer to that question so the hamburger takes the hit.

"Do you think I talk too much?"

"Yes."

"Why?"

"Stories should be like a skirt. Long enough to cover everything but short enough to keep interest. Your stories hit the floor and have a mile long train."

"Are you wearing the same shirt you wore yesterday?"

"Yes."

"Why?"

I take another bite.

"Does this mean I win?" Glenny asks when the food basket is empty save for a few smears of ketchup to commemorate the fallen French fries.

"Nope. Because technically I didn't eat all of it," I say. "You had at least half the French fries."

"We'll call it a draw, then," she says. "You know, I was thinking about driving out to go to Burns' show and see if there were any leads or something there. But this was better."

A livelier band has replaced the slow-song balladeer and a younger crowd swarms back around the stage to pay homage to the faster beat. I think Glenny recognizes a few of the faces in the audience because she's goes rigid and refuses to look over their way.

"Where're you going?" I ask when she stands to leave.

"Home. To my sister's," she adds. "I know you're tapped out on company for the night and she'll be getting suspicious if I stay out much later."

She scuffs a combat boot against the ground. "Thank you. No one's asked me to do anything fun for a while. It was nice."

I decide to do a test, requiring I stay seated and sacrifice the gentlemanly responsibility of walking Glenny to her car. Sure enough, the cold sensation creeps back in, urging me to go after her as she walks away.

"Here. Here. Come here."

That Silvia wants me to stick around with Glenny is clear. The why is much less obvious. If Silvia will only be put to rest if I spend every waking moment hanging around Glenny, there'll be no peace to be had by any of us. There's got to be more to it than Silvia clawing at me from beyond the grave to ensure Glenny has a friend.

"So what is it?" I ask Silvia. "What do you want?"

The cool tugs continue in the direction Glenny left but no revelation comes my way.

The trio on stage draws out the song's ending chorus, keeping the audience in suspense as to what will come next and the lead female singer's stunning alto voice convinces me to stick around. The three musicians change seamlessly from a final croon into a mournful retelling of "Ghost Riders in the Sky."

The minor key in which she sings takes the song beyond a simple folktale and reshapes it into an ominous warning. Staying to listen is one of the better choices I've made in the past few days. It's a nice break from the murmurings and the whispering dead.

My fingers play along to the beat, each tap of the finger against the table sends months of tension flooding out from me. The lead singer absolutely nails the vocalizing leading up to the chorus, convincing me there's still good to be found in the normal things I used to do.

I can do this. I can do normal. I can sit here and enjoy the music simply for the sake of enjoying music. There doesn't need to be anything else to it. Murders and murmurings can wait until morning. I can still—

"Hey, pal! I'm talking to you!"

The man standing over my picnic table must have been talking at me for some time. He's got the annoyed expression folks get when I've failed to give them the attention they think themselves entitled to. He's a beacon of body odor from spending all day under a summer sun, swimming through a crowd of people doing the same as him, topped off by beer-marinated breath.

I blink up at him in an intimidatingly stupid manner until recognition breaks through.

"Oh hey, Penn," I say. Couldn't he have waited until the song ended for this?

I lean around him to see the table across from me. A couple of his guy friends are staring over at us, salivating in hopes things escalate. There's strong similarity running through their features suggesting they're related. Brothers or cousins.

"What were you doing with Glenny?" he asks. Accusation is as ripe on his breath as the beer.

"Who?" I ask more to annoy him than to play dumb.

He gets right in my face, leaning in close. He's about my age, a little heavier, definitely taller, and has a longer reach. "You stay away from her. You hear me?"

"What's it to you?" I ask. I'm tired and testy, making it easy for this clown to get under my skin. And why's he angry at me? Glenny was the one who was obviously stalking him earlier today. I'm sure some guys would have found that strangely flattering.

Parnell-Penn-Tom-Thomas' buddies aren't the only ones watching now. A few more eyes have been drawn to my little table. A group of young women are looking over at us. A few glance around nervously while one is eager for a testosterone-fueled showdown. A curvy bleached blonde leans so far forward she's about to fall out of her low-cut spaghetti-strap dress.

"Well, whatever you're doing with her, you're gonna cut it out," he says. "In fact, why don't you just cut out and leave.

Single guy like you doesn't need to be taking up a whole table like this. You ain't even got a drink."

"You could always go buy me one," I say. "You're more like to get in my pants that way than with this whole tough guy act."

A couple of the women listening in laugh. Penn doesn't share their sense of humor. His face burns red and he shows his teeth.

"You leave Glenny alone," he hisses.

"What, it's not like I can knock her up." I put two and two together and add, "You've already taken care of that."

His telegraphed swing could be seen by a blind man. I slip it easily. Grabbing hold of the back of his neck to slam him face-first into the wooden table is even easier. The sound of skull smacking hard causes my tinder pile of fear, frustration, and grief built up over the last year to catch. By the time I jump to my feet to knee him in the groin, then gut, it's a full blaze.

Penn hits the ground and curls up into a wheezing ball. His buddies all rise as one, fists and teeth clenched. They're all bigger than Penn and now they're twice as angry.

"Well?" I kick Penn out of the way and throw out my hands in invitation for his friends to come forward.

Two of them do. They're drunk. I'm not. They're ticked. I'm just mad.

***

For the first time in a while I take a real look in the mirror.

There's a stranger staring back, face thinner than it should be, even with the swelling. My nose is bloody and I'll have a black eye by tomorrow. The waste basket in the motel bathroom is white and red from all the bloodied tissues.

Sheriff Suarez wasn't happy to see me again. The young women the next table over saw the whole thing and thought it funny as hell it was the 5'9" vagabond wannabe who walked away from the fight. None of the women could make it through the whole story without at least snickering. Flower-Sleeves, the purple-haired waitress from Sawdust, was one of them.

"I've had to eighty-six those guys before," she said to me after the police cleared off. "They've been overdue for some humbling for a while."

With over half a dozen witnesses backing me up on the claim Penn swung first, save for Penn who whined I was crazy and needed to be in a bughouse, the cops didn't have much interest in me after I said I wasn't interested in pressing charges.

"Just a friendly dustup between guys," I said. I'm just glad the reason for the fight never got much attention. Sheriff Suarez would be even less pleased to hear his youngest daughter has been running around with me and I'm already getting into scraps over her.

Before he left the scene, Sheriff Suarez pulled me aside.

"In the old days, you'd be run out of town for causing this much trouble so quick," he said.

"That's how I ended up here," I said. It's half true.

"Son, I've seen you too often for my liking the last couple days," he said. "I don't want to see you again. Understand?"

I plug one side of my nose and snort out a clotted bloody stream. Suarez is a decent guy and I'm sorry to be giving him so much trouble. Especially since I expect to be causing a hell of a lot more.

Chapter 16

A scream catches in my constricted throat. I fall out of bed in a tangle of sheets as I make a blind dash away from the dream where Alec held a finger to his lips. He crouched down next to me among the hostile rock and scrub of Afghanistan, warning me not to make a sound. If they find me, I'm dead.

I clamp my hand over my mouth to stifle the rasp of my uneven breaths. The dream's lingering shadows take the shape of hands reaching up for me through the motel floor. They don't grab at me. They beckon me to follow them down. Down, down into the dark, murmuring waters.

I don't dare close my eyes to shut it out. The retreat into darkness would only give the fading dream new life.

It was there in the dream, the entity, more tangible in sleep than waking. It followed after me through the barren mountains. The rock and dried brush were quiet under my feet but they cracked and withered under its stalking tread and—

And I can feel it, escaped from the dream to wait on the other side of the thin motel door, eager to come in. There's no unnatural bend to the shadow. No scraping noise of something intangible pressing its way into the physical world. Not even a rattle of the doorknob. But I know it's there. It turns the world utterly silent save the unending chorus of murmurs.

I press back against the bed, half-finished prayers hissing between clenched teeth. I want to run but am terrified any greater movement will invite it in. I go stock-still, watching the door for the smallest hint of opening. The morning sun slipping light up the wall does nothing to banish the entity. Its fading away is much slower than the sun's rising and even when my chest stops feeling as if a giant hand constricts it, I don't dare move.

Sound makes a timid return to the world. Only when birds' singing drifts through the open window and I hear the sleepy shuffle of the people in the room next door getting ready for the day, happily ignorant to murmurings and hauntings, do I risk a free breath. The helplessness the entity inspires is the worst of it—I don't know what it is, what it wants, or what to do about it.

I curl up against the bed, pulling my fraying mind back together. Before the entity invaded sleep to wake me to its presence outside the door, I had been dreaming of something else, something important. I try to remember, the shape of the dream dulled by sunlight. A madman's fevered certainty has me convinced it was relevant to Silvia. I swear it had something to do with Glenny as well, and with all the oddities dog-piling onto my life it would be stupid to dismiss it as only a dream.

An angry hum sounds behind me and I whip right round into the bedside table, slamming my forearm against the corner.

"Motherfuck." The sharp pain clears away the last paralysis of panic and adds another bruise on top of the several earned in last night's brawl.

I don't find my culprit cellphone before it stops ringing. A second call right on the end of the first helps me locate it buried deep in the folds of the bed sheets.

"Hello?" I ask.

"You didn't call."

I slide my way face-first back across the bed until I lie flat across the twisted sheets.

"Sorry, Kitty, I got distracted."

"When should we expect you?" she asks.

"I said not for a couple days."

"Yeah, and I know better than to take you at your word anymore."

Ouch. But she's right.

"Logan, if you can't even remember to give me a damn phone call—oh no, sweetie, I said darn—then forgive me if I doubt your ability to handle the more complicated demands in life."

"Your faith in me is a needed strength in my dark hours," I say.

The silence on the other end of the line doesn't bode well. A hollow pit in my gut saps away the ability to navigate a conversation with my older sister. I can't find the needed words to ease her worries and I know the longer I talk to her the more she's going to worry.

"Did you just wake up?" she asks.

"No," I lie. "Why?"

"Because you're slurring your words."

"That's because I'm lying face down on a mattress," I say.

"You said you didn't just wake up."

"Because I didn't. I've just been lying like this for hours."

Again, the foreboding silence. She has zero appreciation for my attempts to lighten the mood.

"Do not make me come get you," she warns.

"I love you too, Kitty," I say and hang up.

I ignore her calling me back and sigh when I see the time. It's well past ten and all I've accomplished so far is falling out of bed and then crawling back in. Lying here for a few hours might not be such a bad plan. I have a feeling today is going to suck so there doesn't seem much reason to hurry the day along.

The phone rings again as I pull out my laptop. By the time I've searched Burns' address, there are three more missed calls from Kitty. She shakes up her attack pattern and sends me a text instead.

Logan, please call me back.

I don't shake up my pattern of behavior and don't respond. Ignoring the buzz of the phone distracts from ignoring the preternatural hiss and hush of the murmurings. There's an ugly hiss to them this morning, setting my teeth on edge as I go over the aerial and street imagery of Burns' address. I explore the surrounding area, get a feel for the terrain, note the placement of neighboring houses, where I'm most likely to be seen by a witness, and where copses of trees provide cover.

I can feel myself slipping into a pit of despondent procrastination as I toggle back and forth along the map, beginning to lose sight of the screen as I stare at it. I shut the laptop before I get sucked into the delay tactic of staring at the same bird's eye view of Burns' roof from varying angles.

I should have gone to his house last night. I knew Burns wouldn't be home. It was the perfect time to make an uninvited call and ransack his place for evidence of Silvia's murder. I really am terrible at this whole paranormal detective thing.

The murmurings crawl over my mind like insects and while

the entity has faded away, the dread it brings has not.

Whup. Whup. Whup.

Hitching my senses onto the fan's rhythmic spin is second nature now. It provides the fortification needed to keep the damned murmurings at a tolerable volume.

Showering sounds too complicated and it isn't as though I have anyone to impress. The clothes I wore yesterday lie in a crumpled pile on the floor, an impossible distance away from me.

"Ah, no." I slide my hands down my face, remembering I'll have to change shirts. Yesterday's is splattered in blood.

I could just lie here. Whatever that entity is, it was on the other side of the door. A smart man would keep it that way. Keep that door shut. The day's mostly shot anyways, it probably won't be worth going out to Burns' place. Besides, he might be home, which would complicate my planned breaking and entering. Being a self-made snake oil salesman of pop psychology, I'm not sure how he spends his days other than volunteering at music festivals and murdering people.

A gentle tug on my arm encourages me out of the otherwise inescapable inertia.

"Come on," Silvia calls, showing me far more patience than I deserve. *"Come on."*

The motel lobby is too busy to stay there long. People ranging from eighteen to eighty wear bright shirts, khaki shorts, and sunglasses perched on the brim of baseball caps as they go over the list of events for the day and brochures for local shops and restaurants.

May waves to me as a middle-aged couple—the man possessing the courage to wear calf-length white socks with his sandals—depart to begin their day of fun and festival.

"Morning, Mr. Dalaguerre," she says. "How are . . . good heavens, if people see you leaving the motel looking like that it's goin' to scare away all my business."

"Like what?" I ask, rubbing a hand over my stubbled jaw.

"Like you and some hussy were shooting up heroin all last night and she blacked your eye when you wouldn't pay," she says.

My too-slow blink and failure to come up with a witty comeback doesn't help my cause.

"I fell," I say.

"Don't sell me that, son." May wags a bony finger at me. "I heard about your scrap at the festival last night. Frank called to make sure you weren't causing any trouble 'round here."

"Frank?"

"Sheriff Suarez," she says.

"I can check out early. I don't mind," I say.

May snorts. "No need for that. Just be glad I didn't tell him you've been running around with his little princess. Oh, don't look at me like that, Mr. Dalaguerre. I'm old, not blind. I can see out into my own parking lot."

Her expression softens as she peers at the dark circles beneath my eyes and she can tell it's not just from bruising.

"Did you have trouble sleeping? Was it too noisy for you last night? I already got some complaints about kids on your floor not settling down until near dawn."

I didn't notice and as much as I'd like to thank her for the concern, the ability to string together a simple sentence escapes me. A stiff headshake is all I get out and I feel her frowning my way as I shamble out.

I blink when I see Glenny waiting for me, sitting on one of the front porch chairs, a paper café bag beside her.

"Oh wow, what happened?" she asks.

"I hit a man's fist with my face," I say.

"Really?" she asks. "Did it have something to do with Silvia?"

I shake my head.

"Coffee?" she asks, offering a to-go cup in one hand and a Danish in the other. She nudges me a few times with the toe of her boot to motivate me to respond.

"What're you doing here?" I ask.

"Waiting for you." She deflates a little as she looks me over, catching my contagious cheerlessness. "You look . . ."

"Dead?" I offer.

She nods. "And like rigor mortis is setting in. Are you okay?"

"How long were you waiting out here?"

"I don't know. Maybe forty minutes? Did you win the fight at least? Does it hurt?" She points to my face. "I think I have ibuprofen in the truck. You're not supposed to take that while pregnant, but I probably still have it in there. Or May would make you an ice pack if you asked. She likes you. And feels a little sorry for you."

"You could've let me know you were out here," I say, feeling guilty my lethargic indulgences kept Glenny waiting.

"I don't want you to think I'm bothering you," she says to her feet. "I'm not bothering you, am I?"

"I thought you knew things," I say, taking the coffee and Danish before sitting down in the chair next to hers.

"You don't need to be rude when people are trying to help," she says.

That guilt trip would've had me land face-first and blacked my other eye.

"You're right, and thank you," I say, toasting her with the coffee.

Squirming in her seat, she holds back her excitement and stays quiet until I finish the coffee.

"So any word from Silvia?" She leans forward on the little wooden table between our chairs to whisper, eyes wide and bottom lip between her teeth.

"Nope," I say.

"Oh," she says, face falling. "So nothing at all on the, you know, spirit front?"

"Nothing to report."

"Oh." She plops her head down on crossed arms. "So then what are you going to do today?"

"Don't know," I lie again.

And this time she calls me out on it. "Yes you do. I can help."

I hold up the empty cup. "You already did."

Twenty ounces of black coffee is waging war on the hollow lethargy that's trying to keep me sitting here on the porch or retreat back to bed. Give it a bit more time and the caffeine will grease the engines of moral responsibility to help me walk the fifteen feet between the porch and my car.

"You know what I mean," Glenny says. "So are we going to tail Burns or something? See if you can get any vibes off him? You don't think he killed her, do you?"

"Could you visit with your dad today?" I ask.

"Why?"

Because that will keep you safe and out of trouble.

"Because he's the sheriff and he might know things. Things that you might be able to pick up."

She huffs, blowing a strand of pink hair off her face. "Yeah, okay, fine."

My eyebrows fly up. I expected resistance or at least some complaining.

"Might as well," she says. "He's been trying to take me to lunch for over a week now. I keep saying I'm busy 'cause I know we'll just end up arguing."

Glenny kicks up her legs to propel herself out of the chair. "But are you still gonna come by later? You don't have to help me move the furniture. We can compare notes on anything we find out or something like that. You could come by my place, I mean my sister's, if you don't want to go out somewhere. I can order dinner or make something if you want. Is that okay? Do you like enchiladas? I make really good enchiladas. Or if you don't want to be around Josie and Jacob, we could go back to the house. And if you're tired, you don't have to help me move, we could just hang out if you want. Adrienne is probably staying at her boyfriend's for the weekend and Nicole has the day off but she's hardly ever at the house except to sleep so you won't have to worry about people overhearing anything. Logan?"

"My brain isn't firing on all cylinders yet so processing is taking a bit longer," I say. "Yeah, we can meet up."

The joy on her face at the thought of company is heartbreaking. "What time do you wanna meet?" she asks.

I can't give her a time but I give the promise to call.

"Great! See you later," she says, managing to do a pregnant waddle-skip back to her truck. She pauses and turns back around, smile fading under a creased brow. "Are you sure you're okay?"

"Shouldn't you know the answer to that?" I ask.

She rolls her eyes. "I do. It's still nice when people ask."

"I'll see you later, Glenny."

The country music escaping from her truck hiccups and skips a couple times before she pulls from the parking lot. The guitar strumming fades as she drives off to be replaced by a hissing blare of white static. My car's engine isn't running, but the radio is running its mouth at a volume high enough to be heard through the closed windows.

"Yeah, I hear you." The static summons and coffee works together to motivate me to walk over to the car and start being useful.

The volume drops and dies when I slide into the driver's seat.

"I must be getting old," I say in a mixed excuse and apology. "It's getting harder to get moving in the morning."

The radio spits a few incoherent burbles before shutting off.

"I know," I say, "I'm trying."

Chapter 17

Driving out to Burns' place takes me well outside Encrucijada's limits. Residential streets become scarcer as they're replaced by ranches and multi-acre lots. Soon, scrub and brush replace the neat fields and rail fences interspersing the homes. Every once in a while a cluster of houses will crop up with crepe myrtles lining the streets behind signs reading "Stone Oak," "Stone Ridge," or the real creative one of "Oak Ridge." The neighborhoods are the rarities. Most homes along the road are solitary sentries pushed far back into the low oaks. Only mailboxes, wooden or wire fences, and gravel driveways hint to a home. It's the quiet country road you'd drive down to visit your grandparents on Sunday, not a place where you'd think to find a murderer.

Which reminds me, tomorrow is Sunday and the end of the reprieve Kitty granted me. I wouldn't be surprised if she swings by to abduct me from the Ranger's Roadhouse tomorrow morning on her way to Mass, stuffing me into the back of her minivan. I'd better sort out this Silvia business before then.

I drive straight past Burns' house without even slowing for a real look. From what I glean as I cruise by, it looks like any other house on this stretch of country road. Not even my supernatural senses tingle as I pass his driveway. I'm not sure what to make of this silence, if it's a good sign or a bad sign. Or if it's a sign at all.

"Nothing to say?" I ask the radio. It keeps to itself as I drive another mile and turn into a collection of homes marked by the requisite crepe myrtle around a stone sign reading "Stone Creek." The neighborhood is decently large and hosts a manicured park, a circle of green lawn and trees around a man-made lake. My silver Honda blends right in with the half dozen cars already parked beneath the protective shade of thick oak leaves.

No cars pass me as I hike the mile back to Burns' place. Other than the heavy thrum of insects and high trill of cardinals flitting through the brush, the county road remains barren.

Reaching Burns' home reaffirms the need for me to stop toting these Hollywood expectations around because once again they're wrong. Instead of the dilapidated grey shack of rotting wood I imagined he lives in, guarded by a pupil-less black dog at the front step, the address belongs to a two-story French country style house. There are no fallen boards in the steep hipped roof, no broken fingernails embedded into the stucco siding, or bloody handprints pressed on the French pane windows. The driveway is devoid of both cars and sketchy vans designed for the single purpose of abducting victims. His front hedge is pretty thick, but not to where it could hide dismembered bodies beneath.

A wide yard separates Burns' home from his neighbors of competing acreage, barely visible through a tangle of oak and hedge of mountain laurel. There hasn't been much done to Burns' land beyond managing a small section for a patch of grass sporting a barbecue pit surrounded by cement squares for sitting. All the better for me. The untamed yucca and buckeye reduces the likelihood a nosy neighbor might see me and take issue with a stranger traipsing around.

Coming up to the front porch, I pause to crouch down and peer through the esperanza flowers lining the gallery. No dead bodies hidden in the garden. Tick off the easy boxes first.

I knock in case he has a dog. The house stays quiet. I knock again in case he has a dog hard of hearing. No bark or frantic scrabble of toenails on tile floor answers.

A quick circle around the house doesn't show any evidence of an alarm system, and there's no warning beep when I pick the lock and open the front door. Knowing my luck, there's probably hidden security cameras recording my breaking and entering. When the police come round and catch me I'll just tell them the God's honest truth: Carl Burns murdered Silvia Lopez and she called to me from beyond the grave to be her inept avenger.

At that point, it's not like there's anything to gain by lying.

Again, I'm slightly disappointed as I step into the foyer. No blatant signs that Burns has a side hobby earning him a special seat on the express bus to hell stand out. The tile leading into the kitchen is free of blood stains. Human heads and body parts are absent from the freezer stocked with easy microwave meals, frozen vegetable packs, and ice cream. His most recent mail is left half-opened on the table. A letter confirming renewal of car insurance sits on top of a cellphone bill and an invitation to a wedding in Louisiana next spring.

The rooms themselves look like they were cut out from a home decorating magazine. The den and dining room walls seem to have been built around the furniture, it all fits so well. A leather couch and matching leather chairs form a perfect right angle to face the flat-screen television positioned exactly to never catch glare through the window, flanked by speakers for surround sound. The Saltillo blankets hanging over the backs of the furniture are neatly folded and creased. The pictures hanging on the walls are ones you'd find in any home—a family reunion, a Hawaiian vacation, a group of dusty-faced men posing in front of dirt bikes. The paintings are equally innocuous, closer to the themes of Cézanne rather than Goya.

The only upset to the orderliness is the small ring on the coffee table from the morning's mug which is made of mundane ceramic, not carved from human bone. I cross my arms and turn on the spot a couple times. The controlled tidiness to his living space is a stark contrast to the chaotic shambles I've allowed my existence to fall into.

"Silvia?" I ask, hoping she'll lend a ghostly hand.

I get no answer. Not even a chill up the spine.

Neat as the home is, there's something unsettling about it. It isn't something that's there causing the unease, it's something that's missing that I can't quite place. There's a hollowness to the picturesque furniture arrangement and the orderliness seems a mask for something sinister.

The bedroom is equally underwhelming. The king bed is neatly made, the spread an inoffensive green and white between two bedside tables topped by reading lamps and a couple more photographs. The only instrument of torture at his bedside is some trash tough-guy-cop thriller novel that would make Dashiell Hammett despair. The opening pages read like an over-dramatic telling of a role playing campaign, and I regret I'll never get back that precious minute of life spent flipping through the book, checking to see if he uses human skin bookmarks or writes confessions of murder in the margins.

I rifle through his dresser and turn up nothing more damning than a couple of socks divorced from their partners. I rifle through her dresser just to be egalitarian and again come up with a big goose egg.

No bodies are stashed under the bed. No suspicious wear on floorboards or wall paneling suggests a hidden room. The closet has nothing more alarming than green nurse scrubs mixed in with sundresses, suits and slacks, a worn leather jacket and a carbon-copy new one. None of the clothing is sewn from human skin and the closet's most offensive occupant is a Hawaiian-patterned eyesore of a tie.

"Well, shit," I say. Other than being haunted by the victim, I've got no evidence that Burns is a murdering psychopath.

I consider eating some of the ice cream in his freezer. Just to stop this trip from being a complete waste and because I don't like this Burns guy much, so joke's on him when he gets back from a hot day of volunteering at the festival full of sweaty people to find he has no more ice cream.

Not quite ready to sink that low, I opt to loot through Burns' belongings again. Force feeding yourself ice cream is almost as much a sin as ordering coffee to go. It also falls under stealing and I've already broken half the commandments, no need to add another mark against me.

I do another sweep through the house and then a third, certain I must have missed something. Some clue or a supernatural trigger that would give me a connection to Silvia and tip me off as to what to do next. I'm a little ticked she's being so quiet when I'm doing all this work for her. The murmurs are the flat, bothersome buzz I now consider status quo. They give no indication there's anything more sinister afoot. Stepping back into the bedroom to search it again, I hear the unmistakable creak of the front door opening.

I bolt down the hall to the back door, cursing myself for missing the sound of a car pulling up. Pressing myself flat against the mudroom wall, I use the glass of the picture frame across from me to watch for movement in the hallway. The windows to the master bedroom and the den give a clear view of the backyard. Unless I want a fifty-fifty shot of being seen making a mad dash out the back, I have to wait and see which way Burns or his girlfriend goes. Hopefully they won't stay long. Or they'll make enough noise, prepping food in the kitchen or taking a shower, that they won't hear the squeak of the back door opening and me slipping out.

A sinister hiss like the shush of dead leaves skittering across stone drowns out the world as the entity moves across the entryway. The fear I had at being discovered by a mortal presence pales as true terror settles in. If it were a natural cold, the chill that sweeps through the house would have made my breath mist. This cold scrapes ice across my soul instead.

My hand seizes the knob to the back door and I reel back in pained surprise. The handle is so cold it burns and the door won't budge.

The entity speaks, too low and quiet for me to make sense of it, but in the unmistakable rhythm of a summons. It calls again and again, requesting I come out.

It's not my imagination as the house darkens. The entity's presence seeps out to suffocate the sunlight reaching in through the windows. I can feel as much as hear it, taking its time as it comes down the foyer. It reels the world in closer, shrinking it down until it's only the house and us inside.

Hard shivers rack through me. I clench my teeth to stop their chattering. The whole house creaks and groans as it struggles to contain the new presence stalking through halls. The buckle of wooden beams and crack of plaster grows louder and louder as it comes closer. I have no doubt it knows I'm here, knows exactly where I am wedged in a corner by the linen closet and washing machine. Fight or flight wages a useless war that only serves to lock me in place. There's nowhere to run, hiding is just waiting for the inevitable coming down the hall, and how do you fight a thing like this?

Logan, it calls.

The house trembles as its hissing step picks up in pace and something comes around the corner, a dark form reflected in the picture's glass.

Whirling, I grab the sliding door to the mudroom. For a second I glimpse it before slamming the door shut. My hands shake so hard it's almost impossible to hold on to the door. There's no lock, no way to barricade myself farther in. The little rationality surviving my mounting terror tells me physical locks and barriers won't do a damn thing, but surrender isn't an option.

The wood of the door groans in toward me. The frame cracks in a slow yield to the entity on the other side as I feel it pressing through the wood. The handle chills and burns beneath my grip. Three inches of splintering door is all that stands between me and it.

Logan.

"No," I gasp as the door begins to slide open. I throw my weight against it. My life's sole purpose narrows down to keeping that door shut.

Slow and deliberate, the door slides open another inch. The

floor tile hums and cracks beneath me, the washing machine shudders, and the glass from the ceiling light threatens to shatter as its presence thickens the air.

My feet slide as the door opens farther.

"No, no, no, no, please," I beg. The handle sears my hand and the door shifts another inch. I turn my face away so I don't have to see it slip through the widening gap and I feel it reaching around the door for me.

Logan. It's a breath away from my face. It demands I give up, let go.

"No, no."

Logan.

"No!"

A sound system blares to life with a jet engine's roar. Static and fury snarls down the hall, the entity screeches and I stumble back, hitting the back door hard. It flies open and I land even harder on the stone back porch.

Head swimming, my eyes water as I stare up at the blinding return of sunlight. Hot summer air flushes out the cold constricting my lungs. Birds chirp, insects hum, and a summer breeze teases through the leaves. Sitting up, I brave a look back into the house. The back door hangs wide open. The sliding door to the hallway beyond the mudroom is open to where a thin man would be able to slip through, but no figure of hell-spawn shade stands in the hallway. There's no one there at all. The floor tiles aren't cracked. The walls are smooth. There's no splintering of the door frame or even a dark stain on the wood from being so close to the entity.

The radio from inside continues to blast out angry white noise.

"I'm fine," I say as I flop back against the unforgiving deck, feeling winded as though I just sprinted a mile.

The heartachingly familiar opening greeting for her morning show is barely audible through the static.

"Good morning, ksshkshh this is Maria ksshak . . . and there's a whole lot to . . . kshh . . . get to . . ."

"I'm fine, really," I say again and the static shuts off.

I might have spoken too soon on that score. The blue summer sky turns rough and grey. The shack's roof materializes above me and I feel the crinkle of plastic beneath me. Shoes sound against the floor and though the shadow that looms over me remains faceless, I know who it is.

There isn't any room for this vision to inspire fear. Not so soon after the entity paid call. But there's plenty of room for anger to harden into resolve.

In a blink, the sky returns. As does a light, cold tapping on my shoulder. I turn around.

The little gardening done to the front yard hasn't been extended to the back. Beyond the weak buffer that prevents the path connecting the front yard to the back porch from being overgrown, the yard has been conquered by the natives. Through the untamed trees and shrubs, a grey shape too boxy to be natural is sheltered far back and hidden among the leaves and knotted limbs. It wasn't there before.

I rub my eyes to clear my sight. Nothing changes. The trees and scrub don't thin out to make room for the little shack. From where I sit it looks like the trees impossibly grow up through the structure without compromising solidity.

Strange, but not the strangest thing I've seen today.

I stand and take a testing step toward the shed. I'm worried it will disappear if I make too quick a move toward it, as if I can startle away the vision. One cautious step, then another, the next more bold. I cross the threshold between grass and overgrown shrubs and sigh with perverse relief when the shed doesn't fade away. It's moved though. The same distance stands between us here as it did when I was sprawled on the porch. A different clump of trees sticks up through it and the shadow pattern of leaves on the roof doesn't match the branches overhead.

"I'm guessing I go that way?" I point at the shed, turning to look over my shoulder back at the house.

The radio cackles back to life and Sinatra singing "Someone to Watch Over Me" sounds out.

I give the radio a thumbs up for both choice of music and message, the back door to Burns' porch swings shut without a visible hand to move it, and I give chase to the apparition.

Chapter 18

Dry twigs tug at my shirt and burrs cling to my pants. Each step brings me no closer to the grey shed. I've lost track of time and distance. I know it's been miles and more than an hour. No matter how far or long I walk, the shack seems just as far off behind the bramble as it did from Burns' porch.

The woods are unmoving and lifeless, there's no breeze to stir the trees, yet the sound of a harsh wind rushes over fallen leaves. It makes me shiver more than the unnatural cold that accompanies it. The murmurings are excited, a lively audience before the start of a much anticipated show.

The entity follows me. I can hear as well as feel it, circling around me. Leaves crunch needlessly as it moves. I know it could move soundless as shade if it wanted. The little noisy theatrics are for me and it works. Sweat sticks my shirt to clammy skin and the effort to not turn my head away from the grey shed makes my neck ache.

It doesn't speak or creep closer. Waiting for it to do so is almost as maddening as its opening the door was terrifying. Perhaps that's all it needs to do, chisel away at what little is left of me until I cave to despair and succumb to insanity or suicide.

A branch snaps within arm's reach and my hands fly up as if to bring a rifle to the ready. I curse at having nothing to defend myself with and then curse again, fed up with this damned thing. I'm not going to hide behind any more doors and wish it away like a child taking shelter under the blankets.

I tear my eyes away from the ever-retreating grey shed to face the spot where I feel my stalker lurking, just out of sight.

"Well fuck you too," I say and flip it off. It's not very articulate, but it gets the point across.

I half expect some dark monstrosity to come hurtling out at me, a creature of sin and hate to barrel through the branches, leaving oblivion in its wake. Apparently my stalker has thicker skin than to be provoked by those childish antics. It laughs instead. The woods catch the ugly noise and echo it off the branches.

The sweat creeping down my neck doesn't dry up after this display of bravado. My heart keeps skipping and I'm still shaking as I throw complete commitment into each step. I'm not able to cast out the terror the entity brings, but I'm not surrendering to it.

A cool, soft hand wraps around mine to give an encouraging squeeze and for the first time since I set out, I see I am closer to the shed. It's stopped moving away and sits perched at the top of the hill. The abandoned hunting cabin stays fixed in a small clearing that the sun can't seem to find. The world's gone silent. It's just me and the murmurings now. The dried leaves and twigs refuse to rustle under my feet as I approach the shack.

A rusted deer skinning rack stands to the side and my stomach rolls when I imagine what kind of prey Burns has used it for. Tracks in the dirt road leading up to the cabin suggest it's hardly as abandoned as it looks. If I follow the tire tracks out, I bet they'll lead me to a farm road that sees more dust than drivers.

My muscles tense into piano wire as I raise my hand and press against the door. The rough wood is solid beneath my fingers and a couple of splinters stick in as I push it open. If this is all a hallucination, then my psychosis deserves to win.

The door breaks the unnatural silence fallen over the woods and creaks with all the cliché grimness I've been waiting for. Muffled streams of light come in after me and filter through the lone window to give shape to the single room interior. The worn floorboards are stained from water damage and the tattered plastic covering the small window shivers as I walk by it.

My hands clench into fists when I look up and recognize the dilapidated roof, corrugated and rusted. This time it doesn't fade back into the ceiling fan at my motel room. Resting a hand against the wall I press down hard. The rough wood pricks against my skin to give me the physical reaffirmation I need that this isn't a vision or hallucination.

Although I'm convinced the walls exist outside my unstable mind, I keep a hand on them as I move around the small shack, reluctant to lose contact with the physical anchor.

There's a metal chair that you'd find at a grade school assembly folded up in the far corner by a locked chest. The chest is decades newer than the shack as is the lock guarding the contents.

Unlike the rest of the shack, the rifle lying atop the chest has been well cared for. I check to see if it's loaded, find that it is, and shoot the lock off the chest. The shot echoes on too long in this otherwise muted corner of the woods.

Flipping up the lid, I automatically shift back, gun raised in case anything jumps out. That nothing moves is only a small comfort. The woods are too silent, the shack is too cold, and an ominous tension hangs in the air, waiting on me to break.

Moving slow, ready to shoot any eldritch abomination that might jump out, I peer down into the chest. Women's clothes, some damaged from the gun shot, lie in neat little piles. A carefully folded dress lies on top of a bright yellow blouse. All the clothes are small in cut, designed to fit a petite young woman, about the size of a nonpregnant Glenny.

More personal and provocative articles, panties, lace bras are stowed farther down in the chest. I use the gun's muzzle to root around through the souvenirs, reluctant to touch something so personal and defiled.

Burns might have collected the clothing as part of a perverse foreplay, stalking the women, breaking into homes to steal private and intimate possessions. Pushing aside the top layers of clothing doesn't support this theory. The clothing below is what a woman would wear out to attract a certain person. Or rather a certain clientele. Only the dress, the yellow blouse, and a couple pieces of the more modest undergarments look to be taken from someone who didn't engage in sexual employment.

The oldest pieces of clothing are beginning to fade. Signs of fraying and wear edge the hems of the fabric. It looks like Burns pays frequent homage to his past sins, stroking the empty clothes, remembering the women who once filled them.

I try to reconcile the regularity of his home with the contents of the trunk. The neatly folded socks of his dresser, the underwear in hers—it shouldn't be any different than the neatly folded clothes of the chest. And materially there is no difference.

The edge of a book peeks out from beneath a skimpy black dress. Using my index and thumb I pull it out with surgical delicacy, doing my best not to touch anything else.

A blank navy cover promises nothing spectacular. Opening to the first page confirms the old adage that you should never judge a book by its cover.

"Oh, God." The word doesn't sound welcome here. It speaks to something that the use of this shack has long worked against.

Drawings in the first few pages chronicle his corruption. Naked women sketched in black ink and dismembered by hard red lines lie across the pages. There's a cruel childishness to the crudity of the bloody lines violently slashed over the black, a petulant wish for destruction born out of a reasonless hate.

I skip over the first dozen or so pages of fantasizing to one made thicker by the polaroid photographs glued in.

The women in the photographs aren't dismembered like the drawings. But they are dead.

The first woman can't have been older than sixteen. There's a sloppiness to the angle of the photos that suggests they were taken as an afterthought and weren't part of the original plan. It was a decision of passion, an eagerness to preserve the rush of the moment, not a careful documentation. Her skimpy black dress with plunging neckline, identical to the one in Burns' trunk, is askew and ripped from a struggle. Bruising is smeared over her mouth and throat beneath blank eyes.

The collection of photos for the second woman is less erratic. More planned. The photos capture her death from careful angles to emphasize the lifelessness to her form, highlight the emptiness in her eyes and thick bruises covering her arms, face, and neck.

This time he laid down a piece of clear plastic beneath her before he started. A little bit of housekeeping to make the mess of strangulation easier to clean up afterward.

The third woman received even greater care in the documentation. This time he took pictures of her alive. Tears stream from her wide pleading eyes, emphasized by the dark makeup tracking down her cheeks. He dedicated a whole page to her living terror. He knew what moments he wanted to capture. Her pages boast a greater sense of order as his ritual became more sophisticated. He posed her in death. Sat her up against the wall, in the metal chair, lay her down with arms and legs at experimental angles.

I doubt all of Burns' earlier victims, if any, were from Encrucijada or even passing through. There's no way he could have gotten away with so many murders, even spaced out over years, if he was preying on locals like Silvia. It would have drawn too much attention. Burns most likely has a wide hunting ground, searching out victims in larger cities before bringing them back here. Silvia is the aberration. Something went wrong. Or perhaps the thrill of the next girl he murdered being someone he knew overwhelmed his discipline.

I turn the page and nearly drop the book. Silvia wasn't the one he was circling in on.

I'm such an idiot—Silvia *did* want me to stick close to Glenny and there was good reason for it.

An entire two pages are dedicated to pictures of Glenny. A cut out from what might've been a yearbook. A photo of her and three other young women in swimsuits at a lake. The first pictures look like they were downloaded from social media, or worse, stolen from homes. The following pictures were obviously taken without consent and from a distance. Polaroids of Glenny walking across the street, climbing into her truck, working behind a diner counter. The photos continue, becoming more invasive. A shot of her leaving her home. Her half-undressed through a bedroom window.

She's not obviously pregnant in any of the pictures, meaning he's been tailing her for almost a year. He invaded her every sanctuary, stole away her every privacy, negating every sense of security and made a documentary of it.

"Here. Here. Here."

Silvia's voice hisses dark and dreadful through my mind. Her echoings of Burns' last words to her make it difficult to maintain the distance needed to look through a photo album Beelzebub would delight in.

Did Silvia catch him taking pictures? Or simply suspect he was stalking her roommate? Did she confront him or did he act first?

I turn the page. There isn't much difference between the next two pages. On the first Silvia's alive. The fog of drugs can't cloud out the fear burning bright in grey eyes. He explored her last moments, recording it with different angles and lighting. Her eyes track him in each shot, staring straight through the camera lens.

The next page is a homage to her death. Her head is tilted at an angle to show the dark bruising around her throat. Her eyes are wide and distorted from strangulation. But they're not empty. There was no surrender from Silvia. Death did not erase the fear. The injustice. Or her fury.

I throw the book away and it hits the opposite wall with

a soft thump. Wiping my hands on my pants, shaking them wildly, I try to get rid of the sick sensation that crept farther up my arms each second I held onto those pages. Floorboards creak as I pace in a tight, agitated circle.

I've seen atrocities before. More extravagant evils than this. I've seen people test how deep they can delve into cruelty. I've had to listen to truly evil men shamelessly revel in their deeds. Smelled the sharp bloody tang of slaughter mixing with the charred sizzle of burning corpses. Heard screams that make you question if there really is such a thing as good or if it's all an empty illusion. After all that, there's a tragic pleasure in knowing I can still be shook by some evils. I can still recognize it as the break from what things should be, I'm not so jaded to accept it as the norm.

I pick the book back up with no intent to open it again. I know there's more information to be gained from these pages. A clue that would give me greater insight into Burns. Give me a tool to more delicately dissect his desires. But I'm not a psychologist. Knowing the why for his evils doesn't mean a damn to me. There isn't a past trauma or repressed memory to justify this. Understanding his motivation, his personal journey into depravity, isn't going to change a thing.

I'm not gonna use the book as a key to Burns' mind, I'm gonna use it as the key that locks Burns away in a cell so dark and removed that the only light he'll see is the waiting hellfire of his eternal damnation.

My vibrating cellphone snaps me out of these unchristian thoughts. An unknown number holds the screen. I ignore it until the number calls a third time. Common sense would favor not talking on the phone while sneaking around a serial killer's murder shed. But what the hell, I'm on a weird high of self-righteous fury that entitles me to answer the phone wherever I damn well please.

"Hello?"

"Good afternoon Mr. Dalaguerre, this is Dr. Joseph Day."

My self-confident high sputters and tailspins down to die in a fiery wreck. The line goes quiet while he waits for a response I don't have.

"Mr. Dalaguerre, are you there?"

"Yeah. This isn't a good time."

"I'm just checking in—"

"Because you got a call from a sheriff?"

"That did influence the decision to call sooner rather than later."

"I'm not in trouble."

"Yes, Sheriff Suarez made it very clear that you were by no means in trouble with the law. But I'm not a lawyer. I'm not concerned with legal ramifications. I'm concerned about you."

"Is this call being charged?" I ask, ready to hang up.

"No, Mr. Dalaguerre, this is on my time."

Dammit. I used my "fuck off" tone and he responded by being the decent man he is. Now I'm irritated and embarrassed.

"Oh. Uh, how you doin' then, Doc?"

"I am well. Thank you for asking."

"Your daughter Anne just graduated?"

"Yes, she did."

"She still planning on going to UT?"

"Last I heard, yes. But she's always been a spontaneous young lady. I wake up every day prepared to find she's left a note by the coffee machine declaring she's decided to join the navy instead or run off to be a missionary."

"There are worse things to run off over. If she's going to take the military route, don't let her go navy. The army is the better choice."

"I'll pass that on to her."

There's a silence as Doc waits for me to try and waste more time through stalling small talk. He knows he doesn't have to wait long.

"Have you been having any side effects to your medication?" he asks after another half minute of giving me the chance to delay.

Nope. Because I haven't been taking it.

"No, sir."

Dammit, I catch the slip too late. Doc picked up pretty quick I only switch from calling him "Doc" to "sir" when I'm trying to dodge around something.

I can almost hear the sound of a pen scratching as he takes notes on the other end of the line. Dammit. Dammit. Dammit.

"Mr. Dalaguerre, are you taking your medication?"

Again, dammit.

"I got it with me."

"That is not what was asked."

I got nothing. I hate lying to him. He's a good man and his patience when putting up with me borders on saintly.

"Logan," he says. Just as I only call him "sir" when I'm on the defensive, he only drops the "Mr. Dalaguerre" when he has something to say I need to hear. That's the thing with Doc. He got every diagnosis wrong but said everything right. "No one is forcing you to do this."

"Never said anyone was." If I recall correctly, and I may not as it was a very unpleasant night that I do not like to revisit, I was the one who voluntarily called and checked myself into psychiatric care. Now every day is a fight to stay out. Involuntary commitment isn't the easiest thing to get. Unless I prove to be "imminently dangerous," the protection of individuals' freedoms keeps me out of padded cells. Still, my record isn't stellar and that may tilt the scales in favor for a judge shipping me back off to orderlies and wards clad in white.

"You did share that you had such concerns three months ago," he reminds me.

The only advantage I have right now is we're talking on the phone instead of in person. My poker face won me enmity from the guys and stacks of easy money to take my wife on ridiculously overpriced dinners. I'd be a broke man if Doc had been at any of those games.

"This is not a weakness, Logan. But neglecting responsibility is," he says.

"Neglecting responsibility is one of the few sins I haven't committed." We've had many similar talks like this before.

"I'd agree with that."

"Then wh—"

"Up until you were honorably discharged."

The doc has a bad habit of bringing that one up over and over again. Turns out even the army understands psychosis isn't conducive to the ability to operate in the field. I respect that, but a prescription of Thorazine wasn't my preferred way of giving notice.

"Have you been eating?" he asks.

I think of the pecan muffin sitting on the passenger seat. Neglecting muffins is not the same caliber of sin as neglecting responsibility. Nope, Doc is getting no compunction from me over failure to eat.

Doc pauses to be sure I'm not going to give him an answer. He's used to me falling into silence and knows when to forge forward and when to hold position. Despite my best efforts, the counter-strategies I've tried out haven't yielded much success.

"Have you had any episodes?" he asks.

He skipped over asking about my sleeping habits this time.

"No." I don't have and never have had psychotic episodes. Maybe.

Doc is quiet for a moment. I don't know if he hears the uncertainty in my voice or just knows by now I'm a lying bastard.

"No one can force you to take responsibility for the hand you've been dealt," he says. "The choices you make on this are yours. But their consequences are going to go far beyond you."

"Yeah," I say to let him know I haven't hung up on him.

Doc takes advantage of the fact I'm not going to hang up on him yet. He lets a pause settle in before asking, "What do you want to do, Logan?"

I don't have a good answer. And what I want doesn't matter. That's not what any of this is about.

"You believe in providence, Doc?"

"Yes."

Old hinges on the shack door creak.

"Me too," I say and hang up.

Burns stands in the shack's doorway. The late afternoon sun silhouettes his bulking frame as he stares at me in dumb disbelief quickly turning to black anger.

Tucking the cell phone into my pocket, I hold up his little scrap book of horrors.

"Looks like you got a type."

Chapter 19

Burns doesn't waste time on pleasantries. He charges. I sidestep and let him go raging past. He slams into the back wall with such force I half expect the whole shed to collapse down on us.

It doesn't, so I move in. He doesn't even have the chance to bring up his guard. His nose cracks under the first hit. He might lose teeth from the second. I help him double over with a low blow to the gut before taking out his legs.

His coming here saves me the trouble of going to the cops. No need for fuss or trouble with the law, I'll just kill him here.

He grabs me and I let him pull me down, falling on top of him to hit him with knees and elbows. He grunts in pain, lets go, and something else grabs hold of me. An inhuman hand darts out from Burns and yanks me into the dead, sepia world. The shack spins into a blur of every evil deed committed within its walls. The women's muffled screams, their pleas cutting off as his suffocating hands clamp down on their throats, their agonized terror, his lust for domination and death slam into me as the entity drags me down into the jeering murmurs reaching out for me from the descending dark. It laughs as it drags me down, down—

I reel back and hit the floor hard. Head spinning, I clutch at anything I can find to act as a line back to the physical world. The clouding reds hanging over my vision fail to hide my seeing Burns has found his feet and retrieved a hand gun from the back closet. I can't clear the distance between us before he'll have it ready.

I roll and run as the first gunshot hits the wall less than a foot from me.

I'm out the door and almost sprint headlong into the black truck he parked out front. I skid over the hood and break the tree line in no seconds flat.

I'm not as far as I need to be when I hear another shot. A tree explodes inches from my head. Fuck. I should've done a better sweep of the place, made sure there weren't any more weapons stashed in the shack. Sloppy, stupid mistake.

The trees flicker in and out of the sepia hue. I don't break stride.

"You little shit!" Burns roars. "Get back here!"

Thanks, but no. I'm gonna keep running this way. Another shot comes after me and hits the tree to my left.

I swerve and crash through the brush. Staying on a path makes me too easy a target. Branches snap and dead leaves fly up. I don't give a damn about making noise. He already knows I'm there. My goal is to be *not* there. The lightness as I move feels wrong. All the other times I've made mad dashes for my life under fire I've always had gear and a gun.

"Move it, Doll!" Alec roared back at me. The concussion of an explosion rocked me forward. Bullets sent up dust around my feet.

Get out of the kill zone. Get out of the kill zone. Get out. The barren openness between the road ambush and cover seemed to stretch from meters into miles. My boots pounded hard against the dry ground and I heard the tear of the assault rifle chasing after me.

Move. Move. Keep moving.

Sharp pain sliced my leg. I didn't break stride. Keep moving.

Alec was a few yards in front of me. A round set off a spray of earth between us.

Keep moving.

A fourth shot shatters a branch. Bark and splinters bite into me. Thank God Burns is as terrible a shot as he is a human being.

"You goddamn son of a bitch!" he yells. "I'm gonna kill you! You hear me?!"

I hear a fifth gun blast through ringing ears but don't see where it hits. Hopefully it wasn't me. Adrenaline has a nasty way of withholding those important updates.

A joyless thrill propels me forward with an intensity I haven't felt in over a year and a hollow grin smears itself across my face.

He doesn't shoot again, and soon his shouting is swallowed up and lost in the thick brush.

Sweat has soaked through most of my shirt. Blood splatters down from where the tree bark peppered my neck. I've had worse scrapes and weigh the consequences of getting it checked out by a doctor and having to explain how it happened, or risk infection as I try to clean out any embedded tree bits myself. After two seconds of deliberation I favor the second option. I spent the last six months in a hospital and need to balance that with at least half a year free from a visit. And I've got a perfectly good set of tweezers waiting in the motel room.

When my heart slamming my ribs is the loudest noise around, I go low to wait and listen. Insects buzz and dried leaves sigh when another of their brethren falls to join the ranks rotting on the ground. A mockingbird changes perch, causing a twig to snap.

But no Burns.

I'm somewhat surprised to find I'm holding onto Burns' book. I can't remember if I had it through the whole scuffle or if I grabbed it before making a mad dash for life and limb into the woods. I stretch my arm out to keep the book at a maximum distance from my bleeding neck as to not risk its evil contaminating me through the open wound.

After a few more minutes of listening I ease my way, quiet and low, through thorns and burrs in what I think is the most straightforward way to the road. More guesswork than I'd like is acting as a poor man's compass. Chasing a phantasm shed through the woods and then running from a serial killer while he's shooting at you can throw off even the best sense of direction.

Being lost in the woods doesn't worry me much. Adrenaline keeps my heart at a steady war drum beat. I feel myself smiling and hard laughter that belongs to someone else threatens to escape out on each short, deep puff of a breath. It's been a long time since I've been shot at. You don't ever get used to it. You learn to live through it and there's nothing else like it. I'm just glad this time I had good tree cover and was on domestic soil.

I keep the setting sun to my back, hoping more than thinking the road is to the east. The light sinks lower and stretches out the shadows running down the gnarled oaks. Bats flutter overhead above the darkening tree limbs. The ground begins a gentle slope down, and I say a quick prayer of thanks when I hear the occasional car engine rumble.

Light on water winks up at me through the thinning trees as

the lake's surface reflects the dusky sky. In another hundred feet, the slope deposits me out on a pavement trail winding around the manicured lawn of the lake where I parked. A couple of joggers are running the wrong direction to see me stumble out of the brush. The older couple sitting on the bench don't notice me until I walk a bit closer.

"You've got something on your neck, dear," the woman says, eyes narrowing behind thick spectacles. At least sixty years of wrinkles deepen as she puckers her mouth in disapproval. Her hand reaches into her bag and for a panicked second I check for cover, thinking she's drawing out a gun. Instead, she pulls out a crinkled pack of disposable towelettes.

"It's nothing, ma'am." I smile but she sees right through it. Even the old man I assume to be her husband is shaking his head.

"Good heavens, child," she says. "What on earth did you do to yourself?"

I shrug and wave a hand to show off how filthy I am to help sell the fib. "I fell and tried to catch myself with my face."

Old joints keep the woman's rise from the bench slow.

"Why would you do that, handsome as you are?" She hands me the pack and I take one because I know better than to refuse. She doesn't back down until I take the whole pack.

"Thank you," I say.

"You sure you're alright, dear?" she asks and I step back when she reaches out to get a better look at my neck.

"Wasn't my worst fall." I've managed to rack up such an impressive ability to eat dirt that almost tumbling under the wheels of the truck yesterday morning doesn't even clear the top twenty. At least this latest dustup didn't involve a near-miss car collision. Only gunfire.

"I'd believe that." The old man nods. I'd guess up until then he hasn't believed a word I've said.

"Thanks again, ma'am." I wave, trying to salvage some courtesy before setting off at a borderline jog. Interacting with people feels wrong while I'm carrying Burns' book. Although there's nothing obviously evil about it, I try to hold it to best obscure it if anyone looks my way while simultaneously trying to keep it as far from me as possible. It's only the thought of the book against my skin that stops me from tucking it in my waistband beneath my shirt to hide something so indecent from the world.

The towelette comes away filthier than I expected when I run it over my neck. A few spots of fresh red from the wounds aggravated by the cleaning dot the mottling mess of dried blood and dirt.

My car is overly hot from sitting in the sun and I leave the door open for a spell to avoid heatstroke. Not only would that be a stupid way to die but it means the murder book would end up in my personal effects and I don't want to be associated with it.

"So, how'd I do?" I ask the radio.

The radio responds with the promise of impending divine judgment through the legendary messenger of Johnny Cash.

"Is that good? Bad? Passable?"

"Come backkshh and we'll do it allshhkshk tomorrow . . ." the radio promises.

"It's a date, then," I say, closing the car door and starting the engine.

To avoid contaminating the muffin on the passenger seat, I pick it up before placing Burns' book down. I decide it's less effort to go ahead and eat the muffin than it is to reach around into the back seat to put it a safe distance away from the book. And I know if I toss it in the back I'll forget about it and then have to go searching for it under the seats when I remember it's rolling around on the car floor three weeks later.

I can tell the muffin is supposed to taste good but it holds all the joy of consuming clotted clay. Instead of curbing the hunger I should be feeling, it stokes the low embers of nausea that never seem to go out completely and are inflamed most whenever I eat without an appetite.

"Well, I tried," I say.

The radio coughs white noise.

"True. But I always was a finicky eater," I remind the radio.

It gives a small puff of static I decide to take as playful exasperation.

Still running high on adrenaline, I drive off much faster than I should. This being Texas, there's a good chance no one will report the gunfire. Someone most likely heard the shots, but they were far enough away that even the most helicopter-parenting-prone mother would think twice before calling it in, dismissing it as someone doing target practice out back.

After my previous run-ins with the sheriff, I'm more than happy to avoid having a meeting with the boys in blue. Breaking into someone's house because you suspect them to be a murderer based off the advice from a ghost might qualify me as "imminently dangerous." But hey, at least I wasn't the one who started shooting.

Chapter 20

An ominous crawl prickles my skin and the ugly feel I get when my entity stalker comes out to play refuses to let up. I keep checking the rearview and side mirrors as I drive back to Encrucijada. That I don't see the entity doesn't mean a damn. I know it's here.

The dull, sepia coloring burns in and out over my vision. One moment the trees are dark green, the next the whole world is cast in a dead reddish-brown hue. The unpredictability of the flicker and flash nauseates me to the point I'm having trouble keeping the car straight.

A patch of gravel runs parallel to the road and I pull off to the side to put the car in park and wait out this sepia spell. Today's fun will be all for nothing if I crash my car heading back to town. I keep my eyes fixed on the empty stretch of road, refusing to let them drift down to Burns' scrap book on the passenger's seat. Having that book sitting so close makes me more nervous than a teenage boy having to explain his browsing history to his mother. It's pushed up against the door, as far away as it can be from me while still in sight.

I hate it being that close to me but I'm reluctant to put it in the trunk or even in the backseat. The thought of letting it out of sight has me equally uneasy. The moment I can't see it, the book will disappear and I'll lose the only physical evidence to prove I'm not imagining this whole thing. Either that or once out of my side-eye supervision it'll sprout legs and become an unearthly horror to better reflect the evils of its author.

Worse than the possibility of carpooling with Kassogtha disguised as a murder diary is that this is probably the last time I'll be driving anywhere for a while. I don't see myself staying out of a mental facility after I take the book to Sheriff Suarez. Though my alibi for Silvia's murder is airtight, my credibility is not. Throw in the lead-up as to how I found the scrapbook by chasing the hallucination of a shack, getting harassed by some dark entity, all while breaking and entering into the Burns' house, and I take a blowtorch to the thin ice I'm skating on.

I could give lying a go, but I know there's no way I'll be able to keep the story straight with all the holes it's going to have if I try to make it believable. And while the book is pretty damning evidence, I can't think of anything other than fingerprints that'll link it to Burns. My testimony as a witness probably won't mean much and that lack of faith could be the needed delay for Burns to get away.

Because if Burns is smart, and I'm sure he isn't stupid, he'd have cleared out any lingering evidence from the shack before I reached my car. Even if I did manage to convince the police to believe me and then was able to lead them back there, we'd most likely just find an old hunting cabin with nothing more sinister than a couple of scorpions sheltering beneath the sink.

For all I know, Burns might've burned the whole damn thing to the ground by now.

"I could leave an anonymous tip," I say to the radio. Leave a note that there's a serial killer shed somewhere within a few miles of Burns' backyard and wish them luck on finding it since I can't provide an exact location. I was too busy suffering through my hellish stalker circling around me and being shot at to make a reliable mental roadmap of how to reach the shack again.

Or I could have Glenny take care of it. Hand the book off to her to give to her father. That still demands trying to sell a bullshit story to Sheriff Suarez for how Glenny got her hands on that book and the more pressing problem of how to keep Glenny from opening the book to look inside.

I sigh and rest my head on the steering wheel. Asking Glenny for help ain't an option. I know what I gotta do. I need to go straight to Suarez. Anything short of that is selfish cowardice. It's me putting my own fears of being locked back up, probably for more than half a year, above what's right.

Although I should give Glenny a call to see if she has any tips for dealing with her father. From the sound of it, she has years of experience of being on the wrong foot with Sheriff Suarez.

I reach down for my cell phone and find my pants pocket empty.

"Shit." I must've dropped it while making a mad dash through the woods. I hope I dropped it in the woods where it can stay lost and not in the shack where Burns might find it.

Maybe it's for the best I can't give Glenny a heads up. She might do something Glenny-ish and complicate things more than they already are.

The sepia flickering dies down to a manageable level and I shift the car back into drive. I make it less than a quarter mile down the road before a dark figure darts through the headlights.

The car's tires screech as I swerve to avoid it and an opaque darkness descends, disconnecting me from the world as I spin out and come to a jolting halt on the roadside. One moment I see the trees and road beside me, the next it vanishes behind a shroud of total nothingness.

The engine sputters and dies in a harsh whine. The murmurings rumble up into an eager, hungry thunder. Metal creaks, sharp and grating as if being pushed in.

It's outside the car.

The radio hisses static in a feeble protest against the entity. Out of the corner of my vision, a darker shape moves against the black oblivion. I flinch and bite back a gasp as the car bounces under its weight. It laughs at me.

Just give up, it seems to say.

And I want to. The hollowness of its presence presses down on me. Breathing becomes a terrible effort.

Give up. It promises how much easier things will be if I just stop struggling. I'm already half-drowned and should let myself sink. It reminds me how pointless it all is. Just like the oblivion engulfing me, there's nothing to hope for, nowhere to go.

Let go. It tells me what I already know—what's been lost can't be restored and I should give up trying.

The front window makes a high-pitched *tink-tink-tink* noise. The glass yields, bending like soft clay, as the entity reaches through and holds an inhuman hand inches from me. I turn away and close my eyes, the only defense I got against it.

The murmurings give ready encouragement to seek a lasting silence. It'd be easy, so easy to sink into the darkness it's provided. I've been here before, and it asks me to do it right this time. Raising the gun back then was little more difficult than it would be to stretch out my hand now.

Give up. It'd be easy.

The opening chords of a song choked by radio static breaks through the deafening dark. Feeble but unrelenting, it holds its ground against the terrible murmurings and that thing hovering in front of me.

The entity's summons harshen from an offer to a cold order. The radio refuses to be subjugated under the screeching static and sings out a song I've avoided listening to for over a year now.

***

"Come here," I said, leading Maria into a side room. The ranch we picked for our wedding reception had plenty of those. "We've got some time."

The guests were busy socializing over appetizers and wouldn't expect the bride and groom for another fifteen minutes.

"You really can't wait to consummate?" she asked. "There's a better room for that upstairs."

"We can do that too if you want," I said, "but this'll do for what I have in mind."

Maria's eyes widened as I showed her in. I'd asked the staff to use any leftover decorations for this side room. I made a mental note to give them a generous tip because they went above and beyond the call of duty. The room's floor had been cleared and the walls lined with flowers. The curtains were closed, leaving only thin slips of sunlight to complement the lantern lights strung over the rafters and walls. My only specific request had been a sound system. The small bottle of champagne and two glasses beside it among a bed of rose petals was an unexpected touch. Either the staff had forgotten or decided to overlook I was a month shy of twenty-one.

"What is this?" she asked.

"Remember how you said you wanted us to have a first dance?"

"And I remember you said that first dances were stupid."

"Because they are. When other people are watching," I said. If the point of a first dance is to dance alone with your wife, it made no sense to have an audience.

"It's something I'll share with you. But only you." I kissed her and she was slow to let me pull away.

I handed Maria my phone. "Pick a song."

She took longer than I thought she would before settling on one. "Don't laugh," she said before plugging the phone into the speakers.

"Elvis?" I raised an eyebrow at the opening notes of "Can't Help Falling in Love" as I slipped my hands around her waist.

"I know, it's a cliché." She gave me a sheepish grin before tucking her head against my shoulder.

"No," I said as we pressed closer together with each turn, "it's perfect."

Our wedding reception was a hundred yards away and we were late to arrive.

***

Elvis croons from the radio. I shake my head and open my eyes.

A twilight sky and empty stretch of road greets me. The hood of my car is bare and the windshield free from scratch or dents. The entity is gone. For now.

When I turn the keys, the engine catches and stutters back to life. Without the entity's presence the song plays clean and pure, and for a moment the music is all there is to hear.

My face is wet and I wait a moment longer for my vision to clear before pulling back onto the road.

"Thank you," I say.

It's bittersweet when the radio hushes and clicks into quiet. The music was a reminder of, not a reprieve from, duty. I'm not done yet.

Light catches in my rearview mirror. The distant headlights bobbing up and down over the low rolling hills prompt me to shift the car back into drive. I imagine the approaching car is a worldly emissary sent on behalf of the entity to do the physical harm it seems unable to achieve. I know that thought is nothing more than the bastard offspring of paranoia and an overactive imagination, but having a sinister entity following me around most days more than excuses the coupling.

Turning on to the state highway leading back into Encrucijada, I check my rearview mirror again. The road is dark for the space of a few seconds then sure enough, the following car also turns. Our following the same road isn't an instant red flag. This is a major road, good citizens and ne'er-do-wells alike have the right to use it without suspicion. Deserved or not, the car earns my suspicion and I shoot increasingly edgy glances back at it.

The radio surges back to life to in a spitting rattle. Again, that makes sense, as much as a haunted radio can. This is the same stretch of road I followed Sheriff Suarez down after finding Silvia's body. There's no need to get carried away and think this an ominous warning. I pick up my speed anyway to get a little more distance between me and the following car.

I wince as the radio gives a high-pitched screech and spits out an angry garble of white noise. An intense cold sends a shiver rippling out to numb my hands. I can't see the entity but I feel its return. Feel its leering smile.

I'm so busy looking for a black form that pales the surrounding night I miss from what shadowed side road the truck pulls out from to get between me and the following car. The truck is much less shy about keeping a courteous distance and accelerates to ride right up behind me.

A hostile *chhk-chhk-chhk* comes from the radio, sepia flickers over my sight, and the deepening cold has me gripping the steering wheel skin-tearing tight. I'm shivering so bad I'm worried I'll lose hold but I'm not going to waste any more time brooding on the roadside.

Just keep driving, I'm almost at the sheriff's office. I can endure this episode for the ten minutes it'll take. I just gotta keep driving.

The truck's engine growls as he swerves over to pass me. He slows down to get a good look at what grandma is driving the speed limit on this stretch of open country road before rocketing off. Within a half a minute he's a distant blaze of red taillights on the road.

The radio screeches, jumping around from station to station in a nonsense mix of music and electric chatter.

I ease up on the accelerator, realizing I had unconsciously sped up to match the truck in front of me. The speedometer drops down from twenty-five to a healthy ten over the speed limit. The car behind me has kept at an even pace, holding back far enough away that I can't make out the driver.

I near sigh in relief when I see the bridge crossing over the dried creek promising only one more mile until I reach Encrucijada.

The headlights of the truck blare bright through my windshield as the driver uses a turn out to do a rapid U-turn. Even at the distance I see the dust kicked up by the tires. He comes back around, engine roaring under the acceleration, and my car's radio snarls in answer, making my ears ring. As the truck barrels back at me and my headlights illuminate the inside, I see why the radio's pitching a fit—Burns is behind the wheel. Too late I recognize the black truck as the one I nearly ran straight into when sprinting out of the murder shack.

A thousand wild thoughts as to how he found me race through my mind. Even if coincidence put us on the same road, there's no way he could have known this car was mine. And then I see his dark passenger.

"You gotta be fucking kidding me!" I slam my hands on the steering wheel. This isn't a fair fight.

The intelligent blackness that grabbed me in the murder shack clings to him like demonic fungi. The entity rolls over him with the grace of a lover's caress, finding him an easy host to sway under its influence and lead him straight to me.

Burns jerks his truck into my lane and I swerve to avoid a direct collision. He clips my car's side instead of turning me into a mashed meat and metal sandwich.

The clip is enough. My smaller car skids out of control.

I try to turn into it and everything dials back into slow motion.

Tires shriek as they shred and burst on asphalt. I see the road and trees tilt rather than feel the car tip. I feel the crunch of the hood instead of hear it. The car pitches and—

Chapter 21

Istared up at a cold, distant sky. Smoke and dust obscured the blue, wafting thick from the ravine ridge high above me. It was too quiet. There was no more gunfire, shouts, roars as the earth was torn apart around me. There was nothing save an ugly ringing in my ears, plunging me into an unforgiving deafness.

I couldn't hear my pained groan, but I felt it rattle my chest as I stared dumbly up, trying to piece together what had happened. Rook had been hit, I saw him go down. And something hard hit me just below the ribs as I carried him over to the joke of a CCP we had set up. That much I remembered. Whatever Alec had yelled was lost in the explosion. I was running back out toward him. Our position was as laughably bad as the intelligence that got us there exposed on that ridge.

A second groan and the accompanying full body pain as I sat up confirmed what I suspected. That mortar hadn't blown me up, it had just blown me straight off the ledge. For a second I thought I was lucky I wasn't dead. The next second I didn't think I was lucky at all when a special hurt flared hot through the bone-bruised ache. I clutched my side and my hand came away bloody.

"Fuck."

Sky and mountain swirled together when I tried to stand. I stared back up the ridge above me, unable to make out any moving shapes through the dusty haze. Where was everyone? I couldn't have fallen that far away.

Reality hit me hard and cold. Never leaving a fallen comrade behind is a difficult creed to hold at the best of times. We had been at our worst when the order to retreat was called out and that mortar round had blown me down the wrong side of the mountain.

Until that moment, I didn't understand the gravity of what it meant to be truly alone. Or the weight it was to accept that I wasn't going to make it home.

My side burned when I jerked my rifle up at the flash of movement.

"Alec!" I collapsed back against the rock in relief as he came into view. I wasn't left behind.

He motioned for me to get low and I ignored every pained protest as I followed the order.

I pressed against the rock cover, and a stray pebble cascaded down, inches from my face. I wasn't alone at all. There were people on the ledge above me. I couldn't hear them, I couldn't hear anything. I could only bite back a grunt of pain as I pulled my legs in closer. Alec crouched down beside me, the rocky outcrop the only thing hiding us from enemy eyes.

He pressed a finger to his lips and I nodded. If they found us, we were dead.

Don't let them hear you.

***

There's something wrong with what I'm seeing but I can't quite figure out what. Blackness spirals in and out around me, free from discernible origin or end. I'm only half sure the car's stopped flipping. My head certainly hasn't. The lobes of my brain are doing their best to run out of my skull and reassemble in completely the wrong order. Spots chase each other across my vision and my right hand feels miles away when I place it against my head. My left hand feels too close. It's a needling mass of shooting pain.

The blood running up my face helps me piece together why what I'm seeing isn't making sense. I'm hanging upside down, staring down at the sky and up at ground. The copper tang of blood fills my mouth and nose. If leaking oil is perfuming the air I can't smell it through my own leaking blood.

"Sonofa . . ." My hands fumble and fail to find the seatbelt latch.

I hear voices through the ringing in my ears. That's nothing new.

No, these sound too close. Too alive.

Burns. It has to be Burns. Strange and male, the voices grow closer and my attempts to get free turn more frantic.

The nagging terror spinning round with the rest of the world comes into sharper focus as my clumsy fingers find the catch and drop me against the crumpled hood. Sharp pain plummets me further down, almost back into unconsciousness.

Broken glass and shattered car cut into me as I crawl through the blown out driver's side window. My whole body is screaming, and moving gives me a more detailed damage report.

Ribs are bruised at best. Each breath burns the bones white-hot. A sick headache and sicker stomach hint to a concussion. Despite the hedgehogs armed with barbed wire flails running around in my left wrist, my arms and legs work, and that'll have to do.

The tinny song ringing through my ears plays an unwanted encore performance and I can't get my bearings. The ground feels like it's above, not beneath me, and I risk sinking off into the empty space below. The male voice is closer now, calling out at me.

It doesn't sound like Burns, but I have no intention of waiting around to find out how accurate my addled senses are. I dig my fingers into the dirt, trying to convince myself that it really is solid ground beneath me. I can stand. I need to stand.

"Get up," I tell myself. I don't listen.

The ever-present murmurings are throwing a riot in my skull, enraged by my survival, thrilled by my pain.

I need to move. The order to find my feet gets bungled somewhere after my knees and I collapse against the ground.

Fine, I'll crawl. I can crawl.

The car's headlights are too bright, a blinding spotlight in a patchwork sea of sepia and black.

"Hey, Dad look! He's alive!"

I twist too quickly and fire blossoms through my chest. The voice calling out is too high to be north of puberty. Two men are running toward me. Neither is Burns. Which means he's still out there somewhere.

"Hey, mister! Hey, hey!" Not two men, one man and a kid.

The kid is the faster of the two. He hasn't grown into his ears and he's stark white under his freckles. The slower of the two holds his cowboy hat down with one hand as he runs. His other hand presses a cellphone to his ear.

"Hey, mister!" Freckles says. "You alright?"

"Ge'down." My words spin into a slow slur. "Ge'down." Can't he see there's a nutcase armed with a pickup and gun?

I motion for Freckles to duck and am rewarded by serrated

spikes slicing hot through my ribcage.

"That guy tried to kill you! He ran you right off the road! We saw it! He tried to kill you, right?"

I scan the scene for Burns, causing the trees and sky to start swooping together again like they've been put into a rinse cycle. I can't figure out where the blood running down my face is coming from. I try to find the source but all I do is smear the mess over my hands.

"Oh man, you're pretty busted up. Huh, mister?" Freckles speaks fast, like this is the most exciting thing he's ever seen. Glenny talks pretty fast too. I needed to call her about something . . .

Freckles stops his dash forward when I vomit. Blood tinges the unappreciated mess of the partially digested pecan muffin.

"Jesus, mister," Freckles says. He hovers and circles with uncertainty, then hollers back at Hat-man. "Dad! Dad, didya call an ambulance?"

Hat-man says something, I can't pick out meaning to his deeper voice. The boy's excitement makes it sound like Hat-man is speaking through syrup.

My vision dips into black. When it comes back, I'm propped up against a rock. Hat-man is crouched in front of me, peering into my eyes. His handlebar mustache sinks his frown farther down.

"I don't need an ambulance," I say. I can't figure out why it's so hard to stay present. I've been through worse but it's a fight to stay conscious. And I'm cold. "Why's it so cold?"

"Okay, son, I need you to stay with me," Hat-man says. "What's your name?"

I shake my head. "Where is he?"

"Who?" Hat-man asks.

Burns. Where's Burns? He's got a gun. He could be at the road edge taking sight and—holy shit, Burns' book is still in the car. The police and probably half the county are on their way and they're gonna find that damn book in my passenger seat.

"I don't need an ambulance!" I need everyone to go away. Need everyone, living and dead, to leave me alone. The murmurings are no longer just voices, they're hands reaching up to pull me down to them. They hold me hostage in this confused, half-aware state.

I make to push Hat-man away but misjudge the distance. My right arm flails wildly between us.

"Son, you need—"

I find my feet and smack my head on Hat-man's chin as I try to stand. It knocks me back down.

"Stay still, son," Hat-man says, rubbing his chin. "You probably can see 'bout as straight as you're thinkin'."

The red and white flashes coming from the road are either fireworks or emergency lights. Whatever they are, they overwhelm my battered senses. I want to close my eyes to shut it all off.

"Hey." Hat-man gently shakes my shoulder. "Try and stay awake, okay?"

"I gotta go." Since standing is not an option I fall back to crawling. I pull at the dirt but can't seem to move.

"Where?" Hat-man drawls the question out into two syllables.

"I gotta . . . gotta . . ."

I'm supposed to do something. I can't remember what it is.

"That's nothing new," I say.

"What isn't?" Hat-man asks.

"I don't know." I can't think. The voices are too loud, crowding out what's left of me.

"Dad, is he . . ." Freckles shifts closer.

"He's just got his head knocked 'round," Hat-man says. "Give him space. He's alright."

There are many men with doctorates hanging on their office walls who would claim a blow to the head is the least of my cranial issues.

"Did you see that guy run into him? Dad, did you see—"

"I saw, Bobby."

"Why'd he do that?"

"Don't know. Might've been drunk."

"Is he gonna die, Dad? Do you think he's gonna—"

"Bobby, be quiet."

The red and white flashes turn out to be emergency lights. An ambulance pulls up and looms over the side of the road. Two EMTs hop out.

"I don't need an ambulance!" I snap as they come over.

The younger of the two stops in his tracks. The older woman cocks an eyebrow and doesn't miss a step, quick to realize I'm all bark and no bite. She's big boned, with bigger hair, and small patience. "Sugar, ya'll take that tone with me again you sure as hell will need an ambulance."

The ringing in my ears is the music to the merry-go-round that refuses to stop spinning. I push myself up into a more dignified sitting position. "I don't need . . ."

"Heard you the first time," she says and pulls back an eyelid to shine a light in my eye.

Darkness takes the place of the light when she turns it off. My vision doesn't clear and noise rolls back into senseless sounds.

"Could you turn off that radio?" I ask. I cover my ears best I can with one working hand to block out the maddening noise. The voices don't stop, crashing down on me like waves over rock.

"Please?" I beg. I need it stop. Please, someone turn it off. The physical wounds are like doorways flung open for the voices to pour through.

EMT Sass is standing over me with arms crossed. EMT Nervous is shifting from foot to foot, holding paperwork in hand. The flash of the lights hurts and I shut my eyes against it. Gravel and dirt crunches under approaching footsteps.

"Come on." Silvia's voice pushes back the fury of whatever lurks behind the veil of this world. It isn't enough.

"He's refusing medical treatment, sir," EMT Nervous says.

Seeking medical help doesn't solve a whole lot of problems, in my experience.

"Bein' a right pain in my ass," EMT Sass says.

In my experience, being a right pain in the ass has only created a whole lot of problems.

"Hey, stay awake."

"Come on. Doing here. Doing here."

"No, not now," I mutter. Her voice is plaintive and low and I cling to it like the drowning man does wreckage.

"He's being very, um . . . adamant, sir," EMT Nervous says nervously.

Footsteps stop in front of me. I jack my eyelids back open to make sure the person they belong to is really there.

Sheriff Suarez crouches down. Again, he doesn't look happy to see me. That's fair. I wouldn't be happy to see me either.

"I'm sorry," I say, having failed to hold up our agreement that he wouldn't be seeing me again.

"They say you're refusing medical service," he says.

I nod and that hurts. "Yes, sir."

"Here. Here. Here."

Yeah, I want to get out of here. But I want everyone else to leave first. I can't think. I can barely see. Sheriff Suarez's shape slips around the edges. If everyone would just leave and stop distracting me I could get a straight thought through.

It's Silvia speaking now. She can't be heard over the din of the murmuring trying to pull me under.

"What?" I ask.

"I asked if you were you drinking," Suarez repeats, sounding like I've already confirmed his suspicion.

"I don't drink." What a stupid question. I shake my head and the motion brings out a feeble second exodus of stomach acid.

Suarez doesn't flinch.

"Alright, Mr. Dalaguerre. You got a couple options. One, you let them load you up and take you to the hospital. Two, you keep being stupid and I arrest you for suspicion of DWI and I haul you off to the hospital."

"Breath test," I say. "I'll take a breath test."

"Come on."

"Come again?"

"I'll take a breath test," I say. I'm not going to a hospital. I'm not going back to any damn hospital. "Breath test, blood test. Do it all. I don't care."

But I ain't going to no damn hospital.

Sheriff Suarez says something but it gets away from me. Everything is happening too fast, the world spins too quick, and I can't make sense of it. If everyone would just be quiet. God, please just make it quiet.

"I'll take it here," I say. "I'm not drunk."

"Come on. Come on."

Sheriff Suarez sighs. "It ain't alcohol I'm thinking had you driving into a ditch."

"I'm not drunk." I meant to say something else but couldn't find the right words. "I'm not . . ." God, please make it stop. Give me quiet.

"He didn't drive into the ditch! Some jackass ran him off the road, sir!" Freckles says. "Tried to drive his truck right into him! We saw it! We—"

Sheriff Suarez directs the power of his mustache at the kid and Freckles goes quiet.

"Come on. Come on."

"Blood test is fine," I say. The ringing in my ears rises in pain and pitch. "Do a blood test. I don't need an ambulance." Just everyone please, go away. Give me quiet. Please.

"Come on."

Someone says hospital. I don't need a hospital. I'm not going back. I think I might've said part of that out loud, because Suarez sighs, pulling at his chin.

"Alright, I'll give you a third option," he says slowly. "You don't choose from one of those two options I laid out, I'm gonna knock what little sense you got left out of you so they have to take you to the hospital, and you'll be eating through a straw for a month."

"You'll need to wait your turn," I say and wave in the vague direction of EMT Sass. "She already said somethin' along those lines, and ladies first."

Sheriff Suarez's voice is a distant rumble. As sound and sight move farther away, the audience moves closer. The swarm of bodies bears down on me. Suffocates me. I can't breathe under it. The dead and damned aren't far behind. They reach through the living veil and take hold of me. The voices grow harsher and crueler the longer I resist joining them.

"Come on."

Suarez catches me as I tilt forward and continue to fall.

Chapter 22

Alec stands guard outside the cave. The moonlight doesn't illuminate him as it should. He's beyond its reach.

The place I'm taking refuge hardly qualifies as a cave. It's more like an indent in a rocky slope. Shrub and brush give sufficient cover but Alec remains outside in the open, an impossibly still sentinel.

I remember my skull had been thundering, pain causing red to streak over my eyes, deaf in one ear clogged up by God knew what. The hasty wrapping job of the gunshot to my side had bled through. The stain was a dark omen as it spread into the tattered remnants of pants and shirt.

I'm not wearing my uniform now like I was then. I'm wearing the clothes I wore this morning and they're intact, no tears or blood spatters. There was hardly room in the small crevice for me to wait and hope to survive another night. Now, I'm not surprised at all to see Glenny comfortably sit down across from me. Or rather a thing shaped like Glenny.

Her eyes are oil slicks, a monotonous empty black that leaks over the lids. Her skin is almost translucent, unable to fully hide the dark something that lurks beneath. But her smile is perversely beautiful.

"Logan," the thing that looks like Glenny says. Trickles of rot leak out of her. From her mouth when she speaks and from between her legs.

I should be screaming in terror, mad from fright. But the fear the entity brings whenever it's close isn't felt here.

I look to Alec. He hasn't moved from his guard.

"Who are you?" I ask.

The thing smiles wider.

"What do you want?"

The entity's laughter sends cold to my core, made even worse that it comes from a twisting of Glenny's. Its teeth are perfectly white despite the blackness dripping out from its mouth.

"What do I want?" It waves a dismissive hand. "That's not why I'm here. What matters is what you want."

The rot leaking out from the thing bleeds into the earth to consume it. Dirt withers and vanishes. The void devouring the ground steadily creeps toward me. I retreat and it smiles pityingly at me.

"Give up, Logan," it says. "Your fight is already lost. Give in, it's what you want."

Alec is watching us now. Head turned back toward us, his eyes filmed over by grey.

"What I want is for you to leave me alone," I say.

The thing's smile widens and more decay slips out from between the lips.

"No, no, no, you brought me here," it says. "*Begged* for me. Don't look at me like that, I heard you. Those nights you lay awake, hoping you wouldn't wake in the morning. Wanting an end and too weak to act. I heard you, all those nights. I am what answers your prayers."

It leans forward. Even though it has Glenny's shape, it's

somehow taller than me. "You asked for me."

The rocks and brush darken and wither as the world crumbles under the spread of its decay. False Glenny survives the dissolution, retaining clarity as it inches closer with a hungry smile.

"Who are you?" I ask.

"You wished for an end to it all, asked for a release. You despaired, called out for relief. I am what follows," it says and all falls into black decay.

***

My eyes are heavy and feel like they're filled by rusted needles as I squint the room into view. There's a vague familiarity to my surroundings, making me think I was conscious at some point here before. A fuzzy memory of a blob in green scrubs telling me to stay awake swims through the murky memories of last night. The cast on my left arm has broken bits of memory associated with it, a haze of drug and headache keeps recall fragmented and faded at the edges.

The numbing medication keeps the past hours distant. It can't keep away the dead. The whispering starts before sleep fully clears.

"I'm not ready. I can't . . . not dead."

My hatred of hospitals isn't solely founded on my own experiences, but that what others have lost in these places is shared with me.

"No, not yet, no . . ."

"I love you, Dad. I lo—"

The witnesses to death who linger in the halls pluck at the tangled strings of my mind. Men, women, children crowd their grief and suffering onto me.

"—and merciful God, we entrust our sister . . ."

The voices of the dead, what they heard, or never got the chance to speak threaten to crack my throbbing head.

"No. No, no, no. Please, no . . ."

I focus on my breathing, my heartbeat, the celebratory sounds of life, to stop myself from becoming lost in the last words of loved ones, lost chances, and the fears that outlived the death of the not quite fully departed.

"I'm not ready . . . please, I can't die . . ."

Focus on the physical. On the surroundings. The sterile cleanliness of the hospital room renders the walls an absurdly immaculate white. Sunlight bounces too bright from the floor tiles, and the bedsheets have been bleached too many times to have the character for feel or scent.

"No, no, no. NO! NO!"

I drum my clumsy, wooden fingers against the sheets in any fragment of a piano melody I can recall, gritting my teeth until the lingering souls of the hospital soften to a manageable level. The voices simmer down from rock concert loud to the volume of chatter overheard at a café, quieting to where I can function.

The lack of handcuffs to the bed is a good sign. I take it to mean that I'm not under arrest and passed blood, breath, and any other test they might've run to check for drugs.

"Son of a bitch," I mutter through a morphine-heavy mouth. A clear drug check might be a double-edged sword. I have no doubt all the tests they ran showed there were absolutely no drugs in my system. Including the ones that were supposed to be there.

I don't know where my privacy rights end. I didn't bother to read what the papers said when I left St. Jude's, what I forfeited and agreed to. I mostly nodded along without hearing what restrictions the doctors and my parents laid out, willing to sign any and all papers that got me out as soon as possible. I only discovered the many responsibilities I had forfeited as I went along—ownership of my bank account, firearms, and my freedom should I start engaging in certain behaviors.

If the doctors here needed to know what medication I was taking to know what they could give me, they must have pulled my records to learn what I am supposed to be on. I don't know if they have the rights to tell my previous host hospital that my system is clear and free of drugs. Too clear. Not taking my medication most likely falls under engaging in certain behaviors that would make people question the wisdom of letting me run amok as a free man. And considering all the hell I've been raising over the last couple days, it's a fair question.

I really should have read that contract before signing.

I close my eyes, trying to remember if Sheriff Suarez was there with the green scrub blob who kept telling me to stay awake. The gap between the memories is too wide for me to fill and the hours remain a blank.

Being a drug delinquent is the least of my worries. What they didn't find in the tests is nothing to what they might've found at the wreck site. If they found Burns' death diary . . .

"Nope, nope, nope," I say. "Vacation's over, we're checking out."

I don't care if I have internal bleeding. I'll swallow a box of bandages if that's what it takes to get me out of here.

I'm not as kind as I should be, ripping the catheter out of my arm. The room spins when I stand, but I refuse to let a dizzy spell trick me out of how I know gravity is supposed to work. Unfortunately, I'm only able to stay upright so long as I don't move. My chest feels wrong and tremors wreak havoc on my legs as they struggle to remember how to do their job.

The air conditioning sending a breeze up the hospital gown doesn't do much to steel my resolve. I've not mastered the self-confidence needed to make a break for it essentially naked.

Any lingering self-confidence goes up in smoke when a middle-aged nurse clad in green scrubs enters the room. I freeze like a kid caught with his hand in the cookie jar.

She arches a pencil sharpened eyebrow as she looks me over. The brow goes up another inch when she sees the still swaying IV line and then another inch more when she returns her gaze to me in the wafting hospital gown.

"Lie back down." She rolls her eyes above a barely professional smirk. "You've got visitors and they don't want to see that."

I have a reply made ready but it isn't something to say to a lady. I meet her halfway and sit down. As if by invitation of someone else speaking, the voices of the hospital's dead come out from the background. They clamor to be heard. I focus in on the pulse of my heart to shuttle them back to white noise.

"Where're my clothes?" I ask, gripping the edge of the bed to steady myself against the relentless hissing voices. My vision tilts from all the up and down motion. Raising a stabilizing hand to my head I feel the skin stretched by swelling. It's like someone shoved a watermelon rind under the left side of my face. Thanks to the painkillers, it definitely looks worse than it feels.

The nurse shrugs. "If they're in the same shape you are, they probably got bagged and ended up in a trash can somewhere. You'll get scrubs to wear if that's the case. Did you do this?" she asks, holding up the forsaken IV line.

"No."

"Alright, smart-ass," she says. "Lie down and behave. You have guests."

Her hand guiding me back down to bed before replacing the IV is much gentler than her bedside manner.

"Take it out again and I'm gonna make a point of struggling to find the vein," she says with a cheery smile. She leaves and surrenders some of her tough demeanor when she brings back the promised green scrubs.

"For when you want to clean up a bit," she says, placing the clothes on the chair in the corner.

When she leaves again, Kitty and Sheriff Suarez walk in.

Which is fine. I didn't think today was going to be fun anyway.

Kitty takes one look at me and turns to the sheriff. "Do you mind if I have a couple minutes alone? Please?"

Suarez gives a stiff nod. His mouth is set in a tight, disapproving line beneath his salted mustache. "I'll be outside."

Kitty thanks him before turning her attention back to me. Her scrutiny of me strikes the perfect balance of disappointment and the selflessness that only belongs to mothers.

Aside from the dark hair, we look nothing alike. She takes after our father with a face shaped for worry, her eyes creasing down at the corners to always look either concerned or suspicious. The dark circles framing her eyes stand out against her pale skin, lightly dusted by the freckles she kept as souvenirs from childhood.

Although she got the black hair from our mother, the early silver streaks running through the dark waves are entirely gifts from our father. A few loose strands fall free from her hasty ponytail as she shakes her head. It isn't a shake of disapproval. It's a weary gesture of surrender.

"You can see now, I had a real good excuse for not calling you last night," I say.

The line doesn't work so I try a different tack.

"Did you have any clients today?" I ask as way of apologizing for disrupting her life.

"I cleared the schedule," she said. Meaning, yes, she did have appointments and someone was not happy about needing to rebook. "Logan—"

"What happened to the car?" I ask.

"Totaled."

"It wasn't my fault," I point out to make sure we've got our basic facts straight.

"Yeah, yeah, I know." Kitty waves away my innocence and rolls up the sleeves of the plaid checkered shirt to her elbows. It must be Mark's. It's a man's cut and much too big for her. She probably grabbed the first thing on hand after getting a call in the middle of the night about some stupid brother of hers forgetting how to keep a car on the road. There's a coffee stain not quite camouflaged by the red and white pattern and I smell stale cologne coming off the fabric.

"Logan," she says, sitting down in the chair by the bed. She knows what she wants to say but doesn't have a clue how to say it. She's missed a shirt button at the waist to show her bright turquoise pajama top underneath.

Movement flickers behind her.

Silvia sits down in the chair in the room's corner. Her dress is white and blue and she wears matching shoes—the outfit she died in. Dark bruises in a mottled semblance of hands encircle her throat. Crossing her legs at the ankle, hands clasped on her knees, she leans forward in tense expectation. Every time she moves I hear plastic crinkle beneath a struggling body.

"I'm not dead. I'm not dead. I'm—"

Silvia stays quiet but her presence breaks the dam holding back the flood of haunting spirits. The room reels under their overwhelming rush.

"He never knew. Never knew. Please, tell him. Please. . . ."

"Can you hear me? Someone, please..."

"Thy kingdom come, thy will be done on earth—"

"I'M NOT DEAD! Please! You hear me? Please, can you hear me?!"

Silvia seems equally irritated by the crowd noise. She was too young for any lines to crease her face and her furrowing brow lacks the depth it deserves.

"Are you okay?" Kitty asks. Her spine is ramrod straight and she sits poised on the edge of the chair as if ready for fight or flight.

"Yeah," I say. "You're just looking at me too loud."

"Logan," Kitty repeats, trying to get my eyes to slide back to her and out from fixing in the corner. I compromise by looking at neither Kitty nor Silvia. The newly reapplied IV becomes an object of incredible interest.

"You're not being charged with anything." The cautious way she shapes her words is out of character.

"Hmm," I say, and one of the smaller knots balled up where my intestines should be loosens. Hat-man and Freckles must've seen enough to clear me of fault in the wreck and I'm willing to bet I'd be waking up under different circumstances if anyone had found Burns' book in the wreck. Which means I've lost the only physical evidence against Burns, but at least I dodged worse trouble than I've already woken up into.

Kitty waits for me to say something. The noise of affirmation I gave didn't cut it. But she has something to say that pushes her outside the needed patience to hold out for me to give a real response.

"Logan," she says, voice soft, "what's going on with you?"

"I'm so sorry for your loss."

"You can tell me. I'm not angry with you," she says. "Please, just tell me."

"Is there anything I can do to help?"

"Could you at least look at me?"

"Can you bring back my husband?"

I grant her a quick flick over before going back to staring at the tube stuck in my arm. My glance passed over Silvia and I feel her pulling at me. Demanding I meet her burning stare.

"Dr. Day put in an order for a seventy-two-hour commitment."

That's more like Kitty. Enough of this beating around the bush.

"I'm so sorry. So sorry. So sorry."

"You're scheduled to meet with a local doctor for evaluation. To get the second opinion."

"Why get a second vote if it's already decided?" I snap. Compared to everyone else in the room I have the least reason to be angry. Kitty probably didn't miss a beat the moment someone called her as next of kin, rolling out of bed to drive to the hospital and wait for me to wake up. Silvia wins the right to be most upset, no contest, on the account of having been murdered.

"I'm so sorry for your loss."

"Logan, I never—"

"Why're you even here?" I'm not being fair and I don't care. Yesterday was terrible, the day before that not great, and today isn't shaping up to be too much better.

An unseen hand pulls my head back to face Silvia. She stares at me with unnerving purpose. I don't know what she wants me to do. Or what I can do at this point. I suppose I could just tell Sheriff Suarez everything seeing as how I'm most likely going back to St. Jude's one way or the other. Thing is, I doubt giving the sheriff the whole truth and nothing but the truth will help Silvia any.

"Is there anything I can do to help?"

Kitty refuses to give up. "I know the last couple days have—"

"To help? To help?"

"Can you leave?" I ask. "Please?"

"Help."

Kitty follows my eye line back to the corner chair. Her frown brings out lines on her forehead that weren't there the last time I saw her.

"Logan, is—"

"Please go."

I don't meet Kitty's eye when she turns back to face me. I can't break away from Silvia's dead grey stare.

Kitty continues to talk at me. She says I should've told her about talking to Sheriff Suarez. Should've told her about finding Silvia's body. As if she thinks finding a dead body would disturb or set me off. Stumbling across dead bodies is nothing new. Hell, I've stepped over bodies I knew were my doing. Bodies are the only thing about the dead that don't bother me.

Silvia's silence turns all sound meaningless. Sweat creeps down my neck and turns my palms slick as my body fails to figure out the proper reaction to having a staring contest with the dead.

Kitty moves the chair closer and takes hold of my hand. The

warmth of her skin feels ugly against the cold wrapping around the room. I jerk away and her wearied hurt is something that'll haunt me later once that slot isn't occupied by Silvia.

If Kitty was waiting for me to look at her before leaving, she gives up and walks away, lingering at the room's threshold, holding out one last hope. I don't look over and the door closes quietly behind her with a disappointed click. She talks to Suarez on the other side, their voices hushed like the murmurings.

Silvia keeps staring at me. I suppose the dead don't need to blink but it'd be a seriously appreciated courtesy if she would.

"What?" I mouth at her.

She taps a slender finger to her left wrist. A shining gold paint coats her nails. I wonder if they looked like that when she was murdered. Her arms had been gnawed off by scavengers by the time I found her and I didn't look too close at the photos in Burns' book.

"Time?" I ask, keeping my voice low.

Her face twists in impatient desperation. She drills her wrist harder.

"Just tell me!" I hiss.

"No one's coming. Come on. No one's coming."

The echoing words don't match the movement to her mouth. Her lips curl up, snarling at the vocal loop she's imprisoned in.

"Just tell me and I'll help," I say unhelpfully. "Just tell me what to do."

She keeps tapping. Faster. Faster. My heart rate jumps to match the harried pace of her finger slamming against her wrist. I don't know if ghosts can become tangible but her frustration and fear knocks the wind out of me.

"Just tell me what to do!"

"Mr. Dalaguerre?"

I startle and nearly upset the IV stand. Pity hangs heavy on Sheriff Suarez's tired features.

"May I come in?" he asks, already standing in the middle of the room.

I nod. There's no doubt he would've invited himself over if I said no, but I appreciate him being polite about it. Over the last six months I've learned to value people in uniform giving you a choice in matters. Even if what you choose won't change what they end up doing.

"If you're up to it"—he scoots the chair Kitty abandoned back a safe distance and sits—"I'd like to hear about what happened last night."

His tone is even, which is at odds with his posture, tensed and ready to spring into action. I'd bet he's wishing someone on the hospital staff had bothered to restrain me with something more than bedsheets and an IV as a safety precaution. The last twenty-four hours has given him every right to be suspicious of my stability.

Silvia stops jackhammering her wrist. She points again and again at the sheriff, hand shuddering in and out of visibility. Her lips move in a frantic fury but not even a whisper escapes her.

I'm about to tell the sheriff everything. Tell him everything I know about Burns, Silvia, his daughter and hand it over for him to deal with but the confession comes up short.

Silvia shakes her head, holding a finger to her lips as Alec did. That gesture I do understand—don't tell him.

I have no credibility. No one has any reason to believe any accusation I can throw at Burns. But if I can't outright accuse

Burns of murder, I can at least lay the groundwork for getting him detained for attempted vehicular homicide.

"Truck ran me off the road," I say and add a shrug to give the story more flavor. All the morphine I'm on makes the movement feel unnatural and sluggish.

If Suarez is bothered by my fixed staring over his shoulder at a seemingly empty chair he doesn't let it show. "What did you do earlier that day?"

"I . . ." Thinking back hurts. My brain protests against being asked to do more than handle basic functions. I close my eyes and pinch the bridge of my nose. All that does is irritate my swollen skin.

Burns. I ran into him at the shack. No, no, I saw him before that. On his driver's license. That might not be the best thing to bring up. Suarez will want to know why I had his driver's license. Why I went rifling through his wallet.

"I was at the fair on Main Street," I say.

"When?"

"Morning? I don't remember when or for how long. I wasn't there..." No, it was two days ago, not yesterday I was at the festival. Snooping around with his daughter.

Thank God I had broken out into an obvious cold sweat before Suarez entered the room.

"Mr. Dalaguerre." The prompt is patient. Almost paternal.

I close my eyes again and count to ten. When I open them, I force my gaze to stay away from Silvia's corner and meet the sheriff's eye. They're the same color as Glenny's.

"I drove out to a park," I say. "Dusky Lake."

"That's a ways out."

"That was the appeal," I say. "Away from all the crowds. That, and it was said to have nice trails."

"And then?"

"I was out there for a while," I say.

"How long?" he asks.

"A while," I say again. "Then I..." Unable to remember when I set out and unwilling to try to fit a fib onto a concrete timeline I grasp at straws for confirmation of my whereabouts.

"Mr Dalaguerre?"

The hospital haunting committee decides to turn up their volume, dragging me down in an undertow of pleas, memories, and mournings.

"Call it."

I watch Sheriff Suarez's lips move, unable to make sense of it.

". . . isn't suffering anymore . . ."

"No! No! NO!"

I need it to stop. To—

"Just stop!"

Suarez goes stiff. A hard wariness replaces the pity creasing the corners of his eyes, that outburst moving me from someone pathetic to a possible threat.

I straighten up in the bed, matching his rigid posture with my own as much as I can muster.

"I was driving back when the truck passed me," I say. The sudden swing back to a level voice after yelling at apparently nothing looks to upset Suarez further. "I thought he might be ticked because I wasn't driving fast enough."

"He?" Suarez asks. "Did you see the driver?"

Oh yeah. "Not really. Driver was male. Middle-aged, around forty with dark hair."

Sheriff Suarez leans forward slightly, and I'm reminded of a wildcat hunching down before pouncing.

"What makes you think he was angry at you?" he asks.

"He passed me illegally," I say. "Made a show of doing it."

"Anything else? Was there anything else that would lead you to believe he'd want to harm you?"

The question is obviously leading. I'm not willing to bite.

"Other than him turning around to run me off the road?"

Suarez dodges the sarcasm. "What did the truck look like?"

"Black Ram 3500 Laramie Longhorn. Didn't catch the plate."

"Did you recognize the driver from somewhere?" Sheriff Suarez asks, and I hope I'm not imagining the clipped tone to his voice suggesting he already suspects who this dark-haired middle-aged man driving that model of truck is. "Someone you knew?"

The temptation to spill the beans, get it all over with and surrender to being thought insane rises up again. A cold clamping over my throat convinces me otherwise. Sharing the full story with the sheriff won't do anything. Except eliminate the need for an appointment with a second physician before I end up committed. Most certainly for more than seventy-two hours.

"I don't think it was anything personal if that's what you're driving at," I lie. "The guy was probably drunk or an asshole who thought it'd be funny to pick a random car to play chicken with."

I never saw Silvia move. One moment she was sitting. Now she stands by the door. She mouths a silent, desperate plea for me to leave. I grip the bed sheet, knuckles going white, straining to hear her voice unscrambled by death.

She paces in front of the door. Her gestures turn wild and she blurs in and out of visibility. A palpable tension twists the air taut and the hair on my arms stands on end.

One moment her features are preternaturally sharp as the emotions holding her to this world manifest in a way they cannot in life. The next she's gone only to reappear in stuttering flashes. Her form hops around the room. One moment clear, the next a whirl of spectral rage.

"Mr. Dalaguerre." Suarez is waiting for me to give an answer to a question I didn't hear.

"What?"

It might've been the blankness to my question that brought out Suarez's sigh of defeat. I didn't have to feign the complete lack of indication I tracked anything he said and have no idea how long I was staring at Silvia. Judging by the pity returning to mix with exasperation, Suarez was speaking at me longer than I thought.

Silvia lets loose a soundless scream. Everything else except for her and the never-ending hum of voices fades away. The hospital room washes away to be replaced by the field I found her in. Her corpse stares up at me, desiccated and empty-eyed, mouth hanging wide in that silenced shriek. This time as I look down at the corpse, the head jerks as it fights to speak.

"No one is coming."

I flinch when Suarez is driven to resting a hand on my shoulder to get my attention, pulling me back to the hospital room.

"Are you alright?" he asks.

No. I'm not.

"No one is coming." Silvia flickers in a frustrated rage around the room.

"I'm sorry, sir," I say. There isn't much else I can offer and the flat apology is a request to be left alone instead of forgiven. I can't be of service to both Silvia and the sheriff, and I've made up my mind who I can best help. I turn a stare flatter than my voice to Suarez. "Are we done here?"

He sighs and rubs a hand over the stubble peppering his chin. "Thank you for your time, Mr. Dalaguerre."

He doesn't bother keeping his voice down as he talks to Kitty outside the open door. She isn't pleased when he suggests stationing an officer outside my room for safety precautions. She insists she can handle me. I'm not dangerous. Just disturbed. Suarez only agrees with her on the last statement.

They're absolutely right on that count. I am highly disturbed by Silvia's increasingly agitated antics. If ghosts breathed she'd be panting. She's beyond desperate and her face is a twisted mask of righteous fury, impossible for a living face to wear.

Her black hair lifts on the thermals of rage rising around her. She flings her arms out at the broken world she can't yet leave as if trying to tear free of the death rendering her message impossible to understand. The lights flicker and my IV bag shudders. Her howl comes out mute and she slams her fists against the wall, sending a tremor rippling through the room.

Suarez and Kitty are too involved in their debate to notice the lights faltering or the chairs jumping and scraping across the floor. The sheriff refuses to budge from his position of taking more secure measures and Kitty gives in. She knows she can't fight a war on both fronts and I've done nothing to win her as an ally.

The bedside table groans as Silvia tears at the physical world muffling her. The room shivers under her efforts. A darkness spills over the walls and floor in defiance of light and structure. I revert back to my original plan and I rip out my IV again as the whole bed shudders under her growing rage. We're checking out of this place.

The corner chair stutters then slams into the opposite wall. Sheriff Suarez and Kitty fall into a sudden quiet. Kitty checks back in the room and her confusion is replaced by the disbelieving horror of witnessing something that she can't explain.

She can't see Silvia or her dark wrath swallowing the room. But she can see my bed trembling and the chairs skittering over the floor. The IV stand topples over. The bedside table splinters and cracks. The lights burst in a shower of sparks and glass.

Kitty screams and throws herself over me as the window breaks. Fortunately, the glass explodes out and not in.

"What the hell?!" The door to the hospital room slams shut in Sheriff Suarez's face. His banging on the door adds a percussion line to Silvia's destructive symphony.

Clumsy from the drugs, I scoop Kitty up and manage not to trip on sheets or gown as I limp-sprint for the window. She pushes against me as if trying to force me back down. There are enough painkillers in my system that my ribs only give a passive-aggressive reminder of yesterday's crash. The bruised bones promise to get me back later as I rush Kitty over to the now conveniently opened window. She keeps screaming, telling me it's going to be okay and to stay calm as she panics.

The now vacant hospital bed flips over and slams up into the ceiling. Dust and bits of ceiling panels patter down and the door rattles, refusing to open under Sheriff's barrage of fists and curses.

"Sorry, sorry, sorry," I say as I heave Kitty out the window of the angry-ghost-infested room. She lands with a graceless thump on the little garden lawn. There's not much more grace to my landing as I hop over the ledge after her. I wince at the popping sensations every twist sets off from my waist to shoulders. The first sorry was for throwing her out a window. The second was for grabbing the keys to her car out of her purse. The third was for everything else that I'm going to end up doing.

I doubt she heard me. She's staring open mouthed into the room suffering Silvia's tantrum. When she snaps out of it I hope she takes the time to appreciate I threw her out the window in the direction of the least amount of broken glass.

I ignore the shards slicing into my bare feet as I hurry through the parking lot. A mother leading her son with his arm in a sling scoops him up as if she's afraid he'll catch whatever I have if he gets too close to me. Which is understandable. A barefoot man in a hospital gown looks bad no matter what parking lot he's hobbling through. I should have grabbed the scrubs the nurse left for me. Too late now, and there's no point dwelling on past mistakes.

Needing to draw more attention to myself than I already have, I miss the unlock switch and slam my thumb down on the panic button for the car.

"Ah, son of a bitch," I say and add, "Sorry," to the woman for cussing in front of her kid.

The blaring car alarm leads me to Kitty's SUV, proudly sporting an honors student bumper sticker.

The boy stares in fascinated delight at the crazy man traipsing through the parking lot as his mother dives into her purse for her cellphone. Probably to call the police. Don't worry, lady, the police are already here.

The car radio welcomes me before I start the engine. Thick static mars the words of a talk show. I don't need to make out the words, I'd know that voice anywhere, transcending death to speak through the garble.

"I know, I know," I mutter. Regret and relief mingle when the radio slides off the supernatural station and goes quiet.

I leave black tire marks behind as I peel out of the parking lot. Me crashing Kitty's car due to a morphine slowed reaction time is of more concern than the glass slivers digging deeper into my foot as I stomp down on the accelerator.

Reaching the highway, I say a quick prayer that if I'm going to crash I be the only one who gets hurt, although it would be nice to avoid a car crash altogether. I think I've already met my quota of life-threatening car incidences for the week.

A female shape blurs in and out of the corner of my eye. Silvia's weak apparition doesn't look like she'll be riding shotgun with me long. At least not visibly.

"Poltergeist jail break," I say to her. "Classic maneuver. They never saw it coming."

I hold up my hand in a high-five gesture and nearly swerve off the road in shock when I feel a hand-shaped pressure slap against mine. Tugs and cold touches are one thing, but I didn't think ghosts could interact with the living in such a refined fashion.

"I . . . didn't know you could do that," I say.

She gives me a look that patiently says "there are a lot of things you don't know," before pointing for me to keep my eyes on the road. Before she dissolves from sight, Silvia taps her wrist with her finger once more, and this time her message is clear. *Hurry.*

Chapter 23

T he road is mercifully empty. No one's around to see me misjudge the right hand turn to get on the county road, swing wide into the opposite lane and spend the next one hundred feet overcorrecting for it. I don't know the town well enough to know where I'm going. Consciously, that is. It feels more like my hands are gloves and someone else is occupying them, controlling the wheel. After a couple miles down an arterial I recognize the strip mall on the roadside.

"I got it from here," I say. The invisible strings pulling at my hands loosen but the secondary anxiety Silvia is pouring on me doubles down hard. The insides of my mouth are raw from me gnawing on them.

A little late I realize I'm drifting into the wrong lane. The car crosses over the yellow line twice before I get it to drive straight again. Urgency makes me want to push the accelerator through the floor. Common sense and a desire to avoid setting a two-for-two car collision streak keeps me driving twenty below the speed limit.

By the time I reach Glenny's place the drugs have worn off, giving me sufficient motor control to pull off a crooked parking job that only puts one of the car's tires in the grass. Her truck sits alone in the driveway. Please let her still be here.

Summoning up as much dignity as a man can muster while clutching the back of his hospital gown shut with the hand not in a cast, I hobble-run up to the door.

"Glenny." I bang on the door. "Glenny, are you there?"

The house is silent.

"Glenny?" I try the door knob and find it locked.

Fluttering movement catches my eye through the windows framing the front door. The white, transparent curtains shiver as a breeze enters the house through the broken sliding glass door leading into the backyard. Shattered glass shines against the kitchen's linoleum floor.

Dread lodges hard in my throat. The blood on my feet leaves thin red streaks on the stone path as I circle around to the back porch. I've got bigger worries on my mind than avoiding the broken glass covering the floor and a few of the smaller slivers join the ranks of their hospital brethren already embedded in my feet.

"Glenny?" I call out even though I know there won't be a reply. At least not from her.

Signs of struggle scar the kitchen. One of the toppled chairs lost two of its legs. The food Glenny must have been packing up was knocked loose from the bags and the refrigerator door hangs wide open.

Sunflowers, stems and bright yellow petals crushed, litter the table and floor. The spilled water from the shattered vase sits in stagnant puddles. I rescue Glenny's phone from the mess. Despite the spiderweb cracks across the screen it comes to life when I turn it on. It's locked and I'm not going to waste my time to figure out the code. There's an emergency function available when I need to make the call.

Each step I take leaves a fresh bloody footprint on a kitchen floor already sporting red spatters. The house is deathly hushed and the silence has become a sound to itself, an outrage against the recently committed evils. The brush of the hospital gown reminds me how starkly vulnerable I am.

The watermelon she had been cutting when Burns broke in sits partially sliced on the counter. Drying bits of fruit and rind are smashed into a pulpy mess over the counter and floor. In the middle of it lies a knife, sticky from something other than watermelon—the drying mess gumming the blade's edge is too thick and red to have come from the fruit.

For a girl whose weight might break into triple digits with the help of the baby, Glenny put up a hell of a fight. Dishes are broken on the floor and counter. The coffee maker is overturned and deep dents gouge the wall where furniture got shoved into the cheap plaster during the struggle.

In the end I don't know if it did her or her baby any good. I don't know whose blood is on the knife and floor. I pray to God it's Burns'. The murmurings delight in the fear hanging thick in the air. Glenny's terror has already stained the little kitchen, the room desecrated by violence. Please, God, let memory be the only thing that ends up haunting this place.

"Glenny?" I ask to the empty house, terrified she might answer. That I get no answer is a dark relief. Please, please don't let her be dead.

"Silvia?" I try the other former roommate of the house.

Straining my ears, I try to pick out the sound of footsteps, voices, anything more than the murmurings rasping through my mind. When all is silent for more than a minute, I start a careful tread down the hall, spreading the bloody prints onto the rough carpet.

Please don't let her be dead.

Static fusses down the hallway from Silvia's room.

"Good mornkssh . . . gangkssh kshh . . . come back to . . ."

The voice torn ragged from interference tells me what I need to know. I'm alone here and can't stay long.

I check Silvia's room first, looting through her desk and dresser in hopes I'll find something of use. The sweatpants with CHEER written on the backside are too short but better than nothing. The shirt she must have taken from Parnell-Penn-Tom-Thomas will probably fit better than any of her other shirts and is a huge step above the hospital gown.

Not until I pull the hospital gown over my head do I realize how banged up I am. Purpling blues and angry reds cover my upper body and make the pale, older scars stand out all the more. The density of bruises thins some on my arms and legs, painting me a mottled mess. A couple small ridged lines on my abdomen show fresh stitching. A few torn black strands poke loose to let out bloody trickling streams.

"Huh." I shake my head when I find matching red spots on the gown's cloth. I didn't even know I had stitches to pop.

Checking my head with a bit more care, my fingers find more sutured ridges on my forehead right below my hairline. I'm more worse for wear than I thought. To be fair, I didn't stick around long enough for anyone to give me a rundown of my scrapes and bumps. Besides, I've collected plenty of scars over the years so these don't deserve any particular fanfare or admiration. And in my experience wounds always start to feel worse after you see them.

"It is what it is," I tell my reflection in the closet mirror. I pretend I'm not unnerved when the closet door closes on its own to shield me from the sight.

I was hoping one of the ladies of the house would be a

gun owner. No such luck. Scrounging through Nicole and Adrienne's rooms, the only thing of use I find is a baseball bat. It'll do.

I unthinkingly do a practice swing and regret it. Hurt is beginning to eagerly break through the fading painkillers. Spots of blood blossom through the white and navy pattern of the shirt as I tear more stitching.

Pressing my good hand over the reopened wound, I rummage through the bathroom's medicine cabinet.

"Oh, thank you, Jesus." The left side of my face tightens, not quite able to pull off the relieved smile.

Behind the ibuprofen and other mediocre medicines is a bottle for a barely expired Vicodin prescription for Adrienne Jorgensen. The wisdom tooth removal or surgery Adrienne had to suffer through is what's gonna allow me to stay halfway functional. I pop two pills back and pocket the bottle. There's a flare of momentary self-disgust that I'm adding stolen opiate consumption to breaking and entering, but the drugs putting out the bonfire burning my body into a bruised mess puts that out as well.

With mission success being a guaranteed impossibility, Glenny will need a secondary extraction team. I take out her phone and the locked screen fizzles as an invisible finger punches in the needed code. I feel Silvia pressing down, cold hands wringing at me.

"No one's coming . . . no one's coming . . ."

It takes me more time to dial Kitty's cell than it does for her to answer.

"Hello?" Worry shoots her voice up a few decibels and I hold the phone farther from my ear.

"Kitty? It's me."

"Logan, where are you?" The panic in her voice hurts.

"I need to talk to Sheriff Suarez. Is he there?"

He's on the phone before I finish asking.

"Suarez." His tone is guarded, stiff and all business.

"Sir, Carl Burns murdered Silvia Lopez." I swallow, there's no point dancing around this. "And he's got Glenny."

He starts to speak but I continue over him.

"There's sign of a struggle at the place she was renting. Nobody's here." I hope that the house being empty is evidence that she's still alive. That if Burns was just going to kill her right away he would've done it here.

"There's a shack a ways behind Burns' property," I say. "It's where he's been committing the murders."

"Murders?" Emotion threatens to break through Suarez's collect. There are fissures forming in the hardened shield decades of being a cop gave him.

"There were pictures."

"What pictures?" he seethes. I wouldn't be surprised to hear his teeth crack under the anger.

"They were in a book," I say. "But I lost it."

"Why didn't you tell me this?" he asks. The real question he wants to ask is, "Well you're a right damn incompetent idiot aren't you?" but using less polite phrasing.

Because half an hour ago you wouldn't have believed it. But now's not the time for a confession. When this is over, I promise that if the sheriff will listen, I'll tell him it all. Well, most of it.

"I don't know where the exact location of the shack is," I say.

"Dalaguerre—"

"I'm taking Glenny's cell phone with me," I say. "See if you can track it."

"Logan, don't—"

I hang up. There isn't anything else I have worthwhile to say and Suarez doesn't sound like he can listen to much more. Passing through the kitchen I grab a butcher's knife to add to my pitiful arsenal. Stabbing might be easier to manage than swinging with the condition of my arm and torso but I decide to keep the baseball bat as my pathetic backup piece. I can't carry the bat in my left hand due to the cast and need to tuck it against my protesting ribs.

Glenny's cell phone rings when I reach the back door. Kitty's cell number lights up the screen.

"Sorry, Kit," I answer. "I don't got time."

"Logan, please. Stop whatever you're doing and just—just stay where you are. Someone will come to help you."

"I can't talk, I'm gonna be driving." I give her the space of the lawn between me and the car for her to do her obligatory and doomed attempt to talk me down.

"Logan, you're not in trouble, don't make—"

"First off, no, I'm pretty sure I'm in trouble. Second, even if I'm not, Glenny is," I say. I slide into the car and turn the ignition.

The car radio is in such a fit I expect to see sparks and smoke.

"Good morning, gankshhhkshhh . . . we've got a lot to gsksh do today . . ."

"I've gotta go," I say. "I'll call you tonight. Really. I promise."

"Logan, are you psychic?" she blurts out.

"What?" Her question catches me completely off guard.

"With the bed and the window . . . was that . . . did you do that?"

"Oh, no, that wasn't me. That was Silvia."

"The dead girl?"

"Yep. That was her."

I'm not sure what the silence on the other end of the line means but it sounds disbelieving, which is grossly unfair since she just passive-aggressively accused me of trashing a hospital room via telepathy.

"I'm not psychic, Kitty. Don't be stupid, there's no such thing." That's not true. I'm pretty sure Glenny counts as some sort of psychic.

"Remington Logan Dalaguerre, if you—"

"Love you too, Kitty. Talk to you in a bit." I feel better hanging up on Mom-Voice Kitty than Oh-Jesus-Save-My-Mentally-Unhinged-Little-Brother-Voice Kitty.

Chapter 24

There are thirty-one missed calls, eleven voicemails, and twenty-three text messages on Glenny's phone by the time I pull up to the lake I parked at yesterday. Most are from Kitty's number. There are a couple I don't recognize and assume are from Suarez or Josie, and maybe even Glenny's brothers joining the attempt to make contact.

Assuming Sheriff Suarez took me seriously, the cops are probably already at Burns' home. In a world where things work as they should, Burns will be there as well, confess to everything, and Glenny will be fine and can eat all the ice cream he has in his freezer.

I don't bother with the notion of calling the sheriff to try and lead the police to Burns' murder shack. There's no way they'd follow me anywhere. Calling in backup only ends up with me handcuffed to a hospital bed and Glenny dead.

That Silvia is waiting for me in the woods is a reminder this is a world where things rarely work as they should. She doesn't walk alongside me, she simply watches as I pass her by. A moment later she's there in front of me again. She waits for me along a ravine crest. Under a stumpy oak. Without word or gesture she guides me to where I'm needed. My own macabre fool's fire showing me the way.

Alec had pointed and gestured. He didn't need to speak, I knew what he was saying. Come on, Doll, keep moving. He waited for me at the crest of a ridge. Motioned for me to duck for cover. Held a finger to unbreathing lips when survival demanded absolute quiet. I never saw the enemy. I only ever heard them, their foreign voices or their crunching footsteps over rocky ground when they came too close to where I hid. They stayed masked behind unwelcoming mountain ridges and gnarled trees. I stayed hidden under Alec's guidance. His refusal to abandon a man tethered him to this world.

Reduced to focusing on nothing more complicated than living to see the next hour, I didn't have the ability put it together then. Operating on instinct disciplined by habit, I followed Alec without question. It wasn't until I stumbled out of the mountains to be picked up by a patrol I learned Alec hadn't been missing as I had been. They'd found what was left of his body.

Sweat works through my shirt, and dizziness competes against my constricted chest to see which can slow me most. Some sick bastard at the hospital replaced my ribs with splintered needles and didn't even have the decency to arrange them so that they all went at the same angle. Breathing shoots the pointed ends into my lungs in a white-hot burn. I consider taking another Vicodin but I'm already high as a bird and my decision making is too dangerously impaired without more narcotics. I've done a great job of eliminating any good choices I could've made. Now I just need to make the least bad ones.

Every step ensures the dozen cuts in my feet stay open and fresh. My feet are slick from sweat and blood.

"Come on." Silvia begs me to hurry. She sounds impossibly close as she continues to urge me forward.

"Come on. Come on. Come on."

Pain ricochets around my skull. Lack of food, water, and blood throws me into a disoriented fog. I stumble and something snaps. I can't be sure if it was a dried twig or me. If it was me, it must not be too vital if I can keep walking.

The sepia haze descends over me with the absolute finality of a closing curtain. I feel the entity waiting behind Silvia. It hangs in the background, amused as it watches my struggles. The murmuring voices wrap around me like physical ropes trying to slow my tired march.

"Come on."

Another misstep sends the ground hurtling up at me.

"Fuck," I mumble into the dried leaves. There's nothing comfortable about all my weight crushing down on my ribs but my body refuses to allow any movement. Air isn't flowing to my lungs as it should. They can't expand as far as I need against the barbed wire encircling them. I'm in no shape to be rushing off to rescue anyone. All I'm doing is giving Burns the opportunity to go after someone outside his usual type.

"You alright, Doll?" Alec asked.

No, sir. I don't think I am.

There's a tugging sensation on my arm. Small hands, nails painted gold, pull to lift me back up. Silvia isn't having any of this dawdling. She alone is unaffected by the sepia haze growing thicker and harsher. If anything, she looks clearer than she ever has. She certainly looks more alive than I feel.

"Come."

"I know, I know." I push myself up through vice-like pain. Nothing works right but I've been here before. I have no control over the signals my battered body sends out. I have complete control whether or not I decide to give in to it.

My mind has long been made up on what I need to do and I've walked closer to hell than these few scrapes and bruises can take me. If by only one working arm I have to drag myself and rap on that shack's door, I'll be damned before I don't.

Chapter 25

Time is lost to me as I stumble through the woods. It takes too long to reach the grey blight of a shack but I reach it all too soon.

There's something different about it. Just as the shadows of the hospital room failed to shape themselves to natural law under Silvia's wrath, the day's warped and dying light doesn't play right across the structure. It sways and shifts like a darkened heat haze, hiding a terrible truth that's waiting for the right moment to reveal itself.

Staying back in a thicket of trees, I search the window for movement. The sepia hue clotting over the world, the distance, and my doubting the reliability of my senses has me unsure if the hulking figure I see move is real or imagined. It doesn't matter, I don't need visual confirmation on Burns. An undoubtable intuition tells me he's in there.

His truck parked in the clearing is also a good indicator.

God, I wish I had my Beretta. I settle to call Kitty instead.

It isn't my sister who answers. A terrible, low voice hisses out to me. Tells me to turn back, give up. I won't win.

I mute the phone and lay it down, hoping it still works despite the entity's interference and if there is a physical body on the other end of the line, they can track the call.

Knowing my body will punish me for it later if I live long enough for it to, I crouch low and move forward. The quiet to my step is so complete not even the driest leaf dares give me away.

I could make noise. It might draw Burns out. Or it might do the opposite. He could hunker down, wait with gun loaded and pointed at the only door. Or he may panic and kill Glenny. If she's still alive.

God, please, let her be alive.

Betting on Burns behaving in any sensible manner isn't a risk I'm gonna take. Not when it gambles Glenny's life.

I hope Burns doesn't know the difference between silence and quiet. Pray he doesn't notice the silence as I crouch low against the side of the shack and edge under the window. All I hear is the murmurings. There's no creak of floorboards, pleading cry, or hints to any life coming from within the shack.

I risk a peek through the window. Movement flashes large and I duck down, heart hammering. I wait for the surprised shout, the roar of being discovered. Nothing.

Slowly, not daring to breathe, I raise my head to check back in through the window.

Burns' agitated pacing carries him around the small shack. He wrings his hands as if he's yearning to find a substitute for a slender neck. A dark slice of red stains the front of his shirt from where Glenny must have slashed him with the knife. Every once in a while he stops trying to break his own hands to wipe at his face, pull at his shirt collar. The whites of his eyes stand out sharp against his black expression. It's the look of a man after his world's been turned upside down seeking to reestablish past rituals, only to fall further down into madness.

Burns is much bigger than I am. He's got more muscle and a

longer reach. On a good day that would be something to stay wary of. Today has not been a good day.

He doesn't pay Glenny any attention. She lies on her side on the floor, legs brought up protectively around her stomach. Hands bound, duct tape circles around her mouth, winding around her head. The skin around the tape is angry and blood splatters the front of her shirt but it doesn't look to be hers. There's no patch of red on her to indicate a wound, and other than bruising she doesn't look too banged up.

No sign of tears stain her face. Her eyes are wide but not rimmed red. They're sharp and wary as she tracks Burns' pacing. Her pinprick pupils are the only bit of her that moves. She looks like she's doing her best to stay as small and still as possible, barely risking breathing.

Burns doesn't see me as his pacing takes him past the window. Glenny does. Her eyes widen more. Before I can make any gesture to try and communicate what to do, she kicks at the chair leaning against the wall. Metal bounces against the hard floor in a jarring clang.

Burns whirls around. Hate sparks from him as he advances toward her. His focus has narrowed down to her and only her.

Two precious seconds pass as I sprint around the corner and burst through the front door. Burns whips back, shock and rage contorting his face.

"You—"

Running into him is like hitting a concrete wall, but it gets him off Glenny. I twist so he hits the ground and I'm on top. Even with the painkillers, the movement sets my whole body on fire. My chest throbs and the breath I need doesn't come. I lose the bat and barely keep the knife tight in hand. The room whirls like a top. Burns shoves me off and I come charging back at him to plunge the knife down.

His last-second lunge puts the knife straight through his bicep. Shit. I meant to get him right below his collar bone. He roars in pain and I can't pull the knife free before he jerks away.

He screams again as he tears the knife out. I torque his wrist, forcing him to drop the blade. He swings, and I move so his fist slams against the wall instead of my head. Adrenaline and instinct are the drugs keeping me moving. It's all I got, and I need it to be enough.

He lunges and I grab the bat rolling on the floor, bring myself halfway up to brain him—and that's all I can do. I hit the proverbial wall with shattering abandon. Adrenaline can't cut it anymore. There's no kindling left for it to burn.

My legs give out and Burns slams me hard against the wall. I hear the snapping sensations race through my body like a string of firecrackers and the world dives into a painful black.

"You little shit." Burns' voice is the line reeling me back. If my ribs weren't broken before they are now. Each breath is a lance of pain yet it all feels so far away.

"You and that Lopez girl. Snooping around where you got no right to be."

I instinctively shift. The fist I didn't see glances off my pounding head, barely missing scattering my teeth across the floor.

"She didn't cause near as much trouble as you've managed to kick up."

A foot sinks into my gut. I grab it but can't move right. Not the way I need to take him down to the ground with me. Burns laughs and shakes me off. He knows I'm beat and it thrills him.

He grabs me by the hair and twists my face up toward his.

"You probably thought things would go a bit different than this. Didn't you?" His lips, swollen and bruised from our first exchange, curl back in a patronizing smile. He keeps talking but I can't hear him. The murmurings are no longer whispers in the back of my mind. They rush to the front of my senses in a frenzied mob. They roar and cheer, indiscernible and deafening. I can't push them away. Whatever veil separates them from my senses is too thoroughly torn. Or I'm too close to tipping through to the other side.

Burns is breathing hard. Exertion and excitement have him flushed. There's a grin splitting his face, and I've seen that expression on men before. The perverted joy in catching the depraved thrill he chases.

His eyes flick to the knife temptingly within his arm's reach. Then to his hands. Then to my throat. Weighing his options.

He takes a testing step back, seeing if I'm able to run or fight. I spit up blood. He relaxes, satisfied I won't be trouble for him. He can take his time.

"I've never tried a boy before," he muses.

I grin up at him. Blood slips warm down my chin. That's right, asshole. Keep looking this way.

"What you got to smile about?" he asks.

Baseball bat clenched in her duct taped hands, Glenny swings in hard. The bat cracks against Burns' skull with unholy might. The tape over her mouth muffles her scream but none of her fury. I doubt Burns ever heard it.

He sways but Glenny's aim is true. She hits the exact same place on her second swing. The lower half of Burns' face stays in place. The top of his skull shifts. His knees hit the floor.

A third strike caves the side of his head in. A fourth sends blood and bone spraying out into right field.

Burns collapses to the floor but Glenny ain't done. Five, six, seven, she screams each time she takes the bat to his head. When she finally stops, the bat drops from her hands, hitting the floor with a dull *thunk*. It all goes quiet and still, save for Glenny panting hard beneath the duct tape and Burns' twitching. His fingers end their jittering scrabble in a half-clenched fist. His mouth freezes in a gape for blood-laced saliva to dribble out beneath uneven, bulging eyes.

Glenny breaks the too-long silence stretching over the dead man.

The duct tape around her mouth hides the articulation but not the cadence of her desperate, "Oh God. Oh God. Oh God."

She stumbles away from what's left of Burns' head. Her shaking hands move from covering her taped mouth to her swollen stomach. Red and less pleasant matter is speckled across her dirty maternity shirt, and tears track through the splattering on her cheek.

"Glenny." Speaking proves harder than breathing. I use each exhale to carry out a tight string of syllables. "When you can, call your dad, okay? Let him know you're alright."

Maneuvering the cellphone out of Burns' pants pocket hurts more than it has any right to. I slide the phone across the floor over to her. After everything she went through, I'm not going to test her willingness to let any man approach her.

Glenny has more moxie than I gave her credit for. Her cries cut off and she nods. Picking up the phone she points to her mouth.

Good point. She might have trouble talking through that.

"Can you breathe okay?" I ask.

She nods. That makes one of us.

"And you're not gonna throw up or anything?" I ask.

Glenny hesitates, considers, then shakes her head.

"Good. Then leave it on. It'll hurt like hell if we try to take that off," I say. We might as well wait for alcohol or at least warm soap and water before trying to take it off her face if breathing ain't a problem. She's probably going to have to cut her hair shorter to get it free from that mess of tape.

And that's a nice thought, being able to think about the future because you know you're going to make it through the day.

"Just dial your dad's number and I'll talk," I say.

Talking that much took the rest of my wind. I'll need to take five before I can make the call.

Glenny gestures at me. It takes another minute of her waving her bound hands about for me to figure out she's asking if I'm alright.

"Am I alright?" I ask, indignant and lying flat on the floor. "What the hell makes you think I'm not?"

Chapter 26

That same strange familiarity of being in a place I recognize but don't remember arriving at gnaws at me. Or maybe that's the drug-suppressed pain in my chest.

And gut.

And head.

And everywhere else.

I blink a couple times and the pieces start to fall into place. I'm in a different hospital room than I was earlier in the day. I wonder if I was purposefully placed in a room with smaller windows on account of what happened to the ones in my last room. As unpleasant as it is to be back among the constant whispering stream of the lingering dead, knowing that Burns' brain is too splattered outside his skull to be doing anything except rot in a morgue is a small, savage comfort.

Glenny should be proud of how—

"Glenny!" I bolt up. Or rather, I try to and end up doing this feeble fish-flop in the hospital sheets.

"She's fine." Kitty grips my hand in hers. "Everything's fine."

I return the squeeze, grateful for the warmth of the living.

"You're not going to ask me what happened?" I ask. Her calm is out of character and can't be trusted.

"Glenny already told us everything," she says. "Multiple times."

My relief at not having to talk to people is short-lived.

"Wait, everything?"

"Every. Thing," Kitty confirms.

Shit.

"Who do you mean by *us*?" I ask.

"Me. And Frank."

"Frank?"

"Sheriff Suarez. He's gonna want to talk to you," she says.

"That doesn't sound good," I say.

"It can wait," she says.

"That makes it sound slightly better, but I'd rather just get it over with if he's around."

Kitty waves to someone in the hall and Suarez switches places with her. The coordination in their movements along with the first name basis confirms they've established a dangerous alliance. Engaging the two of them in a direct offensive is a guaranteed defeat.

Suarez sits heavily in the bedside chair. The space between this hospital visit and the last has aged him ten years. The lines to his face run deeper and there looks to be more salt than I remember flecking his hair.

"No bullshit this time," he says. His nostrils flare, ready to sniff out anything I might try to slip by him. He's out of uniform, but wearing the piece on his hip, Stetson hat, and the don't-try-me mustache, he looks just as much a sheriff as he did wearing the badge.

I tell him about the haunted radios. About Silvia. That I lied about how I found Silvia's corpse but a coyote sounded like a more believable guide than the dead. I tell him about Billy

Davis for the sake of context. I even tell him about breaking into Burns' house, following the hallucination of the shack to its actual location. Tell him that even now I can hear the dead haunting the hospital, whispering through the walls.

I don't tell him about the entity. And I don't tell him about the murmurings that I now firmly believe to have more sinister origins than simply the dead.

He listens without interrupting. Not a spark of emotion flickers across his face to indicate what he's thinking.

"I want to pack you back off to St. Jude's," he finally says.

"I understand, sir." I can't fault him. It's the sensible thing to do.

He sighs and pulls at his salted mustache. "But it's the story that's crazy. Not you."

I pause. Not believing what I'm hearing.

"You sure on that, sir?"

"No. And ask a stupid question like that again and I'll change my mind."

Asking him if I can leave the hospital because I want a break from hearing the dead probably falls under stupid questions, so I keep that to myself.

Suarez shakes his head. "The devil's got your number, son."

More than you know, sir. "Yeah, well the angels got my back."

"You sure on that?"

"Despite my best efforts, I'm still here and if that's not evidence of divine intervention, I don't know what is."

Suarez shakes his head again, a weak grin hiding beneath his mustache.

"Is Glenny alright?" I ask. I figure that question is a fifty-fifty toss up in regards to stupid.

"Yeah, she's . . . she'll be fine. The baby's fine, too," he says.

"She had the baby?"

"Yeah, she's never had a good sense of timing. She went into labor about an hour after we picked you two up."

"Are they here?"

Suarez shakes his head. "I got her down to St. David's in Austin. She wasn't due for another couple weeks and with everything else I wasn't going to chance a lesser obstetrics ward."

Beating a man to death with a baseball bat and giving birth all in the space of a day. Glenny's been busy.

"But they're both okay?"

"Yeah. Little baby boy. Just as tiny as she was when she was born. Screamed just about as loud too." The thought of his daughter and grandchild gives him back a couple of years as a weight lifts off him. His boot heels knock against the floor as he shifts uncomfortably.

"I suppose I ought to thank you for that," he says.

I stare at the wall and make an inarticulate grunt. He knows how to give thanks just about as well as I know how to take it.

"What are you gonna tell people? About what happened?" I ask.

"You mean what story am I gonna concoct to cover up that a psychiatric patient who talks to the dead tracked down a serial killer and then had to have my pregnant teenage daughter bludgeon the guy to death with a baseball bat?" Suarez asks.

"Yeah."

"Son." Suarez gives a wry grin and doesn't look as tired. "I'm the sheriff of this here town. I'm the one people try to sell cover stories to."

Chapter 27

I gave Sheriff Suarez too much grief over the past couple days to push my luck and ask for an earlier discharge more than five times. It was Kitty who snapped first, telling me to shut up and stop asking stupid questions. I didn't take it personally. I heard her later asking if there was any way I could be moved out of the hospital early. I'm not sure she quite fully believes I can hear the folks who never left the hospital, but she believes enough to know it's wearing on me.

The moon tracks shadows across the floor. Low embers burn behind my eyes, but despite being thoroughly exhausted, sleep can't make its way through the undercurrent of ghostly mutterings. Being unable to sleep but too tired to do anything useful is the most frustrating part of it. I don't have the mental acuity to do much more than watch the silver light shift over the room and wait for morning.

I didn't expect closure, for everything to be suddenly alright. That I'd start to feel like the person I used to be. I know better than that. The dead don't come back and closure isn't a gift received in this life.

I'd like to blame sleep playing hard to get on being stuck in a hospital but again, I know better. Something else is keeping me up, this sense of waiting for someone.

And that someone comes. The room cools, prickling my skin but not quite to where it brings out a shiver. Silvia's presence does what the temperature drop does not.

She steps out from the soft night glow to stand over the bed.

"Why're you still here?" I ask and realize that sounded pretty damn rude.

She doesn't seem to mind the poor manners. She gives a crooked smile and winks. I feel a pang at the unfairness that the world was cheated out of her life.

"Are you . . . you'll be okay now?" I ask. It's not a conventional question to ask a murder victim, but she picks up what I'm getting at. She tilts her head back. The bruising on her neck is gone. Her smile widens into a sincerity that can't be expressed by flesh.

"Thank you." Her voice is clear and purer than any earthly sound. An involuntary, but not unpleasant, shudder ripples down my spine.

The kiss she places on my brow has no warmth. I close my eyes under the strangeness of a touch I shouldn't feel at all. When I open them she's gone. The room warms to match the thermostat and an invisible weight lifts.

"Eternal rest grant unto her, O Lord, and let perpetual light shine upon her . . ."

I sink into the bed and a quiet I forgot existed settles in.

"May she rest in peace."

About the Author

When not reading or writing, S.K. Ehra can be found wandering the woods and while skittish, is friendly when approached.

You can connect with me on:
- https://skehra.com
- https://twitter.com/SKEhraAuthor

Subscribe to my newsletter:
- https://sendfox.com/skehraauthor

Also by S.K. Ehra

IN THE SERVICE OF SHADOWS
Book #2 of the Crossroads Series coming soon!

9 7 9 8 9 8 5 1 5 2 2 0 3